Sally Emerson attended Oxford University, where she read English and edited the university magazine *Isis*. She won the *Vogue* Talent Contest for writers and worked on New York *Vogue*. She was awarded the *Radio Times* Young Journalist of the Year prize, a Catherine Packenham award, and a *Yorkshire Post* prize for a best first novel *Second Sight*. She was Assistant Editor of *Plays and Players* magazine, and Editor of *Books and Bookmen*. She is married with a son and daughter.

'SECOND SIGHT is a remarkably well-managed story . . . there are brilliant chapters on the murder case . . . Sally Emerson is a highly original, creative novelist' Eric Hiscock

'In her boldness and confidence of approach, Miss Emerson is to be congratulated' *Spectator*

'I look forward to meeting Jennifer Hamilton again' Auberon Waugh *Evening Standard*

Sally Emerson

SECOND SIGHT

AN ABACUS BOOK

First published in Great Britain by Michael Joseph Ltd 1980
Published by Methuen London Ltd 1984
Published in Abacus by Sphere Books Ltd 1992

ISBN 0 349 10248 1

Printed in England by Clays Ltd, St Ives plc

Sphere Books Ltd
A Division of
Macdonald & Co (Publishers) Ltd
165 Great Dover Street
London SE1 4YA
A member of Maxwell Macmillan Publishing Corporation

To Rosalind

1

Sometimes Jennifer wondered that her mother could bear to go to sleep and part from her own company. She appeared to enjoy it so much. She was not alone in this. Everyone seemed to like her. Her husband was besotted. The local shopkeepers loved her visits. Her cleaner hung on every word she spoke. The restaurant she owned and ran was called Sarah's. It was a great success. She had a wonderful memory for names, an excellent chef and a terrific smile. Her vibrancy kept the restaurant warm in spite of its chrome and smoked-glass tables. Jennifer admired her mother enormously. She also despised and resented her.

A few months ago Jennifer's father, Edward, had been away on a fishing holiday up in Scotland. Sarah had refused to join him. Every night Sarah had gone out, usually to her restaurant, leaving Jennifer alone. They'd moved from suburbia to the house in Westminster three years before but it still seemed a stranger. One of these nights the phone rang, Jennifer picked it up, the pips went and there was silence. Sounds spring out of fear: soon floorboards were creaking, there were footsteps outside, rats pattering in the rafters, something banging on the wall and her heart making more noise than all this put together. At one twenty am Jennifer telephoned Sarah's where her mother said she'd be until late. The number was engaged. Sarah must still be there. Jennifer decided she couldn't stay in the house alone. Disquiet had crept under her skin and her heart was jumpy. She dialled again. It was still engaged. The phone rang. It was the pips and silence again.

Jennifer dressed and ran out of the house into the warmth of

Abbey Square. She hurried along two sides of the square, past the bushy green trees of summer, by windows half open, through lamplight, across Vauxhall Bridge Road and into Pimlico. A staring-eyed car loitered along the kerb beside her but she ignored it, or rather pretended to, and it drifted off. Curiously, outside in the night she felt soothed. There was a velvety quality to the darkness and a rich wistful smell which she couldn't quite recognise. The night blacked out the tawdriness of the grey street and the closed-up shops surrounded by moats of rubbish. An argument was escaping from a top floor window above a supermarket. A couple were kissing on a street corner. The girl didn't look much older than Jennifer, sixteen perhaps. She wore an expression of ecstasy and a skirt shortened by the boy's embraces. A shabby man ambled along by the kerb kicking up bits of paper and cans as if they were autumn leaves. He had his hands in his pockets. Jennifer was pleasantly sad as she walked past the couple, past the man, away from the argument. They were all locked in their lives.

By the time she reached the restaurant her fear had lessened but her loneliness increased. She wanted her mother to come home. The restaurant had a white pebbledash exterior emblazoned with the word Sarah's in scrawling navy-blue letters. She turned her key in the varnished wooden door and entered the main room. It was deserted but the dim wall-lights were still on. Some of the tables hadn't been cleared. Half-eaten rolls, screwed-up napkins, rinds of cheese, littered the tables. The opulent navy carpet was scattered with crumbs. She closed the door. She heard voices below, down the central stairs which led to the basement bar. She walked over to the stairs and looked down. It was pitch black. She heard moaning escalating into a sort of scream. She turned on the basement lights. From the top of the stairs she had an aerial view of a burly man lying between the legs of a naked woman. He leapt off leaving Jennifer with the momentary but unforgettable sight of her mother spreadeagled, a sacrificial victim, over one of the low, obviously strong, drinks tables. The mat of pubic hair, the nipples, the red distorted face all jumped out at Jennifer. She gasped. So did Sarah. Sarah cascaded off the table, shouting 'Switch out those fucking lights *now.*'

8

'I'm sorry,' murmured Jennifer.

From down in the blackness her mother's husky voice continued, 'What is it? What's happened?'

'Nothing. I was scared.'

'Scared ...?'

'The phone kept going. Nobody replied when I picked it up.'

'It's just some crank. You are crazy, you know that? You're fifteen and you act like a four-year-old. *Just get out of here, will you?'* Sarah sounded close to tears.

'I phoned here. It was engaged.'

'I took the phone off the ... the blasted hook. That's why. Now go home. Go *home*.'

Jennifer rushed out of the restaurant, through the empty streets where street lights were reflected in black windows and back to the empty house, which was silent except for her rage. She hadn't realised before how much she could hate her mother. That evening was never mentioned again.

She did not, of course, tell her father. It would have hurt him too much. Edward thought Sarah could do no wrong. Jennifer was amazed that a man as intelligent and understanding as her father could fail to see Sarah's faults. Jennifer could see them well enough.

Sarah had an ego of mammoth proportions. Last year she'd had a full-frontal portrait of herself painted by Lucian Freud. This seemed to Jennifer the height of unjustified confidence, an undiluted ego slammed on the drawing-room wall for all eyes to see. What's more, it was a most unflattering portrait. The presumption was that Sarah was so beautiful no one could possibly confuse the broken debauchee in the painting with Sarah herself but would be impressed that she had the contacts, taste, nerve and money to have it painted. And it was true, people were impressed by the painting. Sarah had the confidence to carry anything off.

She treated herself with immense affection. Her manicure was always immaculate and her clothes well pressed without buttons missing or hems down. Often, sitting in a chair, she'd slowly rub her shoulders against its back. This wasn't, or Jennifer didn't think it was, intended to arouse men. It was an introverted,

9

self-preening habit. There were mirrors everywhere in the house. Sarah could often be found gazing into one.

But Sarah's self-love didn't preclude love for others. Just as those who dislike themselves generally blame others for the unpleasantness of being alive, so Sarah credited others for its pleasantness. She was generous with her time, her laughter, her advice, her kisses. She was always encouraging Jennifer to enjoy herself. She dragged her out on clothes-buying expeditions, invited her to come to parties with them, plied her with make-up, gave her an anthology of love poems for her birthday. All to no avail.

Jennifer found it hard to enjoy herself. It was as though she knew she couldn't do so as much as her mother and therefore wasn't going to try. Instead she buried herself in her work, the one area where she could surpass her relatively uneducated mother. She chose history, her father's great love, in which to excel.

Her interest in history was in part an attempt to avoid the daily barrage of detail. She spent so much time catacombed in classrooms being pumped with knowledge she'd release from her brain the moment the term was over. Jennifer watched the news occasionally, read newspapers sometimes but found 'current events' on the whole confusing. The plot was bewildering, lurching, back stepping, splaying out in sub-plots, bringing in new characters, new causes, new effects, piling into a mountain of newsprint, instantaneous and ephemeral. The attraction of history was that the plot was completed, a cohesive whole with the main characters clearly spotlit. In her home newspapers were read only in the morning, by the evening they were out of date and relegated to a big grey plastic bag collected by a dustman every Tuesday. It was too much for Jennifer to cope with, the present bombarding her from every country in the world, and some of the planets. She retreated into the well-planned past.

Up until the night Jennifer discovered Sarah in the restaurant she had not allowed herself to accept her feelings of resentment against her mother. She had sometimes been irritated when Edward had praised Sarah excessively for her cooking, her conversation, her exuberance, her beauty, but that was all. Now that she had decided Sarah was a deceiver, that her apparent openness hid a cold mechanism of lust, Jennifer allowed her dislike to surface. She found it hard to talk to her mother. She seemed so phoney. Jennifer had thrown herself more and more into her work, hoping in that way to win her father's respect and affection but she didn't succeed. Or rather didn't succeed enough. Her father was hooked. Sarah had caught all his love. She was forty-three, he was forty-eight. They'd been married twenty years and he still treated her like porcelain. And how many more men had her mother had affairs with? How many more? And how dare she?

The other effect of the restaurant incident was to make the idea of sex even more distasteful than it had been previously. She did not want to grow up. She especially did not want to grow up like her mother. She wanted to remain in the safe, no-man's land of adolescence. Jennifer ate as little as possible. She hated the breasts and hair on her once androgynous body. They grew in spite of her. They made her feel helpless. Everything made her helpless, especially the unerring, obliterating, competence of Sarah.

There was, however, one man in her life: Shelley. Before falling in love with him she had been besotted by Rhett Butler from *Gone with the Wind* and Yossarian from *Catch 22*. Never the boy next door nor even a film star. She admired energy. She admired intelligence. Literature and the past were more real to her than the strange miseries of day-to-day life. She also liked to be different from the other girls, to feel herself an isolated, Romantic figure. To have shared some pop or film star with thousands of other schoolgirls would have been abhorrent to her. Instead, secretly, obsessively, she dreamed of more remote figures.

Shelley was everything to her. He had wooed her very gradually over a number of years, with his poems and his prose and his life. Now she thought about him constantly. She invented conversations with him. She wondered what his opinion of various people would have been. Would he have liked her father, her mother, would he have disliked her

11

schoolmistresses as much as she did? When the sunset was beautiful as she walked across nearby Vauxhall Bridge she wished he were there to see it, and worked out how she would describe it to him. She felt she was, in a way, living her life for him. Sometimes she felt his presence by her, sometimes she even saw him standing over her or lolling in a chair, watching her. But when she spoke the image would disappear. She longed above all things actually to meet him in the flesh, to talk to him, just as she used to long to meet Rhett Butler and Yossarian. This time, perhaps because she was older, perhaps because she was reaching a point where fantasy was no longer as satisfying as reality, her longing was more acute.

Her invented conversations rang so clearly in her head as she hurried along pavements or through shops or across St James's Park that she would occasionally think other people *must* hear them. In these conversations Shelley would usually be flattering her and flirting. He would draw closer and closer until the world disappeared and all that remained was his interest in her, making her feel she mattered. She told him her handwriting was awful. He said 'I'd have thought it was lovely. Show me some.' She took out a scrap of paper from her handbag and suddenly realised it had a love poem to him on it:

Shelley
I want to write poems of love,
Of absence
Of need
For you
But in a year will I still want
Will I still want
to and will I still want
you will I want you so much
so much that I do
I want to write poems of love,
Of absence,
Of need
For you.

12

'I hope so,' he said. She blushed and looked down, feeling the intensity of his eyes all over her body.

Most of the conversations were equally silly but all were very pleasurable. Occasionally he would become jealous because she was surrounded by men at a party. When he came to take her away she would slap his face. They would stare at each other furiously – like cats, backs arched, ready to pounce – then the anger in his eyes would change, he'd grab her by the arm and kiss her violently as his strong hand squeezed her arm tighter and tighter.

Her image of Shelley was not that of the gentle, persecuted angel presented by enamoured biographers such as Trelawny. She saw in Shelley something crueller, more vital.

Women were drawn to him and a few were destroyed by him. He married Mary Wollstonecraft Godwin only weeks after his first wife Harriet Westbrook drowned herself in the Serpentine. In that same year Mary's half-sister Fanny killed herself, also, it seems, for love of Shelley. Mary loved him in spite of everything, his flirtations, his love poems to other women, his selfishness.

And of course Jennifer could see why. He had wit, charm, vitality, sympathy, he was a great poet and a great and unconventional thinker. For a man like that – a breaker of laws and creator of new ones – would inspire devotion from any woman with an ounce of nerve. They didn't love him for his goodness, although they might kid themselves they did; they loved him because when they were with him they seemed to matter. He made the world dramatic, their emotions important, he transformed everything. And for a few hours of that, of seeing the world brightly, of feeling acutely, what wouldn't Jennifer do?

Jennifer was nearly sixteen now and had just taken her O levels. The idea of taking them had terrified her but once the papers were actually before her she'd found them surprisingly easy. In the week leading up to the first exam Sarah had taken her to see a doctor. Her symptoms were acute and continual headaches, refusal to eat, hands which couldn't stop shaking and tears for no apparent reason. The doctor had spoken of

13

work pressure, sensitivity, adolescence, proper diet and had prescribed tranquillisers.

She hadn't mentioned anything about Shelley to the doctor. And of course neither her mother nor her father had any idea of the clarity with which she saw Shelley. She doubted whether Edward would have thought it all that odd. He had just completed a biography of Aphra Behn, the female Restoration playwright and novelist who was every bit as outrageous as Shelley. At one point, when he was deepest in his book, he'd sometimes mutter – while watching television or reading – 'Aphra wouldn't have stood for that' or 'Aphra went there' or even 'Aphra would have enjoyed that.' Sarah became rather irritated, perhaps slightly jealous, of this Aphra who was acclaimed for her mind as well as her body. If he hadn't had Sarah, who lacked the brains but had the verve of Aphra, Jennifer imagined that Aphra might well have befriended Edward as Shelley had befriended her.

2

It was a Sunday early in July, one of those sweet-smelling summer days alive with faint breezes. The square looked its best with the sun brightening the white terraced houses and turning the detached ones into country paradises. The great plane trees which lined the square rustled their waterfalls of leaves and butterflies skimmed the flowers in the pots by the doors. A cricket match was in progress on the central green and Jennifer was trying to watch it from their first floor balcony, out of the way of her parents' visitor. But the visitor's voice was insistent. He was telling Edward what he thought of England, how charming it was and how much he liked the people.

The sky was a peaceful mediterranean blue.

Jennifer suspected that he was the man she'd seen with Sarah at the restaurant a few months before. It had all been so quick and so shocking she wasn't certain. But she was nearly certain.

14

He'd seemed slightly embarrassed when they first met, but soon got over that. His name was Saul. She couldn't understand what Sarah saw in him. He was a gargoyle. But people said women go for men's characters, not for their looks, so perhaps he had a marvellous character well concealed. It did not seem very likely to Jennifer. She had strong feelings about people, and in Saul's case her feeling was distaste.

Jennifer doubted that Sarah had invited Saul here for the sake of drama-mongering. Both Edward and Saul were writers. With her usual largesse she had probably thought they might enjoy meeting each other.

Jennifer returned to the room and sat hunched up in an armchair watching Saul and Edward blackly. She wished Sarah would finish mucking around in the kitchen and help out with the conversation. Saul and Edward were not getting on well. Saul would keep making points.

'Ed, I want to tell you something. We are all potential criminals,' said Saul. 'And that's your answer. That's why I write crime novels. I understand criminals, you know that? I really do understand criminals. Take my greatest creation, Jeff Bent. You know the books?'

'I'm awfully sorry but I can't say I do and, actually, my name's Edward.'

'What?'

'Edward as in Edward the Confessor.'

'I know that, Ed. I know your name.'

'Terribly sorry. I'm just a little sensitive about the name Ed. Sarah calls me Ed, sort of spits it out, when I'm being irritating. Sorry, do go on.'

'I was just saying that I relate to my hero Jeff Bent. And you know why? The same reason as all my fans. He's free. He fulfils himself. He does everything we'd like to do ourselves but daren't. That makes me a potential criminal, right? Because I'd like to be one.'

'Dear me, I see what you mean.'

'He doesn't give a fuck – sorry to use bad language in front of your daughter – doesn't give a fuck about anything or anybody....'

'They do well?'

'My novels? Ed, I'm a rich man. I live in Beverly Hills. My taps are made of gold. I have a maid. I have a swimming pool. I have cacti outside my window....'

'And you can actually afford to eat at my wife's restaurant.'

'Awh Ed, it's not expensive. It's cheap. I find it a terrific place to eat, Ed, I really do.'

Saul Goodman had a splayed-out nose, little lecherous eyes and a blotchy red face. The knuckles of his hands were lost in fat. Strands of greying hair loitered over his head, semicircling the shiny bald patch above his forehead. Under his chin his flesh was a poor fit. It drooped flaccidly in three tiers. He was chunky and pugnacious. He wore a short-sleeved checked shirt, beige cotton trousers and sandals. Jennifer thought he ought to have been a butcher. He had so much flesh showing.

'And why are you visiting England?'

'I'm researching my latest Jeff Bent book. He comes to England. I haven't written it yet but I've sold the film rights. Now Sarah was saying you were working on something really interesting?'

'I've just had published a book on Aphra Behn. A remarkable woman.'

'What does she get up to, Ed?'

'She's dead, actually, but she was the first English woman to live by her pen. She wrote bawdy Restoration comedies, translations, poems, political satires, even novels. Difficult book to write. She tended to fictionalise her life. But Jennifer enjoyed reading it, didn't you?'

'I loved it. I think it's probably the best thing Edward's ever written.'

Edward smiled his vague, distracted smile.

'Jennifer is my writing's greatest fan.'

'I'd really like to read it, Ed.'

'No problem about that, it's in most bookshops. I'm afraid I've run out of spare copies.'

'That's all right, Ed. I'll buy it. I really will.'

'Thank you,' said Edward.

'Sarah said you were writing something else though, something about crime?' said Saul.

Edward ran his fingers through his magnificent crop of grey hair which raced in all directions. He was tall, spindly and sprawling. His stretched-out legs revealed the colour of his socks. One was brown, the other black. Edward was exceptionally forgetful. Beneath sickle-shaped brows, gentle blue eyes blinked in an aristocratic, narrow face. He was shabbily dressed in a sports jacket, a paisley shirt fraying at the collar and corduroy trousers which were just a bit too short. Sarah had often told the story of how, during his brief career as a journalist on a local paper, an important visiting politician had been coming to see the editor. The editor was delayed and Edward sent to welcome and entertain his visitor for a few minutes. When the Rolls drew up in front of the newspaper office he ran out and, as the politician was about to get out of the car, said 'Hello, Lord Maddox, what about a cup of tea?' Lord Maddox had rifled in his pocket and given Edward a handful of coppers.

Edward's dress sense, she pointed out, had not improved much since then.

'Something about crime ... Oh *that*, I haven't even started that yet. It would be a new departure for me. Don't know whether I'll do it. History's my field. Biographies, one or two historical novels, you know the sort of thing. They sell well. I must say that always surprises me. Never thought one could actually make money from writing *books*. Writing articles, news pieces, that I understand. But not *books*.'

'Now tell me more about this crime novel of yours. There's money to be made from crime.'

Edward laughed. Saul's fat, chipmunky cheeks raised themselves in an approximation of a smile. The eyes stayed lifeless.

'Really, Ed. I would like to hear about your novel.'

'It's not a novel, actually. The idea is to write up a number of the murders which are tried at the Old Bailey in a year, this year. I'd have to do some work with newspaper cuttings and interviews to sketch out the ones that are already over. But there's one coming up soon which the chap whose idea it was, a barrister friend of mine, wants me actually to attend, and I suppose there'll be others.'

Edward, his legs out before him, stared at his shoes. The pose and the thoughtful, almost wistful, expression recalled that of Alice as she grew tall and her feet distant. Edward always seemed a long way from anyone or anything. Except, of course, Sarah.

'It sounds a good idea,' said Saul.

'Quite honestly I'm not keen. The barrister friend is though. But of course he doesn't want his name mentioned as he's the prosecutor in this forthcoming trial. I must say I'm not at all sure about the project.' Edward wrinkled his nose as if at an unpleasant smell.

'Professional assistance. Terrific.'

'Actually, I doubt if I'll do it.'

'I really am interested, Ed. It's one of the reasons Sarah introduced us, you know, to discuss our work. Perhaps I can give you some advice. I'm quite a professional when it comes to crime stories. What is this trial?'

Edward took his glasses from his pocket and started polishing them with a red handkerchief. He seldom actually wore the glasses.

'Well, it's not that exciting really,' muttered Edward, 'I'd in fact just be recording the trial of a young man charged with murdering his girlfriend.'

'How?' asked Saul, leaning towards Edward.

'How what?'

'How did he kill her?'

Edward polished more fiercely and said, 'We don't know that he did.'

'Really, is that so?'

'Yes it is, as a matter of fact.'

'Well, go on.'

The talk about the trial made Jennifer extremely uncomfortable. It gave her a kind of tingling under the skin. She had had the same sensation before.

'You don't know anything about the law,' she said.

'I told you – Geoffrey would be helping me.'

'Geoffrey is a very disagreeable man. He just thinks you might portray him flatteringly in the book.'

'I doubt if that's true,' said Edward.

'What's he like?' said Saul to Jennifer. 'Why's he so disagreeable?'

'He has shifty eyes and his skin isn't just greasy, it's covered with blackheads. What's more his voice is slimy. He oils his way through conversations. I'm always surprised he hasn't stained the sofa after he's sat there.' She smiled pleasantly at Saul.

'You do have an imagination,' observed Saul. 'Now Edward, please, tell me a little about this trial. Sarah said it was intriguing.'

'All right,' said Edward. 'A girl was stabbed in the bath and died by drowning.'

'In her own blood?' proffered Saul.

'If you like, yes. She was only eighteen, a highly talented violinist studying at the Royal Academy of Music. She was shy, very quiet and thoughtful, with fair hair and wistful eyes.'

'What was the girl's name?' said Jennifer.

'Jane. Her name was Jane Thomson. From the photograph she looked a bit like that friend of yours – Rebecca.'

'Like Rebecca?'

'Yes.'

Jennifer's clothes clung to her hotly and she could hardly breathe the humid air. The outline of the room seemed affected by a trembling haze. A bee caught between the curtains and the french window buzzed lazily and outside all was blurred, an impressionist painting. She felt very peculiar, very drowsy, unbearably sweaty, unbearably weary of it all.

Rebecca had been Jennifer's best friend at school. She'd been killed in a crash a couple of years ago, when she was only thirteen. The moment Jennifer had seen the bike on which Rebecca was to die, she had felt the tingling sensation which was running under her skin now.

'I must admit I enjoy murder trials,' Saul was saying. 'It's real excitement. Life at its most heightened. And this sounds a good story. But Sarah said something about incest … '

19

'It happens to be a real case,' said Edward, 'not a story. If you don't mind, I'd rather not discuss it any further.'

'I'm sure you'll treat it with great taste. But don't treat it with too much, Ed. Sarah said you were into a project which might make a packet and, Ed, it might just do that. I know the market; I'd go for it, Ed, I really would.'

As Saul spoke Edward did not look at him. He methodically smoothed down the arm of his velvet buttonback chair as if to comfort it, make it better.

'Thank you for the advice ... another whisky?'

'Thanks. I'd take the advice, Ed. It's a good scheme.'

'I'll mull it over a bit before I decide.'

'Right, you do that. But don't lose the chance. Make sure the barrister knows you're his man. I don't think you'd ever regret getting involved.'

'By the way, did Sarah ask you to persuade me?'

'Ed, would she do that? Of course not. But I understand. You don't want to discuss it. That's fine. If you don't want to discuss it further ...'

'I don't. But it's kind of you to show so much interest.'

Saul's glance shifted, embarrassed, from Edward out across the square. It was clipped velvet and fringed with plane trees. At the sides of the green tottered squat little children, mothers sat chatting on tartan rugs and men strode angel-white through the cricket ritual. A breeze toasted the leaves in golden sunlight, swaying them up and down and from side to side.

'I just love this square. What's going on out there?'

'They're just starting up an afternoon's cricket. It's a Burnam Old Boys match against the sixth form I believe. My old school, you know, Burnam.'

'And this match, they play one every Sunday?'

'Oh no, once or twice a year at the most.'

'You play cricket, Ed?'

'Used to. Bit out of practice now....'

'It's a quaint game. Very slow. It looks very slow. Do you think Sarah needs any help with lunch? Can I give her a hand?'

'No, I wouldn't do that. Sarah copes marvellously.'

'Of course. Do you ever help in the restaurant, er ...'

'Jennifer,' said Edward.

'Jennifer?' said Saul.

'No, I don't like it.'

'Aren't you proud to take your boyfriends along to your very own restaurant?'

'Jennifer doesn't have boyfriends.'

'And why's that? Come on now, I want you to stop staring with those lovely big eyes. I want you to tell me all about yourself.'

'I've just finished my O levels.'

'Did you flunk them?'

'Sorry?'

'Did you fail them?'

'No, I believe I did rather well.'

'Why are you looking so miserable then?'

Jennifer frowned. She didn't know whether it was a rhetorical question or not. Saul leant forward, sympathetic.

'You know, everyone gets a bit glum in adolescence. It's just a stage. Adolescents are always serious. I was. I wrote poetry.... *I* wrote poetry when I was young. Can you imagine? It was lousy of course. I'm glad to say I can now see it was lousy. At the time I thought it fantastic. Adolescents get everything all wrong, just remember that, Jenny. Take my advice. Grow up. Have boyfriends. Have fun. Get your ass out of adolescence just as quick as you can. Adolescents can't think straight.'

Jennifer was scarlet. Her lower lip stuck out childishly, as if she might cry or be rude. She did neither.

'Jennifer is academically very bright. I think she does think straight.'

'Sorry, sorry. I didn't mean to be rude about your daughter. She's cute. Just giving some advice, that's all.'

'Saul!' drawled Sarah's contralto voice, 'You're not doling out advice again?' She stood at the door, hand on hip, smiling expansively, a touch possessively, at the two men. Sarah, thought Jennifer, was a spider. She drew everyone to her and made sure they didn't escape.

Orange lipstick glistened on the broad curves of her mouth and her dark eyebrows were unkempt. To Jennifer there was

21

something unpleasantly suggestive, almost obscene, about those shaggy eyebrows. She couldn't understand why Sarah let them get like that; the rest of her appearance was completed with such care. Glossy black hair veined with the occasional white thread was piled up in a heavy bun which artfully gave height to her wide, sultry face. Sarah had radiant skin which mattressed the strong cheekbones and gave a sponginess, a flexibility, to her expressions. But it was the mouth everyone noticed. It was a Sophia Loren mouth, big and beautiful. Jennifer had a smaller version. People said it was her greatest asset. Slanting up from Sarah's eyes were slight wrinkles, the feet of crows, but the lines were hardly visible under her light but efficient foundation. Sarah's figure, like her skin, was well looked after. The breasts and hips were fulsome but not vulgar and her legs long and slim enough to allow her both grace and sexiness. She wore a fire-coloured silk shirt and black linen trousers. Although her bearing made her look tall, she was in fact of medium height, only an inch or two taller than her waifish daughter.

Sarah burst from her momentary stillness into chatter ending with the words: 'Anyway, you must all be starving. *Do* come down, Saul.'

Saul leapt eagerly to his feet. Jennifer remembered how quickly he'd moved that night at the restaurant.

They trooped downstairs, Sarah chattering all the while. The light from the chandelier transformed the yellow-ochre hall into a corridor of gold. The whole house was decorated in flamboyant colours which gave it a Florentine air. The main bedroom was scarlet, the drawing room a reddy-brown and the dining room dark pink, laden with Flemish floral paintings and four cherub wall lights. A bay window looked out over the square. Jennifer had insisted on her room remaining simple, with tiny floral wallpaper her mother despised.

In the window was an armchair from which Edward's terrier, who recently had died of old age, used to keep an eye on the street and bark at other dogs, black men and one particular roadsweeper he detested. Although the room was crammed with antiques Sarah had never objected to the terrier having the run of it. She told him not to scratch the furniture and smacked him

22

when he broke a porcelain figurine, but that was all, and soon forgotten.

A glass-fronted cabinet contained the remaining figurines – which had belonged to Edward's mother – and a complete set of Dickens which had been given to Sarah by an aunt who always gave Dickens to those she loved. Sarah believed the leather-bound set to be valuable and Edward did not have the heart to disillusion her. Sarah had never read the books but thought she had because she knew the stories from television and from her aunt. Whenever asked to name her favourite author she replied 'Dickens.' Sarah was actually a far keener fan of Harold Robbins, Jacqueline Susann and even Saul Goodman.

Jennifer sat with her back to the window facing her mother who was spooning avocado mousse on to white china plates. What would Shelley have done with this oaf Saul? Would he have teased him, ignored him, argued with him?

'Do pour the wine, darling,' said Sarah to Edward.

Jennifer poured herself some water from a flowery pitcher Sarah had discovered one Saturday morning at Pimlico market. It was slightly chipped but cost only 20p. Sarah loved a bargain.

'It's so wonderful you two could meet,' said Sarah. She passed a plate to Saul and gave him one of her flashy smiles as she stretched. Jennifer noticed the darkish ruby stain of sweat under her outstretched arm. 'I hope you've persuaded Edward.'

'Persuaded him?' said Saul.

'Oh you know, to do this crime book he's so snooty about.'

Saul lowered his eyes, embarrassed.

'Sarah I ... ' Edward's sentence finished in a sigh of hopelessness and a defeated shrug. 'I'll do it. Promise.'

'But Edward ...' said Jennifer.

'Oh *good.* I knew you'd see sense,' said Sarah. 'That's settled then.'

'It will be quietly factual, not sensational, I want to make that clear.'

'Of course, of course darling,' Sarah reassured him.

'Boy,' said Saul, 'this mousse is good. Doesn't Jenny drink?' He peered at Jennifer's glass of water with an air of trepidation, like a cat examining a saucer of milk laid down by a stranger.

23

'She neither drinks nor smokes. I try to corrupt her, God knows I try ...' said Sarah.

'My kids don't need encouragement I'm afraid. Sharon's younger than Jenny and she's out on a date every evening. She has a good life, my daughter. Knows how to live. What are you going to be when you grow up, Jenny?'

Jennifer's lips tightened angrily. She found this a patronising, infuriating and obliterating question. It suggested that only her adult life mattered, that at present she was a nothing, a mere foetus sucking its thumb. She replied, as always, that she didn't know. Another equally frequent question was the hobby one. But people didn't seem interested in her replies. They were merely, so they thought, being polite. If she'd said her hobby was poisoning they'd probably just have nodded their heads, taken another sip of gin and turned their glazed eyes elsewhere.

'*I'll* tell you,' said Sarah, 'Unless something radical happens she'll end up a fusty academic bicycling from some dingy Oxford college to some even dingier library.' With that, Sarah spooned the last morsel of mousse into her mouth as though that were her final statement on the matter.

'I can think of worse fates,' said Edward.

'Edward was educated at Oxford,' explained Sarah, 'It's where we met. I was on a secretarial course.'

Jennifer's head was bowed over her food but she knew Saul was watching her. Her mother's lover was watching her. She wondered what he was thinking. Jennifer was overcome by self-consciousness. She shifted uneasily in her chair.

'The academic life is no life for a girl,' announced Saul, 'Especially a girl as cute as your daughter. You know, Jenny, you must decide what you want, what's best for *you*, then you must go all out and get it. Don't betray the self. Enjoy yourself. Get in touch with your feelings. You have a right to happiness. It's the human birthright. Take it.'

Saul's face was filling out Jennifer's vision as if it were being pumped with air. What shocked her was that this man's views were not really so different from Shelley's. They might even have got on rather well. He was leaning at her again. She shrank back and remembered the fat young man at a party who had

24

tried to kiss her with his horrible slobbery lips and his breath stinking of beer. The smell of beer had seeped from the walls of the rooms where girls and boys snogged. Red crepe paper had covered the light bulbs to give out a sexy pink light. Her friends had called her a prude because she'd only talk to the boys and wouldn't allow any to touch her. She had left early, alone and by taxi to the station, although more than one boy had offered to drive her home. But Jennifer hadn't liked any of them. They either seemed to erupt with spots or with confident leers. Unlike Shelley. The parties were so degrading, so different from the 'grown-up' parties she'd imagined when younger, so much less sparkling and intelligent than the gatherings at which Aphra Behn had charmed, back in the colourful days of the Restoration.

'Shall we have the next course, darling?' said Edward. He watched Sarah collect the plates and carry them out.

'You do see what I mean though, about Jenny, Ed? I'm talking about freedom. Happiness. The freedom of the individual. She must grab what she wants when she wants it. I'm free, and look where it's got me. I'll tell you where it's got me – to the top!' He jerked the butter knife upwards into the air.

'Quite,' said Edward coldly. 'This looks delicious, darling.'

Before long Saul had the tomatoey remains of paella round his lips. Vampire mouth, thought Jennifer. His looks and manners made her discount everything he said. Edward listened attentively to Saul. The chill in his voice and in his eyes made it clear that he found his opinions as disgusting as his personality. The sun was searing through the window behind her and sweat dribbled down her spine and from her armpits.

Now Saul was watching Sarah. He was staring at her with absorption. The look of someone sticking valuable stamps in an album, gloating and intense and careful. His balding patch gleamed like the dome of a mosque in the midday sun.

Soon Jennifer excused herself, received a leery handshake from Saul and went up to her room at the top of the house. She washed her hands and dried them on the white towel which hung over the aluminium rail of her bathroom.

'That man Saul is a monster,' she confided to Shelley who was

25

slouched in the chair by her desk, his hair wild and eyes bright in his feminine face. As usual he was dressed in a dark suit and high white collar.

3

Jennifer sat down beside Shelley at her pale green desk. He was in one of his silent moods but his presence made her skin feel warm. The desk had golden lion-paw feet and was decorated with pagodas, black streams and Chinese women holding parasols. She wrote the name APHRA BEHN on blotting paper and watched the letters blur.

'You'd have liked her, I think,' said Jennifer. For the umpteenth time she picked up her father's biography of Aphra. She read out loud the dust-jacket:

'This is the extraordinary story of a Kentish yeoman's daughter who, by the force of her daring and personality, dazzled the wits of the Restoration and became the first Englishwoman ever to earn a living by writing. Verses, novels, plays, poured from her pungent, bawdy pen. Before enlivening the London stages with her comedies she had been a darling of the court, a spy in the service of Charles II and a prisoner at Newgate. The name of Mrs Behn was notorious. She had numerous lovers, opinions that would shock today, and friends both disreputable and famous including Rochester, Otway and Dryden. But she had her tender, generous side, well-documented by her love letters to the rakish John Hoyle. Love, sex, marriage are the themes which run through her work, amply quoted and assessed by the biographer and expert on the Restoration period, Edward A. Hamilton. To read this is to meet a woman who didn't dilly-dally in the shallow end of life but dived headlong into the pain and the pleasure.'

Certain phrases had kept nagging at her since she'd first read the blurb – 'dived headlong into the pain and the pleasure'

... 'the force of her daring and personality' ... 'but she had her tender, generous side.'

'Compared with me,' said Jennifer to Shelley, 'She was a very vivacious character.'

Jennifer knew she inhabited the shadows of life. From there she dreamed, thought, and observed the bright figures out in the sunlight. Her mother, the gaudier girls at school, the inhabitants of the square and their gossip, all intrigued her. But they existed at one remove from her. They were the actors, she was the audience, endlessly sitting in passive greyness while everything happened before her, nothing to her.

Her school friends rushed eagerly up to perform in the show. With hardly a blush one had got engaged, another an abortion, a third had left to become a model, another decided on a career, plenty had boyfriends and a few smoked in out-of-bounds coffee bars at lunchtime. They made life look so easy. In a way she envied them their breezy approach to decisions which would have had her in a turmoil.

As a child Jennifer had been dreamy. She had suffered from anti-school tummy aches every term-time morning and from excruciating shyness justified by a stutter, losing her way to prep school and to classes, wearing odd socks and occasionally forgetting to wear pants so the school chairs felt cold on her bare bottom and she feared a gust of wind or a jocular friend lifting up her skirt. She retreated into a marvellous imaginary world where she always played the star part and was never shy.

At night when she couldn't sleep she became a gipsy who only pretended to be crippled. Beneath her fairground tent where she lay in bed was an underground labyrinth of computers enabling her to listen in on any conversation in the world, buttons which if pressed would blow up whole countries, others to assassinate anyone she chose, potions which gave immortal life, others which gave a lingering death. From here she rearranged the futures of her clients for better or worse.

In childhood it had been easy to be significant. For one thing, she'd been sure no one else existed. She remembered walking from the kitchen of their former house into the breakfast room where her mother sat at a formica table spread with papers. Under the table were the blue crayon marks she had scribbled when she was tiny and the table huge. On the wall above was a glass-fronted box of bells marked dining room, drawing room, first bedroom ... bells which rang for servants in the old days. She stood in front of the table. The window was black with night.

'Mummy,' she said softly. Her mother looked up.

'Please darling, do stop calling me Mummy. My name is Sarah.'

'Sarah,' she continued, 'Promise you'll answer my question truthfully?'

'Of course I will, darling. Now what is it? I'm getting into such a muddle with these accounts.'

'Cross your heart and hope to die if you lie?'

Her mother crossed her heart.

'It's just that, well, when I can't see you do you vanish? Do you disappear when I leave the room?'

Her mother smiled. Or maybe she didn't smile but she seemed kind and understanding.

'No, Jennifer darling, I don't disappear. We all remain, we all continue living, even though you can't see us.'

'Really?'

'Really.'

She opened the varnished pine door which led to the back stairs, once servants' stairs, and closed it on her mother. She thumped up the stairs and then tiptoed down and, holding her breath, quickly pushed open the door and, sure enough, her mother hadn't vanished. But Jennifer had still not been convinced.

Jennifer used sometimes to flounce round the house in a black gipsy skirt twirling with coloured specks. Her father laughed at her admiringly. He often teased her about her dressing-up games.

Edward seldom teased or admired Jennifer nowadays. He hadn't even remarked on the dramatic change in her appearance since the storm of spots, which had volcanoed over her face since the onset of puberty had calmed down. She had been a pretty child but a plain adolescent. Now she didn't know what she was.

At school the girls hardly bothered with her because she was so strange and aloof. The teachers, however, made much of her academic excellence.

It was Jennifer's friendship with one girl, Rebecca, which had helped to dislocate her from normality, but it was also a sadness that the infinite possibilities of childhood had gone. She could no longer be whoever she pleased. Time had sneaked off with all the chandeliers, the magic rings, the gipsy, the dancer, the mountain-tops, the caves under the bed and left her just herself.

Rebecca drew beautifully because she noticed everything around her. If asked what colour were trees she'd never have said green. Sometimes she'd skip lessons and sit out by herself in the garden behind the playgrounds just staring at the flowers and trees. Occasionally Jennifer would join her. Once she found her staring at a rose bush.

'That yellow rose is an Indian dancer, don't you see?' Rebecca said. 'The leaves curl out like hands, graceful, dancing but not stirring. And the petals aren't just yellow. They're pink merging with gold. So soft and shadowy.'

There was a dreamy look in Rebecca's green eyes. Her head on one side, she was like Hans Andersen's Little Mermaid watching a ship at sea, longing for something out of reach.

'Such perfect beauty,' she said.

Rebecca couldn't draw people, only flowers, trees, plants, pebbles. She didn't understand people, liked them all, trusted everyone. Her drawings couldn't catch likenesses because she was blind to imperfections. To her the whole world was joyous, still but moving.

But one Saturday, a few weeks before she left the school, Rebbeca seemed sad as they walked on the local Common together. The trees were daubed with the colours of autumn and the ground underneath was a wonderful mush of pinks, coppers, yellows and browns.

'What's the matter?' said Jennifer.

'Oh nothing. Just me.'

'There's nothing wrong with you.'

'There is. I'm so stupid. I don't understand people. I don't even understand literature. I enjoy it, I don't understand it.

'That's because you're innocent. I wish I was more like you.'

'You don't. I'm just blind. Melinda said Valerie's desperately jealous of my drawing. I never noticed. There's something else too ...'

Rebecca was walking with her head, as usual, in the air. Her hair was tied tightly back off her face and her long nose protruded. She was a pre-Raphaelite beauty with a mane of hair and a pure pale skin. The drab school uniform and grey socks looked good on her and today, even in clumpy lace-up shoes and baggy jeans, she was exquisite. Rebecca, like Jennifer, never wore make-up.

'I'm not interested in men. Everyone talks about them but I've never been interested in them in the least.'

'I'm not either.'

'Everyone has boyfriends, they talk about them all the time, and I haven't even had periods.'

Rebecca's cheeks turned ruddy when she mentioned the word 'period'.

'I haven't either. And I haven't a boyfriend and don't want one. And lots of people don't have periods until they're fourteen or even fifteen. Don't worry.'

'I'm flat chested. You're not.'

'Rebecca!'

Rebecca used to show Jennifer poetry, written in beautiful black italic script. It always described objects and places, never emotions. A pond was pea-green soup, a pebble was varnished with rain. . . . They were like Japanese poems, pinpointing and celebrating one moment.

One day Rebecca was given a fold-up bike to ride to and from school. She painted it bright yellow. The bike filled Jennifer with unease. She thought the unease was because Rebecca had no traffic sense. She'd wander straight across roads looking neither left nor right, detonating an explosion of angry horns. Jennifer doubted she'd be much more sensible on a bike. The thought of Rebecca on the bike gave her a sense of panic: her palms sweated and her heart beat fast. There was a tingling under her skin.

'Why don't you come by bus if you're tired of walking? Buses are great fun if you sit on top.'

'I have been on buses.'

Rebecca had moved with her family to Leicester two years ago, when they were both thirteen. Jennifer missed her very much. She wrote to Jennifer twice a week for a month and then, one Saturday morning, Jennifer had a phone call.

'Hello, Jennifer?'

'Yes?'

'It's Rebecca's father. Rebecca had an accident yesterday. She was knocked off her bike by a lorry. She was unconscious until she died two and a half hours later in hospital.'

'Oh God.'

'She'd written to you recently?'

'Yes.'

'We thought so.' And there was something accusing in his voice. 'Could we have the letter please, do you think? There's so little left of her.'

'You do mean Rebecca *Morrison*?'

'Yes, my daughter,' he said. 'The funeral's next Thursday in Leicester at East's crematorium, at three pm.'

'I can't believe it. I'm so sorry. Terribly sorry,' said Jennifer.

'We all are. I must go,' and as he put down the phone he left Jennifer with only the picture of Rebecca lying by the roadside, bleeding, which blew itself up in her mind to poster size, a poster which she swore would hang by every bed she slept in, every desk she worked at, for the rest of her life. A terrible silence swept through her until her mother called from downstairs 'Would you like to go shopping?' and it seemed incredible that lives should continue jogging along while Rebecca's had stopped. Rebecca had had such hopes and none of them fulfilled. She was hoping to go to Cambridge and then become an archaeologist. Rebecca was a potential revolutionary: she could have changed some part of the world because she really wasn't like others were.

Rebecca's death turned the faces of passers-by into skulls covered with a thin layer of skin. Jennifer felt herself dying every moment, dead any moment, inconsequential.

She realised her parents had lied by omission all these years. They had presented a world without death and now that

Rebecca had died that world, the one she had trusted, was shattered.

Every time she went to the lavatory she was disgusted. The sight of her mother, with grease on her chin, chewing a chicken bone like a jackal nauseated her. Her own hunger pains and mouth-watering when the smell of meat permeated the house infuriated her. Most of all she detested having the periods which, perversely, had just started. They confirmed her helplessness, the fact that she was a slave to the inevitability of growing up, having babies and dying. Rebecca's death had concertinaed Jennifer's life, brought her up sharp against the blackness. Jennifer, at thirteen, had begun to dread the future.

Rebecca's mother's blotchy face and stifled sobs at the horrid modern chapel, the father's bowed and silent head in prayer, had been miles away from her as she sat behind them at the cremation. On the bunches of flowers and wreaths were cards to Rebecca. She thought it odd that people should send cards to a dead person. But then everything seemed odd now. She stood at the roadside as she looked out of the enormous glossy car and watched it and her own pale, black-dressed self go by. Everyone, including herself, was suddenly so tiny.

It was after this that Jennifer had become obsessed by the distant past.

From the shadows of the present she could watch heroic figures strutting through their lives, affecting the future, fighting against tradition. Her father was right: compared to this the present was dull stuff. What's more the past couldn't murder your best friend, couldn't hurt you, couldn't grab you by the arm and try to kiss you or tell you to write a crummy book on a sordid trial. But sometimes, just sometimes, when she imagined so hard that she could almost hear the fluttering of fans, the laughter of flirting courtiers and the brilliant talk of her heroes, she wanted to be part of it all and not apart from it all. She wanted to be important, take part in important events, have important emotions, be something more than an animal. She wanted to dance in the arms of Charles II, inspire Shelley and be herself a witty, inventive figure as Aphra Behn had been.

On the wall by her desk she had sellotaped a postcard of sloe-eyed, boyish Shelley, his face pale amid a whirl of hair.

The space round it was plastered with other pictures of the dead: a death-mask of Shelley, cut out of a colour supplement, a drawing of the haggard Branwell Brontë, a photo of Ivan the Terrible from the film, pictures of Rasputin, a monkish profile of Virginia Woolf, the mad John Clare and the Brontë sisters.

More than once Sarah had remarked anxiously on the contrast between the pictures Jennifer had on her wall and the photos of pop stars, rows of make-up and piles of magazines she had seen in the bedrooms of some of her friends' daughters.

On Jennifer's desk was her father's biography of Aphra Behn, Shelley's poems and letters bound in flaky brown leather, Trelawny's *Recollections*, and a 1724 edition of Aphra's plays. Its rough paper was tobacco yellow and the words hard to read, but Jennifer enjoyed the struggle. It concentrated her mind.

Many of the front covers bore an egg-shaped label marked 'London Library, St James's Square, SW1'. On her fifteenth birthday her father had bought her a life-membership of the library and every month or so she went there and returned with a hefty basket of books. She liked the atmosphere. It was like a graveyard; peaceful and with rows and rows of monuments to the dead. The books looked musty and drab but when you opened them up their dead creators jumped out merrily, wrily, passionately, wisely, alive. Everyone in the library – from the young scholars to wealthy retired men – seemed to have left the traffic of Piccadilly far behind. In the silence it was they who were wraiths, neither in life nor out of it, while the dead ruled over this small portion of the world.

The death of Rebecca had shown her that death could easily one day squash her flat. What was the point of huffing and puffing through life just for nothing at the end of it? An eternity of nothing.

That fear, of eternity, was reflected in many minor fears. She dreaded travelling on the underground in case she got off at the wrong stop, was pushed against by a man, stepped on toes, couldn't work the ticket machines, was approached by a drunkard, lost her ticket or was noticed reading the back of someone's newspaper. While other girls marched up to counters and demanded a packet of Tampax, Jennifer would spend long minutes outside a chemist's shop arranging her features into confident ones and working out how she'd put her demand. Even then her sentence would come out mangled by shyness. She hated the thought of everyone staring.

Going out, growing up, growing old began to frighten her in a way it never had before. But she was nearly sixteen, in the mid, stultifying seventies and everything – parents, friends, teachers, clocks, newspapers, even the air – seemed to press in on her, crush her, force her into the future, mould breasts and hips out of former puppy fat, oppress her with period pains, treat her as victim not heroine.

Childhood had been spacious not just because she was small while everything else was big. There had been room to grow in, a sense that she could expand into whatever shape she pleased. There had also been space to dream, to play a hundred parts, and there was time. A year was for ever and a summer holiday only slightly shorter.

4

'Can I see your notes?' asked Jennifer. She had knocked on Edward's study door. Saul and Sarah appeared to have gone out. 'Your notes on the case?'

'Why?'

'I don't know. That girl.'

'I know. It upset me.'

He took the notes out of the top drawer of his mahogany desk. As he closed it petals fell from the overblown roses on its leather top. The study smelt of roses and tobacco. The curtains were half-drawn, making the room dark although outside it was light.

'There are quite a few. You're more involved than you say.' The notes were in brown ink on thick white paper.

'They're based on the committal proceedings. And Geoffrey's

account. And my imagination. Some bits are a bit personal ... '
He leafed through, 'I think I go into why I'm attracted to
women like Lucinda and Aphra ... but it doesn't matter. Take
them away, please. I must get on.'

Jennifer took them to her room. But at first she couldn't bring
herself to read them. She turned her thoughts away from the
trial, back to Shelley. When she was lonely and worried and not
at home in herself, in her home, she needed Shelley most. He
was, she felt, her other half, her brother born in the wrong time,
and only with him could she feel whole.

She imagined him, books under his arm, waiting in the
cloister at Eton to go into the upper school for supper. Boys
buzzed like black flies, shoving, whispering, chatting, while he
stood a little apart, leaning on a pillar and watching the rain
drum down in the courtyard. In his small head he had
bush-baby eyes, brown seas of thought, and his mouth was
sensitive and feminine. While most of the other boys stood
square or tall, Shelley's shoulders stooped and hair curled. A
burly lout with a spreadeagled nose pushed his way to the pillar
facing Shelley and leant against it, fixing him with rude, staring,
sneering eyes. Shelley's lips curled disdainfully. The lout
reddened and walked bulkily towards Shelley. With one swipe
of his hand he knocked Shelley's books out into the courtyard.
The boys crowded round, craning their necks and laughing. If
she'd been there she'd have fought them. Shelley hurried over to
the books, head forward like a battering ram. It was raining
hard and his books lay muddy and soggy. Shelley crouched by
them, the rain straggling his hair into rats' tails, and a large shoe
kicked the books from his grasp. Shelley looked up and saw the
grinning red face of the bully above him.

From the cloisters came a shout of 'Shelley, mad Shelley' and
the cry was taken up until the courtyard echoed thunderously.
Shelley slowly stood up shivering, his hands clenched white as
he watched the many-headed crowd of boys, jeering, shouting
and pointing at him.

He'd shown them all in the end. Shelley had not been
destroyed by suffering, he'd turned his oddness into genius, his
isolation into glorious freedom, his unpopularity into fame. He

was a great man, and like so many of the great, he had had an unhappy childhood. She too had an unhappy, imaginative childhood. He was like her, he would have understood her sadness, her love of solitude. After Rebecca had died Shelley's poem to Keats, *Adonais,* had comforted her. She remembered the lines now that she cherished most:

> Peace, peace! he is not dead, he doth not sleep –
> He hath awakened from the dream of life –
> Tis we, who lost in stormy visions, keep
> With phantoms an unprofitable strife,
> And in mad trance, strike with our spirit's knife
> Invulnerable nothings. . . .

> He lives, he wakes – 'tis Death is dead, not he;
> Mourn not for Adonais.

She could feel Shelley with her, standing over her, breathing softly, smelling somehow of the sea, as she made herself read.

ROUGH NOTES ON THE TRIAL OF CHARLES GRIGSON

Main protagonists: Charles Grigson, accused. Jane Thomson, murdered. Others of interest: Lucinda, Charles's half-sister. Jane's friends and relations.

Charles Grigson is a tall, handsome chap of about thirty. His great round arms are packed with muscle and he has a shiny, cheery face. Habitually he wears plimsolls, corduroy trousers and tatty shirts or T-shirts. He's an architect who does a spot of teaching at the Architectural Association. People who know him, like him. They say he is a decent and merry young man, if rather scruffy. He lives in a house in Stoke Newington with his half-sister Lucinda and spends his spare time either gardening their huge and wild garden, reading Anthony Trollope, playing all manner of sports or mending his motor bike. His father died soon after Charles was born, his mother married again, and Lucinda is the child of the second marriage. Their mother had only one child from each marriage – Charles and Lucinda. His father was a commercial artist, his mother is a rather successful dress designer. His stepfather, Lucinda's father, is a psychiatrist. Lucinda cooks directors' lunches for a living. She is high-spirited, vivacious and outrageously extravagant.

When I was waiting for Geoffrey outside the Old Bailey a week or so ago there was a girl waiting too. She was leaning against the wall and humming quietly. She was tall and dark and had a wild tousle of urchin-like hair which she kept pushing from her face to no avail. Her white dress was dotted with blue spots and had a shiny belt round the waist which matched her navy stockings. She was meticulously scruffy. Her shoes looked very expensive. I couldn't stop watching her. She was one of those people who demand attention wherever they go. Her straw basket was full of books, yogurts and vegetables.

One foot rested against the wall in a model-girl pose. Then she changed to the other foot. Perhaps it was not so much her beauty but her restlessness which made her so entrancing. She looked as though she'd run round the block any minute, she had such pent-up energy.

When Geoffrey came out of the doors the girl was beside him, holding his arm, in a few seconds. She was staring at him beseechingly. Geoffrey was shaking his head. But from the way his eyes were on her I could see he found her attractive. Perhaps a mixture of irritation and attraction. I pretended to read my *Evening Standard* as though I hadn't seen him. They were an odd sight: the wide, greasy-haired Geoffrey with this tall beauty towering above him, while the courts disgorged workers and visitors all around. His face was set firm, lips pursed, and so were hers. She even stamped her foot at one point. Finally she scowled – there is no other word for it – and for a second I thought she was going to stick out her tongue. Instead she swung round and flounced off down the street with her head in the air.

Geoffrey shambled over to me.

'Damn that wretched girl,' he said. 'Did you see her? Causing a scene right outside the court. How dare she? It really is the limit.' His face was puffed up red, disgruntled. I asked him who it was, and he told me it was Lucinda Brown. It was then that I first became interested in writing about the trial of the lovely creature's half-brother. Geoffrey had mentioned the idea to me before, but it had bored me.

'She is such a nuisance,' he continued, waddling along the pavement. I hailed a taxi. Geoffrey is the kind of person who doesn't seem right on a pavement, walking. He might at any moment be overcome by the heat or exhaustion or a heart attack. And anyway, he's too self-important not to be in a taxi or a car. 'She's a terrible girl, terrible. Keeps trying to see me. Sends letters as well. She insists that her brother's story is true, that it must have been a burglar who killed Jane. She claims Charles could never kill anyone.'

'Where was she when the girl was killed?'

'Oh, she has a reasonable alibi. She was with some boyfriend all morning. My God, she's determined though. My wife said she actually came round one afternoon demanding to see me. Fortunately I was out. Can you imagine? Aemilia was scared stiff of her but also very concerned. The girl seemed so upset, she kept saying. You know how Aemilia repeats herself?'

'I hadn't noticed.'

'Lucinda is a very tiresome girl, though I admit she does have a certain charm.' And a rather dreamy look infiltrated his small eyes.

The incident disturbed me. I wonder why I am drawn to women like her. Is it because they provide the life that I lack? Their energy and zest. We pale thinkers on the edge of things love colour. Arthur Miller loved Marilyn Monroe. But I wonder if they are good for us. Moths throwing ourselves against the light.

But Charles doesn't *seem* burnt up by Lucinda. He seems as independent as she is. Their mother and her second husband live in a large flat in Wimpole Street. They are always busy meeting designers, artists, etc. Lucinda visits them frequently but Charles has no time for them, says they're absurd caricatures, social butterflies. He despises the psychiatry of his stepfather and the vast fees he charges. Living with his stepfather constantly analysing everything maddened him. Lucinda enjoyed it. Apparently she can't even get hungry nowadays without analysing why she's hungry. I suppose with that to cope with, it's no wonder Charles was attracted to the simple grace of Jane. But men like Lucinda because she analyses other people just as closely as herself. She concentrates utterly on their problems, often even suggesting solutions. She believes very much that people should fulfil themselves, learn to live with what they are, not crush themselves under the weight of convention. Rather like Jennifer's beloved Shelley. How long will it take this generation to see the limits of Sixties' Romanticism? She's always advising people to leave their wives, move countries, move jobs. Geoffrey has talked to her a number of times, although of course not about the trial, and he says she's immensely attractive but very disruptive indeed. She advised him to leave his wife, poor Aemilia. She said she sounded stultifying. But what about Aemilia?

Geoffrey actually seems quite taken with the demoniac Lucinda! Jane Thomson was a much quieter, more reclusive figure. Perhaps Charles was drawn to her because of this quietness. He himself is undoubtedly an extrovert although not without, Geoffrey says, a degree of thoughtfulness. I can't imagine Lucinda putting up with his burying his nose in Trollope for long. Jane has had a number of boyfriends in the past, and not surprisingly. In the picture I saw, her wistful expression and thick fair hair made her look like a fairy princess up in the castle tower, trapped in a dream, out of reach. Her parents are wealthy farmers up in Lancashire. They gave her quite a decent weekly income, they were so proud of her having won a scholarship to the Royal Academy. Come to think of it, violin music – so plaintive – expresses something of her quality, a yearning, an innocence and a sadness. Like that girl Rebecca, Jennifer's friend. Terrible to have those limbs emblazoned with blood.

So, to sketch out what is thought by the police and by Geoffrey (prosecuting) to have happened:

Lucinda and Charles are devoted to each other. Charles has an affair with the quite wealthy Jane. Lucinda is very extravagant. She buys shirts for £80, dresses for £100, although she only earns about £70 a week and her parents give her no money. They bought the house for Charles and Lucinda, and consider that's quite sufficient. Lucinda often has boyfriends who buy her presents but in the last few months before the murder hadn't had one, and therefore asked Charles for money. He kept borrowing from Jane and lending it to Lucinda who swore she was lending it to a dear friend who would repay. Of course, she was just spending it. But Charles could deny his darling Lucinda nothing. Eventually Jane discovered – or thought she'd discovered – that Charles and Lucinda were having an incestuous affair and it was this that prompted her to write Charles the letter. He received it in Birmingham while he was at an architectural conference. It brought him back to London at once. Lucinda swears she did not tell Jane but it seems likely that she did. Charles and Lucinda of course deny this incestuous 'affair'.

Charles received the note on Wednesday morning at his hotel in Birmingham. It was waiting for him at reception and he took it to read over breakfast. It was eight am, and he sat in the garish dining room overlooking the car park at the long table reserved for the party of architects. Waiters bustled around, piling plates, rumpled napkins and butter-smeared knives on to their trays. There were one or two others sitting at the table. He chose to ignore them. He ordered cornflakes and toast. He was nervous of opening the letter. He knew by the writing that it was from Jane and he had been quarrelling rather frequently with her recently. She wanted him to marry her and he didn't wish to. I presume he thought he was happy with the position as it was, living in Stoke Newington with Lucinda and Jane living in her rented Knightsbridge flat. He did not wish to be married yet. He enjoyed being free. Why did she always have to be so serious? He opened the letter. This is what it said:

Dearest Charles,

When I was an adolescent I wasn't searching for permanence. It never crossed my mind to ask myself whether or not a relationship would last. But it does now. Now I want more than a few weeks of love-making, I want love. If you can't give me the commitment of marriage I'm

40

not interested. We argued about marriage before you went away and now I see why you seemed so against it.

Your sister and you are having an incestuous relationship, aren't you? She told me. I met her today, in Harrods. I warn you – and I can hardly believe I'm writing this, but I am, and I mean it – I am going to tell your parents about it. Unless something is done soon this affair will ruin both your lives. I'm sorry.

Lastly, please, I should like the money you owe me returned or else I shall call the police. She told me about that too, how you gave it all to her. It's over £1,000 now and I need it. I plan to go on a holiday to take me far away from you. I must have it by the end of the week.

I mean all this, you know, Charles, darling. Don't think I won't keep my word.

Why do people fall for each other, what trick of the tongue or heart wins the game? If some remark were left unsaid, would lives be changed? If an intonation were different?

All my love,
Jane.

Jennifer stopped reading. She was remembering Rebecca again. The tone of that letter. The sweetness. How can such people die so dreadfully? She found her lips were trembling. What happened to them, she wondered, and recalled what Mary Shelley had written after her husband's death. 'We have lost him – not, I fondly hope, for ever; his unearthly and elevated nature is a pledge of the continuation of his being, although in an altered form.' She read on:

Charles never ate his cornflakes. He phoned Jane and received no reply. He left a note at reception for the organiser of the conference, saying he was unavoidably called away, packed his bag and drove on his motor bike back to London. As he rode faster and faster through the haze of the countryside he discovered he was becoming more and more angry and worried. How dare she threaten him? What would his parents say?

Would she really dare phone the police? He had been kind to her – even loved her – it was cruel of her to treat him like this. He felt indignant. Nearer London, the traffic was bad. He was stuck in a jam. He hated Jane.

He arrived outside her Victorian block of flats just behind Harrods. He parked his bike. He hurried into the stone-flagged entrance hall and up the stairs, two at a time, until he came to the second floor. He knocked at her door. There was no reply. He could hear the radio playing. He unlocked the door with his own key and entered the main room, where the dining table held the remains of breakfast including half a loaf of bread with a large knife beside it. It was an elegant flat, meticulously tidy. The carpet was a rich blue and the walls a pale yellow. The bathroom led off from this main room. The door was open. The music – Stravinsky – was playing loudly. 'Jane … it's me ..,' where are you?' 'Get out,' she yelled. 'Just get out of here. Get back to that little whore of yours. Get back to your sister.' Suddenly something turned his stomach over, curdled his mind with fury, he picked up the bread knife and walked into the bathroom. Jane was lying there in the bath, her back to him. If he'd seen her face it may never have happened. He stabbed her. Again and again. She was screaming. Suddenly she wasn't screaming. He was holding the knife in his hand. He wiped the knife clean and hid it behind the long curtain in the bathroom. He stood there, looking down at all the blood and the poor girl. The whole of his insides seemed to be sinking away with horror as the blood gushed.

He walked slowly to the phone and called the ambulance and then the police. He waited.

When they arrived he denied he had killed her. He said she was like this when he arrived. He has stuck to this story …

The doorbell rang. After a minute or so it rang again, for longer. Jennifer was shaken by what she had read, by what Edward's imagination had invented. But she didn't quite trust it. Rebecca would never have called anyone's sister 'a little whore'. She would never have been coarse or in any way verbally exasperating enough to provoke murder. And would this girl Jane, who

42

seemed so like Rebecca? She wondered how often Shelley had gone over in his mind the suicide of his wife Harriet, at night in the Serpentine, or of Fanny – Mary's half-sister – who took an overdose of opium in a small upper room of a Swansea hotel. Had those deaths preyed upon his mind, as Rebecca's preyed upon hers, as even Shelley's own death distressed her?

Again the doorbell rang.

5

Jennifer opened her door. The house was silent. She hurried downstairs in time to see the lanky figure of her father skulking down the corridor towards his study.

'Oh, Edward,' said Jennifer, 'Why don't you answer the doorbell when it rings?'

He turned, put his finger to his lips conspiratorially and whispered 'Shh. It's Aemilia Robertson. I saw. Out of the front window.'

The bell rang again.

'We'll have to let her in.'

'Oh dear. Well don't leave me alone with her, that's all.' He nervously jingled the change in his pockets.

'All right,' said Jennifer, walking to the door. 'Where are Sarah and Saul?'

'At the Tate Gallery.'

Jennifer opened the door.

'Hello,' said Aemilia. She was in her early forties with far apart eyes set in magnolia skin. She wore a smocked dress and a pale pink smile. 'Is your father in? I have a book, you see, to give him ...'

'Hello Mrs Robertson. Yes, he's in. Do come in.'

'Thank you. Well, just for a minute, but I know how ... Put it this way, he is very busy isn't he?'

'Sorry if you've been waiting long.'

'Oh no, not at all.'

'Edward,' shouted Jennifer, 'It's Aemilia Robertson.'

On cue, Edward came striding down the corridor with his arm outstretched. Aemilia put down her carrier bag to free the right hand at which Edward's body appeared to be aiming. He shook her small hand vigorously.

'How marvellous to see you.' He looked at his watch. 'Do you want some tea?'

'I ... I ... Yes please.'

'Right, I'll make it. Jennifer, you take Aemilia upstairs, will you?'

Aemilia bent down to the carrier bag and took out a legal tome.

'Edward ... I came to bring the book. Geoffrey was going to come with it but I said I would, you see.'

'Terribly kind of you. Now you two sit down upstairs and I'll bring you the tea in a minute.'

'Oh, thank you. But can I help?'

'Wouldn't hear of it,' said Edward.

The ceiling of the drawing room was high and the tall french windows gazing out on the square were draped in creamy silk curtains with brown stripes. Round the top of the walls a cornice of flowers and fruit patterned its way. Dutch still-lifes, vigorous modern paintings, pastoral scenes poised elegantly on the walls and a gold carpet floated on a sea of honey parquet. Edward's graceful little piano stood apart·from the chairs and sofa gathered, as if in admiration, round the carpet. When Jennifer was alone the room seemed gentle, but the presence of guests or her mother hardened its outlines, made the corners of the mantelshelf sharp, the piano spindly, the chairs uncomfortable and the reddy-brown walls oppressive.

'Your mother really does have a way with colour,' said Aemilia dubiously.

'She's always telling me that one should never be afraid of it.'

'Quite. Jennifer, tell me, how are you?'

'Very well, thank you.'

'Are you really? Your mother was saying you seem awfully depressed, you see.'

'Oh was she? She thinks studying is being depressed, that's all.'

44

'I wish I was working. I get so bored.'

Aemilia was forty-two and had been married to Geoffrey for twelve years. They had no children. Geoffrey blamed her for everything. He shouted at her if he couldn't find his car keys, if there was a gas leak, if the phone stopped ringing before he picked it up. After a nervous breakdown five years ago, she had given up her work as a speech therapist. He used to jeer at her job, and complain when she wasn't at home on his return from work. But as soon as she gave it up, he jeered at her for not working and complained that she was always at home and anyway what did she do all day? Did she just spend his money? Why couldn't she get a job like other women?

'Oh dear. I'm sorry you get bored,' said Jennifer.

'It doesn't matter much, I suppose. One just has to make the best of things.'

'I don't really see why,' muttered Jennifer.

Aemilia was fiddling with her handkerchief, tugging and kneading and rolling it nervously. 'You're young, of course, you don't know. But you are right. Quite right, of course.'

Edward stumbled into the room, nearly dropping his tea tray. Aemilia hovered somewhere between sitting and standing. Jennifer took the tray from him and poured out the tea.

'Well, how are you, Aemilia?' said Edward, lounging back in the sofa with his hands behind his head.

She sighed. 'Very tired. I've been house-hunting all last week, you see.'

'But you house-hunt every week.'

Aemilia's head nodded slowly. Everything about Aemilia – the disconnected way she spoke, her vague movements, the dreaminess in her soft face – was wistful and resigned.

'It's true. I've been house-hunting most days for two years now. Nothing's ever right. Do you find that?'

'Actually we saw this place and bought the lease just like that. It was so much nicer than our place in Wimbledon.'

'That's the problem. Our house is nicer than the ones I visit. If I do find something better it's terribly, terribly expensive.'

'You could stay where you are,' suggested Jennifer.

'Ah yes. But, well, I like looking at other people's houses. One

45

afternoon last week I viewed a house in Belgrave Square. A party was still going on from the night before. I had a lovely time. They gave me champagne, you see. I came home quite tipsy ... Geoffrey was absolutely furious.'

Edward scratched the side of his nose. 'And of course I suppose it's a good idea to keep an eye on the market.'

'Yes, I suppose so ... only I'm not sure if Geoffrey really wants to move. Or if I do, in fact.' She smiled to herself. 'It's just that – as you know – I'm just not settled and living conditions make such a difference to a marriage.'

'Oh Aemilia. Be realistic.'

'What? What do you mean?'

'Nothing, just that your house is not a slum. It couldn't possibly harm a marriage.'

Jennifer thought of Geoffrey's nylon polo neck sweaters and the way he lifted them to scratch his blueish-white stomach. She hated his suety voice. Why did pretty Aemilia ever marry him?

'But I just don't feel settled there. I'm nervous all the time. If I felt settled I'd go back to work. Last week I was offered a job at a clinic in Kennington. I am a qualified speech therapist. I could cope with it. I could. If I just felt more settled.'

'Of course you could. It's just a matter of getting yourself out of the doldrums and back into life.' Jennifer was amazed to see Edward so authoritative.

'Do you really think that?' she mused. 'You think I could?'

'You must take the job.'

'Perhaps I will,' she said. 'But Geoffrey says I couldn't cope.'

'Of course you could.'

Aemilia gazed at Edward with a smile of dedication, as though sucking him into her memory, listing every word and every movement to dwell on in quiet moments. The drained expression had gone from her face and she looked rather happy. Her lips were moist from her habit of running her tongue over them repeatedly and her eyes shone bright.

The fuchsia-pink plastic bracelet round her left wrist matched the flowers in her dress and the sandals on her brown legs.

'Why is everyone so much more able to cope than I am? Sometimes I ...'

46

Jennifer walked out alone on the balcony, leaving Edward and Aemilia to talk. She could smell summer on the warm air and in the rustling of the trees. It was strange the way they rustled even when there appeared to be no wind. The occasional blobs of cotton wool cloud were still against their background of blue.

She looked out over the square. Before the dissolution of the monasteries the square and surroundings had been open fields belonging to the Abbey of Westminster. One of the old enclosure walls still remained in the back garden of Aemilia and Geoffrey's house. Occasionally a scholar or learned tourist would ring their bell and ask to see it. This would enrage Geoffrey and please Aemilia.

Jennifer started as she saw the tiny round man turning the corner. He waddled heavily along the pavement. Every day, at about this time, he took his walk. Sometimes he had a brown walking stick, but not today. He didn't even have on his customary hat. His red, balding head was exposed to the sun.

His clothes looked secondhand: baggy trousers and ill-fitting jacket, as if bought for someone else.

There was something immensely ordinary about the shabby little man and also something extraordinarily odd. His blue eyes were cool and piercing in his circular face.

He was one of the square's 'characters': Mr Davidson, the spiritualist medium. Sarah's cleaner, Maureen, had had a sitting with him once and been impressed. He had, she claimed, made contact with her dead grandfather.

Jennifer, too, would have liked a sitting. She wanted to talk about her own premonitions and imaginings. But she didn't quite dare. Mr Davidson had been thrown out of the spiritualist church because, he had told Maureen, he 'went too far'. Now he just gave private sittings and the occasional group seance. Maureen had not liked to ask what going 'too far' actually meant.

Spiritualism interested Jennifer. She knew she had some special powers, powers which spiritualists would call 'psychic' powers. Often she knew the telephone was about to ring before it did so. Sometimes she knew who would be phoning. She

47

would frequently know things that apparently she hadn't been told, ranging from births and deaths to whom Sarah had invited to dinner. And that uneasy feeling of hers warned of danger. Her imaginings, or visions, of the past were also inexplicable, part of her darker, childhood world.

As Mr Davidson passed by the house, on the opposite side of the road, he looked up at her. She smiled, he stared, but he didn't seem to see her. Mr Davidson's stare unnerved her.

He lived over the other side of the square in a Victorian block of residential flats. An arch topped with the words Abbey Court in black iron led into the courtyard round which the flats were grouped. The walls of the building were laced with pigeon droppings and inside, in the courtyard, was a pond of sludgy weed flashing with red-gold fish. Jennifer liked its air of seedy grandeur. The flats echoed with the atmosphere of former, better, times. But now there were only a few sparrows and the occasional window-box of geraniums in the courtyard.

Jennifer stepped back into the drawing room.

'I don't know why that young lad doesn't plead diminished responsibility,' Aemilia was saying. She pushed a few stray bubbles of her hair behind her ears and straightened her back.

'What's that?' asked Jennifer, as she rearranged the roses in the bowl on the television, her hands trembling.

'It's a defence to murder,' said Edward. 'The law decrees a man whose impulse to kill is uncontrollably strong bears less responsibility for his act than someone whose urge isn't so powerful.'

'How silly,' said Jennifer. She couldn't get Mr Davidson's rotund face out of her mind. He kept looking up at her from that eternity of blue eyes. She wanted to attend a seance.

'But he's not pleading diminished responsibility because he's pleading not guilty,' said Edward.

'Do you think he is guilty?' said Aemilia.

'I don't know,' said Edward. 'I wouldn't like to say before hearing the evidence.'

For all Edward's liberalism, thought Jennifer, there was a kind of puritanism in his make-up. Unlike Sarah, he did not make a virtue out of self-gratification. Instead he held to certain values – such as kindness, gentlemanliness, generosity, honesty and respect for the sanctity of all life – without which he felt his life would be worthless. Jennifer could not understand how Sarah could bring herself to deceive such a man. It was easy to see why he was deceived: he assumed others behaved as honourably as himself. Aemilia's obvious liking for Edward came as no surprise to Jennifer.

'I think criminals should be pitied, not punished,' said Aemilia. 'Put it this way, they're rebelling against the dreadfulness of their lives. They're trying to make a mark on a world which won't let them affect it any other way.'

'Because I understand why someone does something it doesn't mean I therefore acquit him of guilt for that action. One has to draw the line somewhere.'

'But ...' Aemilia had wandered into a discussion without realising it. She was so unused to anyone listening to what she said.

Aemilia sighed.

'You know Geoffrey takes no notice of my views about the trial. Says they're dotty.'

'Geoffrey is never very enthusiastic about other people's opinions. More tea?' offered Edward.

'No thank you. Sarah will be back soon, I suppose?'

Edward looked at his watch. 'Any moment now. If you wait you ought to catch her.'

'No. I have a house to see at six fifteen. Just off Sloane Square. The house sounds pretty but there's no garden so it's out of the question, you see.'

'Oh dear.'

'I hope you'll contact Geoffrey soon. I mean, the trial starts two weeks on Monday, I think.' She stood up.

'I will.' He stood up.

'Oh, and you know there's someone new just moved into the square?'

'No.'

'That's odd. I saw Sarah talking to him yesterday. Number twenty-five, on this side of the square. He's a trainee architect.'

'Really.'

'She said he might be doing some work on the restaurant for her.'

'I wouldn't have thought it needed it.'

'She said something about needing him to design a patio at the back.'

'You mean in that tiny yard?'

'I suppose so.'

Edward shrugged. But he did not take his eyes off Aemilia.

'The young man inherited the house from Mrs Saunders. He's her nephew, you see. I was hoping to buy it when she died ...'

'It's not an especially nice house,' said Jennifer and broke the current flowing between Edward and Aemilia. Aemilia turned her head slowly towards Jennifer and said, 'Isn't it? I've never seen inside.'

'We went there for Mrs Saunders's horrible Christmas party,' said Jennifer. 'She ate nearly all the food herself.'

'Yes,' said Edward, 'she subsided into a dark corner and gobbled. A dirty, depressing house. It made me drink far more dry Martinis than were good for me. If I remember correctly, I became quite maudlin.'

'About Sarah,' proffered Jennifer.

'Really?' said Edward. With a vacant expression, he ran his fingers through his hair.

After Aemilia had gone, father and daughter sat together in the drawing room. Edward poured himself a strong whisky and switched on the news.

'She's very sweet, isn't she?' said Jennifer.

'Aemilia? Yes, very sweet.'

'She likes you.'

'Yes, she needs a spot of guidance sometimes.'

'You like her and yet you avoid her, why's that?'

'Your mother once said that Aemilia's like a sticky toffee wrapper, you manage to get her off one finger and she's clinging to the next.'

'Oh, she doesn't seem too clinging. She left promptly enough when you mentioned the name Sarah.'

'Mmm. I'm always scared the dam will break and the secrets of her soul will pour all over me. Don't want that.'

'Really?'

'What? Look, can you wait a second until the news is over?'

She waited. It ended. Jennifer was pushing back the skin around her nails. Before she could say anything he stood up and walked to the windows, jangling the money in his pocket.

'What time did your mother say she was coming home?'

'She didn't say anything to me.'

'The Tate's well closed by now. I think I'll get on with some work.'

He switched off the television. He was tall and bony and wearing brown carpet slippers and suddenly Jennifer felt acutely sorry for him and for herself. She so wanted to talk to him properly.

She felt depressed by Aemilia's passivity. Must women be docile? Or was it just Geoffrey who submerged Aemilia's spirit?

Alone in the drawing room, Jennifer imagined Aphra in Newgate Prison. She suffered but she wasn't oppressed. She broke free. She knew it wasn't impossible to escape.

Jennifer saw the stone walls slimy with green moss and stale rushes matting the floor. Rusty chains reached down from the huge ring bolts to the women sprawled like rag-dolls beneath them. Their wrists and ankles were trapped in iron bracelets. The bright eyes of rats darted through the dimness of the cell searching for scraps.

Aphra sat shrouded in a brown woollen cloak with her knees hunched up. Her face was pale in the dull light of the tallow candle. She had a long face, with firm black eyebrows and heavy-lidded eyes. Her hair draggled down on either side of her face in ringlets.

Two rats began to fight just by her and Aphra's expression sharpened as she kicked out. But the chains restrained her feet and she scowled.

'God damn the rats, the King and Lord Arlington,' she muttered.

The woman beside her emitted a dainty cough. Her cornflower-blue satin dress and low-necked bodice were ridiculously out of place in the gloom.

'What brings you to this hell-hole?' said Aphra.

51

The woman coughed again. She smelt of heavy-sweet perfume and bad breath.

'Who are you, may I ask?'

'Aphra Behn. Mrs Aphra Behn.'

'My name is Mrs Goodman. It was the fire which brought me here. It burnt most of my possessions and the rest paid only some of my debts. But I have friends. I'll be out soon.' She looked Aphra up and down coldly.

'I have friends too,' said Aphra. 'And I wouldn't trust them as far as I can see in here, and that's not far. Take, for instance, the King.'

The woman looked more interested.

'I spied for him in Antwerp, worked hard, discovered valuable secrets and my reward is this. Prison. So much for the King's beneficence. He paid me a paltry sum for five months' government service. I could not but spend far more. But when I had no more money, did he help me? Did the head of the secret service, Lord Arlington, help? Did any one of my dear friends or honoured superiors bail me out? No. They left me to drown. Trust no one. That's my motto. Remember it, just you remember it.'

Aphra straightened her back and tilted her chin upwards. Her mouth was pursed and tiny beneath the grand sweep of her nose.

'Dear me, and you were on government service,' said the woman with a hint of disbelief.

'Yes, I was a fool. But by God I'll not rot here for my foolishness. I'll not be caged up.'

A woman laughed to herself as she scratched her ribs. Pock-marked breasts exploded from a cream bodice stained dark beneath the arms and her maroon woollen skirt was ripped up the front to reveal a dingy grey petticoat.

'You'll have to find a man then. I've been here five times and I know. Stealing and laying with rich prisoners always got me out. It's the only way. But now they have no need of me. What with the clap and the pox I'll be here for ever.'

'The difference is,' said the lady in satin, 'I am not a common whore. I would never lie with a criminal.'

'All women are whores, how else would we live?' said the pock-marked woman.

'I know many a person of quality who would be glad to pay my debt.'

'At a price, my fine lady, at a price. Have you heard some of the things Buckingham does to women?' She leered in the darkness, her tongue running over her bulbous lips.

'Be quiet,' said Aphra. 'By God, I shall not be a whore I'll not be kept mistress nor wife. I've had enough of that. I'll rely on myself. I'll not depend on men again.'

'Impossible,' announced the fat whore.

'Impossible,' admitted the lady, brushing her dark hair from her painted forehead.

Jennifer stood up quickly and went out on to the balcony.

6

On her way down to the station from school the next day Jennifer was one of the hurrying people, swept along as if on a moving pavement. No one even walked defiantly: some dragged their feet, some moved like clockwork toys with brisk steps, others waddled. Women carried shopping bags, men briefcases, school children satchels: all fixed in the pattern of their lives. On the grey pavement were wisps of sweet papers blowing like dust in the breeze. The sky above had clouded over and the day was dull. Jennifer crossed the road, dutiful as ever, on the zebra crossing.

Jennifer arrived home to find Maureen in the kitchen with Sarah.

When Maureen first came to clean she was massive and had brown hair set in predictable housewife curls. But since then she'd lost stone after stone, grown her hair and dyed it black. She had gradually acquired a wardrobe of Sarah's old clothes: today she wore brown linen trousers and a matching checked shirt. Her hair was piled up into an untidy bun which was on the brink of collapsing.

Sarah stood leaning against the sink with her back to the window and the garden. Maureen sat on the kitchen stool. She had a cup of tea and a biscuit in one hand and a cigarette in the other. Both women looked up at Jennifer as she entered. Maureen's face was downcast. She managed a smile. Her eyes were moist and red. Sarah's were bright as ever. She had the sleeves of her shirt rolled up to the elbows and the buttons undone to midway between her breasts: just the right blend of capability and warmth. Maureen's shoulders sagged down and her knees were bent up as if trying to assume a foetal position on the stool.

'Hello.'

'Hello dear,' said Maureen.

'Haven't seen you for a while. Are you all right?' asked Jennifer and regretted it.

Maureen perked up a little.

'Terrible, terrible. My mother went into hospital yesterday. Gastric ulcer. That's why I'm eating this biscuit. I don't usually touch biscuits.' She glanced from daughter to mother, as if daring either to gainsay her. 'And what's more this is a digestive biscuit. Eighty calories at least. That's how bad things are.'

'I'm sorry.'

'You're not looking so well yourself. You're thinner than usual and a bit peaky. Isn't she Mrs Hamilton? I wish I was as slim as you Jennifer. How much do you weigh?'

'I don't know.'

'You don't know?' Maureen sighed. She'd told Jennifer once how she weighed herself every morning without fail and feared the least quiver of the scales over nine stone twelve pounds.

'Did you have a good day, darling?' said Sarah.

'Fine. And you?'

'Not bad. I've been at the restaurant. Dropped back for tea and a bath and who should I find?'

'Me,' said Maureen dolefully. 'I just hope you appreciate your mother, Jenny. You know it was the empty slippers that really got me, Mrs Hamilton. They'd taken her away and her slippers were by her bed – red ones – and empty. Horrible somehow.'

'Yes, I can see that,' said Sarah.

'I just hope you appreciate your mother, that's all I can say, Jennifer.'

Jennifer smiled bleakly at Maureen. She was glad she had never met Maureen's mother.

'Your mother's a good woman. She always knows what to do. Whenever I have a problem I know where to turn. I hope you appreciate her, I just hope you do.'

Why, Jennifer wondered, did people think they had a right to lecture her? She stared out past Sarah to the lawn beyond. For London, it was a big garden. The lawn trailed away to a greenhouse and a row of tall poplars which barricaded the garden from the road behind. But there was more to it than that. When you came to the greenhouse at the end of the garden, with its patio, lawn and borders of flowers, it wasn't the end. You turned right along a narrow path lined with lavender bushes and came to a square with a giant chestnut in the centre, yew hedges on three sides, a willow and the cherry tree and the wall climbing with roses which shut off this secret garden from the road. While the main lawn and borders were carefully tended to impress visitors, this one was hardly touched and yet here the roses were sumptuous and the bushes a jungle all the year round. Jennifer loved the garden. It suggested to her that the improbable was possible, that perhaps there were many hidden gardens. Jennifer decided that once she'd had a coffee and changed she'd go and read on the bench beneath the chestnut tree. In spring the chestnut held creamy torches: now its fires had died down.

'I was her only child,' sniffed Maureen. 'She couldn't have another, poor thing ... Oh, I didn't mean ...'

She fumbled to light another cigarette.

An affectionate smile flooded over Sarah's face and her eyes lost their authority.

'Oh Maureen, don't look so embarrassed; you haven't hurt my feelings, I only wanted one. We haven't tried to have another, immoral as that might seem to you.'

'Sorry, Mrs Hamilton,' said Maureen.

'Excuse me,' said Jennifer, 'I must go and change.'

Upstairs she put on jeans and a T-shirt. The jeans were baggy and hung round her legs like a frail old Frenchman's trousers. She had a delicate, oval face framed by russet curls and illuminated by thoughtful brown eyes. Beneath her small nose the mouth was almost too full, too sensual. Jennifer rather resented it. She didn't like to see her mother's expression creeping over her face when she smiled.

When she went down for a coffee her mother was still leaning against the sink, blocking out some of the light and some of the garden. Maureen had gone, leaving her saucer soggy with half a digestive biscuit. Clearly Sarah had been of some comfort.

'It's curious isn't it, the way Maureen eats when she's unhappy?' said Sarah.

'Not really, I often eat a bar of chocolate to cheer me up. It never does of course but I always think it will. Do you want a cup of coffee?'

'Jennifer. You know you *are* looking peaky. I've noticed it for some time. I believe you work too hard.'

'Did you want coffee?'

'What? No thank you. I really do think you should make more effort to enjoy yourself. You read too much, fill yourself up with fancy notions and phrases. It worries me. You're always in.'

'You wouldn't understand of course, but I actually enjoy working,' said Jennifer.

Sarah stubbed her cigarette out fiercely into the saucer of her coffee cup. She grappled in her handbag for a peppermint. In a way, she wished Jennifer young again. Her big eyes had been quaintly solemn, her stocky body adorable and her long red hair a pleasure to brush. Everyone had admired her and the exquisite smocks made by Sarah's dressmaker. Jennifer had even been chosen once to present the headmistress with a bouquet at prize-giving. Sarah had occasionally put mascara on the little girl's long eyelashes when she was out on show, at friends or at home. Jennifer had had a gift for amusing herself and hadn't been much trouble. But even then she'd been secretive, frowning when anyone interrupted her dressing-up. Obsessively secretive. If there was a drawer or a box she could lock, she'd lock it. Sarah had discovered, under a loose floorboard, a number of exercise books sealed with coloured wax. They were

56

carefully dated and, presumably, were diaries. Once when Jennifer was all dressed up in her school uniform, standing in the drive of their former house waiting for Edward to give her a lift to school, an acquaintance passed by and asked, inanely, where she was going. She refused to tell him. She'd been ten years old then and had grown more secretive since. Whenever she went into her room or out of the house her face assumed a rather shifty expression. Sarah never dared ask her what she was doing or where she was going. When Jennifer had all her long hair cut off soon after moving to Westminster, Sarah didn't ask why. Jennifer could be extremely rude. Edward claimed it was mere shyness on Jennifer's part, but Sarah wasn't so sure. All the same, she couldn't help but love her. There was something so brave about her solemn urchin face. After all, women had to be secretive. Even as girls some felt they had to hide the secret of their monthly haemorrhage, soak stained sheets at night, wash pants out so their mothers wouldn't see. They also had to learn to get their way by subterfuge, not strength.

Jennifer's head was bowed and her eyes averted from Sarah as she slowly tipped a teaspoon of coffee into her mug.

'I know you like working but you also know quite well that *normal* girls of your age, and, incidentally, looks, have boyfriends, or at least go to dances and parties. You don't know the fun you're missing. Why don't you invite some people back here? You could have a dinner party. I'd arrange it all, you know that.'

Jennifer did know that.

'There is nobody I want to invite,' she said and realised it was perfectly true.

'Well, I'll even invite the guests if you wish. My friend Clara has a son at Burnam who's very charming and about the right age. The daughter's fun too. Then there's ...'

'No thank you, really. It's very kind but I wouldn't enjoy it.'

Jennifer wished the kettle would boil.

'It seems to me you don't enjoy anything but working.'

'You're probably right.'

'Look Jennifer, won't you, for my sake, just make a bit of

57

effort this holiday, arrange to see just one or two people? Girlfriends, anyone. I wouldn't mind if they dressed in black leather and drove motor bikes. I wouldn't mind if they were chronic shop-lifters, nymphomaniacs, drug addicts, just so long as you saw *someone*. I hate to see you so morose cooped up in your room or out in that garden with your wretched books. Even a dreary blue-stocking bookworm for a friend would be better than *nobody*. You'll go balmy. You know it makes you neurotic. Why else did you have to take those tranquillisers?'

'I was worried about my exams, that's all. The exams are over now.'

Jennifer poured water on the coffee, added milk and made for the door.

'Jenni*fer*.'

'Yes?'

'Shall we go to the sales together this summer?'

'Let's wait and see, shall we? You know how busy you are.'

'All right ... and Jennifer ...'

'Yes.'

'I'll make your and Edward's dinner and leave it in the fridge. I'll be at the restaurant all evening. He'll be back from the library six thirty-ish as usual.'

'Fine,' said Jennifer.

Sarah was left, staring at the door. She worried about Jennifer. She was such an odd, withdrawn little girl. As a small child she was always seeing 'ghosts' and 'shapes' in the corners of the rooms. Often she'd lock herself in her bedroom and not come out all day. Sarah would hear her chattering to herself as she passed the door.

Sometimes she'd seem to know things she hadn't been told.

The day Sarah's mother died she found Jennifer weeping in her room. But Sarah had received the call at work. There was no way Jennifer could have known. But she knew. She said she didn't know how.

Sarah's memories of her own childhood were of brown lino, dark corridors, damp on the walls and of fear. Sarah had hated and feared her father. She used to lie in bed, unable to sleep, trying to decipher the angry tones of her father in the living room below. Was he complaining about her, about her mother, or was it just someone at work?

She was glad to leave home and go to secretarial college in Oxford. She met Edward there. He was gentle and considerate, the complete opposite of her tyrannous father. She married him.

For a time the marriage was wonderful. She felt safe and adored. Then she began to feel too safe, too adored. She had an affair with a chatty, goblinesque solicitor who cornered her at a drinks party. Drunkenly she made the appointment and soberly she kept it. They made love in Edward and Sarah's king-size bed after a leisurely lunch in a nearby restaurant. He was a wiry dynamo who talked all the time, flattering, cajoling, gossiping, joking, except when he was actually making love. Then he was silent and his face ecstatic. Immediately afterwards he was chattering again.

Sarah found she enjoyed the adventure, liked its danger. She feared Edward finding out, and that fear gave her a curious pleasure. It made her feel alive.

Edward was always kind, always generous, never bad-tempered. He had worked hard on his journalism, now he worked hard on his books. He would do anything for her, to keep her quiet. All he wanted was peace and time to think.

Sarah did not find Edward an exciting person to live with. All the excitement went on inside his head. Like his daughter, he was a thinker and a dreamer. She couldn't share his world of literature, the past, poetry. Her occasional attempts to enter it had failed. She had fallen asleep over important essays and thrown poems in exasperation across rooms.

Her world was the public one of conversation and love and holidays and money.

She never gave her heart to any of the men to whom she gave her body. Her heart was Edward's. But he wasn't enough. He was too reserved, too private, too respectable. He wasn't much fun.

Saul Goodman, on the other hand, had been fun. Saul had been all over her, adoring her, admiring her body, telling her she was beautiful, confiding what other women were like in bed, confessing his fears. She had liked the touch of his coarse skin and his tongue and his hands.

Just a day or so after they met, Saul invited her to lunch at the carvery of a hotel near Paddington. The meat was tough. The carpets were brash orange. The waiters were slow. He told her he'd booked a room there for the afternoon, for the two of them. She thought he was joking. He wasn't. She was appalled by the tastelessness of his proposed method of seduction. She was also amused. She went with him to the room. For a moment they stood in the room, both embarrassed. Sarah wanted to turn and go. The light through the window was bright. The double bed had a pink cover. The carpets were purple. She was also a little frightened. After all, she hardly knew Saul. She entered the bathroom and marvelled at the gold taps, then exclaimed girlishly at the smallness of the people below. He stood with his arm around her while they discussed pleasant views. He kissed her gently, then harder, and Sarah began to lose her embarrassment.

They made love on the pink cover in the harsh light of a London day. Afterwards, he kept kissing her long back. He said it was the most beautiful back in the world. She liked his lips. They made love again. He ordered brandies from room service.

She decided Saul was entertaining as they explored each other's bodies once more.

But now she had wearied of Saul.

He had been pleased to be invited to lunch. He hadn't realised what a put-down it was. By meeting Edward and Jennifer, he was being dropped into the position of friend. He had been sterilised of romance by sitting and chatting in the drawing room. Saul could be so naive. She could not respect him the way she respected Edward. Edward had dignity. When anyone else entertaining his wife's lover would appear ridiculous, Edward hadn't. He had an inner quietness which armoured him against ever appearing absurd.

At the moment she was feeling uncharacteristically romantic about a young man she had met a few days before. He lived just down the road. He had made her think. He was bubbling with enthusiasm and ideas.

She felt she was so busy achieving, so busy being a success, so busy enjoying herself, fulfilling herself, that she seemed often not to be noticing what she was doing. She was always too concerned with the last or the next meal, about how good the holiday would be, about whether her partner was enjoying sex, about bills and timetables. The rag-bag of the past was filling up and weighing her down. It seemed that she spent her life transferring the rags from one bag to the other, from the future to the past, and that she was so immersed in her task that she wouldn't notice if a diamond tiara shone from amid the rags.

7

That weekend Jennifer thought and worked on Shelley, as she had all week. She browsed through an anthology of early criticism of him and his work. One English essay announced he was a 'fiend-writer', a 'blaster of his race' and the 'demoniac proscriber of his species'. She was intrigued that the Americans had at once received him more sympathetically than the British. His ideals of freedom had been close to those of the new America, released like Prometheus from its chains. She thought of that American Saul and his talk of freedom. She remembered his warm moist hand clutching hers.

On Sundays her father didn't work at the London Library and her mother didn't open the restaurant. That evening people were coming to dinner, including Geoffrey and Aemilia. 'Why can't one ever invite *one* member of a couple?' moaned Sarah. 'Aemilia is so tedious.'

Weary of the poetry, with only a few bright quotes left in her memory, Jennifer was reading Hogg's biography which took her into Shelley's early life. Her mother was busy with dinner party preparations and left her in peace. Her father pottered in the garden all day, pruning roses and humming. He wore a white Christopher Robin floppy hat.

The day passed without Jennifer noticing. She was so immersed that in the evening she could see her hero leaning, dead still, over a microscope in his shirt sleeves.

She could imagine the leaded windows behind him, the patch of green quadrangle and a chapel spiked with pinnacles. It must be University College Chapel, he must be in his college room and the date must be ... 1810 or 1811. His rooms certainly were a mess. His carpet was a riot of letters, clothes, periodicals, unwashed glasses and hunks of dry-looking bread. Electrical and chemical apparatus covered the oak table. From the greyness of the light which filtered through the dusty windows, Jennifer knew it was late afternoon. A fire flickered in the grate.

There was a knock on the door. Shelley brushed his hair from his eyes and shouted shrilly. 'Who is it?'

'Hogg,' said a solid voice.

Shelley rushed to the door, his head thrust eagerly forward and shoulders still stooping slightly. His bright eyes shone as he opened the oak slab and let in a thick-set young man wearing a black gown and bearing a bottle of wine.

'Take a seat. Take a seat,' said Shelley frenetically. 'Or don't. I have something to show you. Under the microscope. Mites crawling in cheese. The invisible made visible. Go on, have a look.'

Hogg had a look while Shelley paced up and down the room, a tiger in a cage, with his hands behind his back and words avalanching forth.

'These dull Oxford dons with their love of classical learning endlessly repeating the past make me want to blow the whole place up. Shock their sedate faces and trim Fellows' gardens. They don't experiment, don't try to unveil the secrets of the mind and the universe. They merely study words and phrases, the names of things. They ignore the things themselves. But the physical sciences enlarge man's vision, show us those mites, reveal suns invisible to the naked eye. The balloon lifts us above the earth and soon intrepid aeronauts will be charting the uncharted regions of the earth, revealing how much more there is to life than we know now. Do you see? New sources of power, balloons, electricity, magnetism, are weapons to fight stagnation, slavery, tyranny ... '

Hogg blew his nose loudly and Shelley swivelled round and

62

glared. Hogg had ensconced himself in the chair by the fire with a glass of wine.

'The fire's gone out,' said Hogg. 'And you're standing on your new olive coat.'

Shelley had no laces in his shoes and his waistcoat was undone and he was so beautiful. . . .

She hurried downstairs and half-way down remembered about the dinner party her parents were having. But perhaps she could have a seat by Edward, for coffee, or he might happen to come out of the dining room and she could take him aside. It was important to know whether or not he felt the same and whether the past was as vivid to him as it was to her.

Jennifer went into the kitchen which led into the dining room. The door was closed but she could hear the voices clearly. She stopped and listened before realising the mistake she had nearly made. What would Edward care about her imaginings? But, oddly, it took her a while to drag herself away from the conversation of her parents and their guests.

'I'm just so bored with it all,' said a voice which Jennifer recognised as Anita's, a divorcee with cropped ginger hair and a fashionable cockney accent. 'I haven't found being free such fun. At first I was overjoyed when we split but now, well, I wonder about the carefree life. It's fine as long as you're not screwing anyone – all the admiration and none of the intensity – then that begins to seem futile so you screw them and get VD and that's the end of that. A sordid clinic and a spatula up your insides to round off the affair.'

'Perhaps you pick the wrong men,' said Edward, rather too pointedly for Jennifer's liking.

'Perhaps I do. You see I'd really like the perfect lover who could provide loving kindness, intelligence and charm and conduct me to grand, operatic orgasms. But my occasional block-busting orgasms are always delivered by the most unsavoury men. You see,' she continued remorselessly, 'it's always the same. There was this squat little man only a few days ago with a horrid leather jacket and an overhanging forehead which gave him an anxious expression. I met him at a party and he smelt dreadful. He pushed me against the garden wall and,

63

whoops, I was in ecstasy. He still looked worried though. But whenever a man with charm, good looks, kindness, intelligence takes me to his bed – perhaps after dinner, probably after a period of courtship – I feel totally unsexy. I wouldn't mind a chat, a naked cuddle but the thought and fact of him pounding away on top of me seems absurdly undignified. So I flounder from lover to lover always searching for the little death of orgasm but more often getting VD.'

'Well, I don't know if it's altogether relevant but can you remember, I mean can you ...'

'Oh come on, Aemilia, spit it out,' said Geoffrey's heavy voice.

'Well, what I was going to say was that, I mean, who was your first ever lover?'

'A lorry driver who picked me up when I was hitching on the motorway in the days when nice girls didn't hitch.'

'Well,' said Aemilia, 'I don't know if you know but people, psychiatrists, do say that one's first sexual encounter is crucial to one's sexual development.'

'I think you're probably right, Aemilia,' said Edward. 'It is reasonable to suppose that one signposts life's route in early, adolescent years and follows it afterwards.'

'Aemilia,' said Geoffrey, 'had an awful first experience....'

'Geoffrey ... please don't.'

'But you really do think one searches for replicas of one's first love throughout life?' said Edward hastily. 'I must say my first love didn't look like Sarah.'

'Mine was very similar to how Edward used to look, when he was twenty-five and I first met him,' said Sarah.

'Really?'

'Oh Edward, I *told* you.'

'And what did Edward look like?' drawled Anita, 'I can't imagine him looking more delightful than he does now.'

'He was gentle, gangly, very clever, very educated and had the most beautiful smooth skin. It's rougher now. I was awfully impressed by his breeding and his incredibly hairy chest. For someone with such girlish skin to have such thick hairs seemed so sexy somehow. Don't see why now. But *then*.'

'Well I certainly hope little Jennifer chooses her first love well,' said Edward. 'We don't want a succession of ... National Front roadsweepers tramping through the house year after year ...'

Jennifer turned and walked slowly upstairs.

How dare he talk about her behind her back like that? It was so sordid. How could he understand what had happened to her? He wouldn't be interested. He was more interested in dirty talk.

She lay down on her bedspread. It was all so pitiful. Sarah talking of the Edward she'd lost. Edward recalling his first love. Aemilia remembering hers, perhaps. Geoffrey jeering. She wondered who Anita's silent companion was that evening, some shy young lad, perhaps. Or maybe someone hadn't turned up, maybe that's why she'd talked so much, to cover up the emptiness. How Anita went on and how sad it was, 'Floundering from lover to lover always searching for the little death of orgasm but more often getting VD.' There had to be something more to life than that.

Shelley had been right when he used to say that earthly love corrupted. She wondered if her father found that tarty Anita attractive. She was sure he liked the gentle Aemilia. Or did he? She didn't know. She bet all those adults were sitting round the table eyeing each other. Geoffrey eyeing Sarah, Aemilia eyeing Edward, Edward roving his eyes from Anita to Aemilia and back ... it was all so fetid.

Juggling with their time, getting nowhere, playing with the same experiences in different years. Jennifer wanted more than that.

Suddenly Jennifer yearned to see Rebecca so much. Her red apple cheeks, her Pinnochio nose, her courage, her complete lack of cynicism or guile and, above all, her innocence. The windows of the room at home wide open, to let in the fresh air. Striding forward, wind on her face, wearing such unwieldy lace-up shoes and such thick socks and such a baggy sweater. Her high-pitched nervous laugh which would have been irritating if it hadn't been hers. Always making notes in that beautiful writing of hers. Pressing flowers. Collecting stones. Scouring the local paper for news of jumble sales.

Jennifer undressed and, as she lay in bed trying to sleep, the disembodied voices of her parents and their friends rang in her ears like sounds in a desert and the remembered image of Shelley had the strangeness of a mirage floating just out of reach. Was that all it was, wondered Jennifer, a mirage in a desert? A fragment, like the rest of her life? Pictures on the wall telling her something but not enough, incomplete memories, half-grasped ideas, friends who drew away when you drew too close, parents who are always distant. And herself, was she just a mirage in the desert? People treated her like an insubstantial trick of the light. If she vanished tomorrow who'd care, who'd really care? Her desk at school would soon be filled by someone else, her absence at home would soon heal over, nothing would remain of her because it was true, she was not substantial. There was nothing she could point at and say 'That's me': her face wasn't her, her work wasn't her, her conversation certainly wasn't her and all those things together didn't even add up to her. They were fragments.

8

At school on Monday Jennifer was depressed. She was sure it was the kind of place which manufactured useless women, oppressed by passivity, fears and men. But most maddening of all was her own passivity. Of all the girls, she was one of the least rebellious. She had never retorted to any of her teachers, never refused to go to prayers and mime religious feelings, never even gone to school without her hat. Her father once said, 'One only really dislikes characteristics which one shares', and she supposed her aversion to the quiet, meek girls supported this theory.

But it was hard to be tough in the real world. Some of the teachers were so fierce. Most terrifying of all was Miss Roberts. She had a square jaw, booming voice, niggly eyes, yellow irregular teeth, frizzy hair and shoulders like a boxer. When glimpsed in the staff room she always had a cigarette stuck to her bottom lip as if with glue. She stalked round the school venomously, always out to criticise, to reduce girls to gibbering pulps of obedience. Her particular forte was gestapo interrogation. She hated resolute girls, preferred ones who quickly broke into tears when she tortured them with public accusations of laziness, sloppiness, bad spelling and broken elastic on their hats.

Jennifer feared that at any moment she might be chosen for persecution. She sat at the back of the class with scrupulously clean dress and a heart which fluttered when Miss Roberts was in the room. But Miss Roberts seldom picked on Jennifer. She was far too quiet, tidy and clever.

The classroom that morning, as usual, was filled by the din of banging desks and nattering girls. The noise stopped when Miss Roberts sat at her desk out front and frowned at the class. Jennifer could see she hated the neat rows of desks being disordered by the messy presence of thirty different pubescent girls. Miss Roberts, she suspected, would like them all to wear their hair exactly the same, all have identical faces. She never addressed anyone by her right name anyway, so that would be no problem. Although she was always muddling names she was never corrected. The girls meekly accepted their changing identities.

She took the register.

In prayers the staff flanked the block of girls. Miss Roberts's chair was in front of the black varnished door of the staff room and her eyes roved over the assembly hall, up and down the rows of girls, round the surrounding gallery. She was on the look-out for scruffiness, whispering and gum-chewing. Her hand rubbed up and down her thigh clothed in tweed.

> 'Our father which art in Heaven
> Hallowed be thy name....'

The girl in front of Jennifer pulled up her socks for the fourth time.

But as the week continued Jennifer cheered up. By Thursday, the last day of the term, she was positively bouncy. The holidays stretched before her. From 17 July to 1 September: six weeks without school.

The last day of the summer term wasn't just like any last day of term. In it was concentrated all the hat-throwing exhilaration and release she had ever felt at the end of the school year.

During assembly one or two former pupils sat up in the gallery watching the miniature versions of themselves sitting in rows below. How slow and painful the journey had been from little girl at the front to eighteen-year-old way back by the leaded window at the far end of the hall. The headmistress had seemed so important, towering above as they sat, cross-legged, by the raised stage. But as the years swept them back she had become a smaller figure, not so different from them. Most of the girls, once they left the school, never returned except in dreams or in nostalgic memories of intimate schoolgirl conversations by the dustbins, lessons outdoors beneath the weeping willow, being voted prefect, eating chocolate at the bus stop on the way home, passing exams and hearing the swack of the rounders bat in the daisied sunshine of the playing field.

Jennifer bolted joyfully out of the cloakroom, clutching her report, as if she never again had to return to the tedium and restrictions and the bad temper of teachers.

It was sultry weather. More than one man carried his jacket over his arm as he walked through the sauntering streets.

As she crossed Vauxhall Bridge the sun dazzled the Thames. She loved crossing the bridge. The river was so changeable. In the mornings it could be grey and Dickensian, in the evenings blood-stained with sunset. She leaned over the side of the bridge and looked down. She imagined leaping to her death; the long fall and the sudden, stunning cold. Jennifer imagined the news of her own death: her parents' white faces and disbelief, self-recrimination, the tearful funeral and its speeches. But then the grief would fade soon because she was irreplaceable to no one at all. Probably Sarah would be quite pleased to adopt some pretty Vietnamese orphan. Jennifer softly kicked the newly painted bridge. Seagulls floated easily through the air and cried out to each other. The towers of Battersea power station stretched upwards into the blue sky as if considering themselves

68

a wonder of the world. Everything seemed unreasonably pleased with itself.

Sometimes she thought that Shelley had planned his death at sea. It had finished off his life so superbly. He'd become immortally young by drowning before he was thirty. Perhaps it was his death which was his masterpiece. Never learning to swim but always obsessed by boats, his death in a storm at sea with a folded-back copy of Keats's poems in his pocket was so perfect it was almost pretentious.

In *Adonais* he'd written what turned out to be an elegy to himself although written with Keats in mind.

> He has outsoared the shadow of our night;
> Envy and calumny and hate and pain,
> And that unrest which men miscall delight,
> Can touch him not and torture not again;
> From the contagion of the world's slow stain
> He is secure ...

Harriet's death had not been so satisfactory: a swollen figure floating face up in the cold Serpentine.

Jennifer walked slowly home over the glittering pavements past people she didn't notice and who didn't notice her.

She unlocked the avocado-green door, put her straw hat and blazer on a peg and hurried upstairs. She had her report in her hand. Some of the other girls had opened theirs in the cloakroom but that was against the rules so Jennifer hadn't. She heard voices in the drawing room, pulled up her white socks and peeped round the door. On the olive linen sofa sat her mother and one of the most beautiful young men Jennifer had ever seen.

'Oh,' said Sarah, 'You're back early, darling.'

'It's the end of the holidays, I mean the term.'

'Paul, this is my daughter Jennifer.'

Paul catapulted out of his seat and seized Jennifer's hand. He shook it firmly while Sarah said, 'Jennifer, this is Paul who lives in number twenty-five and is going to help me redesign the restaurant. He's an architect.'

'How do you do?' said Jennifer.

'Very well, very well,' he answered shrilly as he retreated into an armchair with a quick, noiseless movement. He had a slim figure and a slight stoop. Reddy-gold hair curled round his face with shaggy brows over delicate features. His nose was small and neat and his skin girlishly clear. She had the odd feeling occasionally experienced when meeting the brother or sister of a friend: the face looks more or less the same but the voice is different, or the hair's the same and forehead different, or perhaps it's the manner, something in the way they gesture when talking, which makes you forget you're meeting a stranger. But Shelley was a hero not a friend and self-consciousness swamped her. She didn't know what to do with her head, her hands, her arms and her feet. How did people usually stand, she wondered, did they cross their arms or leave them at their sides? She pulled up her pulled-up socks. Paul was staring at her.

'So we're neighbours,' he said.

She nodded her head.

'I see you haven't lost your report?' said Sarah.

Jennifer shook her head. The long manila envelope was clutched firmly in her left hand.

'Have you ever?' said Paul.

'Oh yes,' she said in an odd, throttled voice.

'You're like me then. I lose everything. Plane tickets, passports, money, my way. I mean, none of my biros ever have tops.'

'I never lose anything,' said Sarah. 'Why don't you sit down, Jennifer? Suddenly you look awfully tall and you're giving me vertigo.' Sarah's voice had the slightly manic pitch and momentum often present when she was disturbed. She took a drag of her menthol cigarette. She smoked with an air of controlled decadence, her eyes turning inwards with pleasure as she slowly inhaled and out as the smoke emerged from her glossy lips. She tapped her ash into the mother-of pearl ashtray which conveniently complemented the varnish on her long nails. Jennifer considered Sarah's tight black and gold shirt vulgar. It was lunchtime, after all. The shirt slunk over her breasts and gold

70

chains glittered round her neck. Her white silk trousers had knife-edge pleats and on her feet were dainty French sandals.

Shyly, but somehow, Jennifer arrived at Edward's button-backed velvet armchair and sat down without incident. Mother, daughter and Paul formed a triangle on the gold carpet, with Sarah on the sofa facing the windows. On the wall above her, Sarah's body, painted by Lucian Freud, sprawled open-legged. Jennifer wondered whether Paul found the juxtaposition of Sarah dressed and Sarah undressed as obscene as she did.

Jennifer sat with her back straight, knees together and arms crossed.

Sarah stubbed her cigarette out, then popped a peppermint into her mouth. She kept a packet in her handbag and sucked them to obliterate the smell of stale cigarettes.

'Have you read it?' said Paul.

'What?' said Jennifer.

'Your report.'

'Oh no.'

'I always did. Don't know why. I mean, even horoscopes are more revealing than school reports. What are your best subjects?'

'History and English.'

'Why?'

'I suppose I'm best at them.'

'What subjects were you best at ...' drawled Sarah with her head on one side, lips pouting and eyes sexily melting. She smoothed out the trousers over her thigh in one of her self-caressing movements '... when you were at school?'

'Art and Maths.'

'And now?'

'I enjoy what I'm good at. I mean, I don't really know what I'm good at now. Architecture I suppose. I like building, creating something. It's only the detail of it I find tiresome.'

Paul examined the middle finger of his left hand then bit into its nail.

It was odd, thought Jennifer, that someone like Paul should bite his nails. But the devastatingly charming often had strange habits. Her friend Stella had once met a gorgeous young man with fair Grecian curls, an Etonian voice and a talent for mimicry who turned out to be an ivory-smuggler and heroin addict.

'Don't you really know what you're good at?' coaxed Sarah. Paul smiled jerkily back at the innuendo in her voice as she rubbed her shoulders slowly against the back of the sofa. She looked attractive now, thought Jennifer, but when she was depressed lines drooped from the sides of her lips to her chin, accentuating her jaw, making it that of a ventriloquist's doll.

'Have you had the results of your final exams yet?' Sarah asked.

He ran his fingers through his hair and Jennifer remembered a passage Hogg had written about Shelley, '... his hair was long and bushy, and in fits of absence, and in the agonies (if I may use the word) of anxious thought, he often rubbed it fiercely with his hands, or passed his fingers quickly through his locks unconsciously, so that it was singularly wild and rough.... His features breathed an animation, a fire, an enthusiasm, a vivid and preternatural intelligence ...'

'Not yet. Five years of studying at that wretched place. I certainly hope I have passed. And I won't be fully qualified even then. Have to spend another two years at an office before setting up on my own.'

Jennifer wished her mother would ask to see the report. She knew it would be excellent and it might impress Paul.

'And what rung are you on the educational ladder?' he asked.

'Just finished O levels,' she blurted out.

'So we're both in the same boat. What does your report say?' His speech was slower now. 'Why don't you open it now?'

Jennifer put the report on the coffee table in front of her mother. She returned to her seat feeling as though she'd just done the cat walk for Miss World.

Her mother reached forward, not for the envelope, but for her glass of whisky.

'I'll read it later, darling, when I can give it my full attention.'

Paul was watching her, Jennifer knew he was, and she could feel in his stare something she couldn't explain. It was immensely interested but also oddly predatory. Perhaps it was the shaggy brows which gave his features a somewhat animal quality. She found it most peculiar. When actually talking to him he seemed unthreatening and boyish but now he seemed more dangerous. She kept her eyes fixed to the ground and experienced a murmur of unmistakably sexual excitement through her body. She blushed.

'Was one of your teachers a young man called Charles Grigson?' said Sarah somewhat tartly. Jennifer looked up.

'Yes. Why?' said Paul.

'Well you know he murdered his girlfriend?'

'I know he is accused of doing so, yes.'

'Did you know him well?'

'Yes. Very well.'

'Were you friendly with the murdered girl?' said Jennifer.

Paul's eyes opened wide, startled. His eyes were grey, like the sea. There was a gold cross round his neck.

'How did you know that?'

'I don't know …' she shrugged her shoulders.

'Jennifer is a witch,' said Sarah drily.

He was gazing intently at Jennifer.

'Charles was a good friend of mine. At one time I went out with his sister Lucinda, later with Jane, the girl who was murdered. After we split up she began going out with Charles.'

'What was Lucinda like?' asked Sarah.

'A spoilt brat.'

He stood up and began pacing up and down the room in a nervy fashion extraordinarily reminiscent of Shelley. Jennifer felt a mixture of surprise at his similarity to Shelley, attraction to him, fascination that he knew this triangle of death and a rather disagreeable curiosity. Why had he been out with all these women? What had they meant to him? Why was he with her mother? What did he want from her, she from him? He was talking and talking as he strode back and forth.

'She was abominable. She always had to be the centre of some drama. And funnily enough people always rallied round her. She'd either be hopelessly in love, or stricken because she had sexual fantasies about her father, or worried because she decided she was incapable of love, fevered because she'd caught the clap,

73

desperate because she'd put on two pounds in weight. She made these things sound enormously important and would demand, and receive, sympathy. She had something. A kind of vulnerability. Also good looks. And a restless quality which was intriguing. I loved her for a while, I suppose. She lived life at such a pitch.

'But eventually I became fed up with her histrionics and her self-absorption. On a steaming hot day, I remember, she looked at me very seriously, put her head on one side, squinted slightly and said, "It's amazing. I feel ... I feel ... terribly hot." "How interesting," I said coldly and decided she was not, any more.

'She could also be bloody infuriating. She was always throwing Lady Caroline Lamb-type scenes. Once her sports car chased my little Volkswagen right across London. She'd screamed she was going to smash my car to smithereens. Fortunately I managed to lose her by nipping into a side-street.'

'She sounds very, very childish,' said Sarah.

'Yes. Since then I have been attracted to more mature ... people.'

'What about Jane. Jane Thomson?' said Jennifer. She wanted him to go on talking. She had never met a man before who talked with such freedom about such personal things. She was sure Shelley had been like that, intensely interested in people, intensely interesting about them.

'Jane was a darling.'

'Edward ought to be hearing all this. He's writing about the trial,' said Jennifer.

'Edward?'

'My father. Sarah's husband.'

'Oh yes,' he smiled quickly and wickedly at Jennifer, laughing at her disapproval. She stared back at him stony-faced.

'Well ... I'm only down the road. He can phone. Sarah knows the number.'

'You were saying, about Jane?'

'I was fond of her. She was so gentle and ... alive ... so full of excitement about sounds and sights and smells. She left me, as a matter of fact, for Charles. She adored him. He was more her type, more wholesome.'

74

'What do you mean?' said Sarah.

'She liked her men to be faithful,' said Paul. 'And I am incapable of that.'

'Have you been interviewed by the police, since you knew them so well?' said Jennifer.

'Yes. But others are testifying to his good character.'

'I hope they don't find Charles Grigson guilty,' said Jennifer. 'I'm sure Jane wouldn't have wanted that.'

'You're right, she wouldn't.'

'I'm so sorry to badger you about the trial,' said Sarah. 'It's just that both Jennifer and Edward have bees in their bonnets about it.'

'That's OK. It's on my mind quite a bit too. It confuses me. I don't understand it. I dream about it. But none of it makes sense. I still can't really comprehend that Jane is dead. She was so *good*. It doesn't seem possible. I knew Charles well. I respected him. I cannot imagine his killing Jane.'

He was standing in front of the french windows with his back to the women, and his hands in the pockets of his jeans.

'I'm sorry, we have upset you,' said Sarah. She glided up and slipped in front of him to open the window to the balcony. Jennifer noticed he didn't move even though Sarah was close to him. They stepped out and as Jennifer came to join them she saw that their elbows resting on the balcony touched. Their backs were to her, they were talking softly and she turned to go. But Paul's voice called her.

'Jenny!' He was leaning on the balcony facing her. He was watching her from the sunshine while she looked out from the darkness. The glorious trees behind him and Sarah's thin back beside him. Golden skin and freckles and those hairs straddling the triangle of his open-necked shirt. How strange that he should look so slight and girlish and yet have that mat of hairs.

'Yes.'

'Where are you going?'

He had such depth to his eyes. Such intensity. Grey, drowning seas of thought.

'To change out of my uniform.'

'We're going to lunch. Are you coming?'

'Well ...'

She saw Paul lean towards Sarah as she whispered something to him. His eyes swept the ground and returned to Jennifer's slightly abashed.

'Oh well,' said Paul, 'If you really are too busy....'

He walked from the balcony and back into the drawing room as if drawn by Jennifer. Sarah was left outside.

'Do you go to the restaurant much?'

'Not much, no,' said Jennifer.

'Why don't you sell the house and buy a flat? That house looks too big for one,' said Sarah as she stepped on to the golden carpet.

'Oh no. I mean, I couldn't do that to a house I have loved. Used to visit my aunt there and consume too much Tizer and too many jam tarts. Anyway, it's such a mess it's quite unsaleable.'

'Talking of food we must be off now. I've booked a table at the White Elephant for one thirty. We have to talk business, you see, darling,' said Sarah to Jennifer.

After they had gone, Jennifer stood in front of her bedroom mirror to see what he had seen. She wore an apple-green and white check shirt dress with white socks. She couldn't recognise herself in the girl who stood before the mirror. She quite liked the look of the alert face, the tousled hair and the bright big eyes. Jennifer practised a smile like her mother's. It was interesting, thought Jennifer, how much her face reflected her moods. When she was happy the very texture of her skin changed from drab parchment to satin. Her hair only responded to her emotions in so far as she washed it into shininess when content and left it lank when sad. It was the conscious reflection of her state of mind, but her face unconsciously reflected the most evanescent of her emotions.

She ran her fingers through her hair. How strange that all the strands were apart but part of her.

Little fragments of the meeting kept returning – the sight of him in the sunlight; her own self-disgust as she stood inside and watched; her mother anxiously tapping her cigarette ash away.

76

What had he thought of her really? A silly schoolgirl suffering from adolescent shyness?

Her checked shirt dress suddenly seemed absurdly childish, with its long white socks and beige sandals. Ugh. She pulled a hamster face, screwing up her nose and baring her front teeth, and turned away from the mirror in disgust.

She went back down to the drawing room where the french window to the balcony was still open. She stepped out and breathed in the faint smell of her summer sweat, felt the breeze and heard the high voices of choir birds in the cathedral trees where swaying leaves presented stained-glass windows of blue sky.

She wondered what Shelley would have thought of her. Would his penetrating eyes have gazed right down into her mind and realised there was more to her than others saw? He made the invisible visible, saw mites in the cheese, poetry in the west wind, revealed the dormant talent of Mary, lifted Harriet from obscurity, why shouldn't he have seen wonders in her, Jennifer Hamilton?

In the drawing room she put Dvorak's cello concerto on the turntable and turned up the sound. She sat in the chair where Paul had sat.

Jennifer turned over the record and caught sight of her face in one of Sarah's many mirrors. She smiled. She had an attractive, mischievous smile. The mirror belonged to a pair with ornate frames which matched the gold carpet. The other was on the wall facing so when she stared into the first she saw a repetition of herself. Where *did* it all end? *Did* it all end?

She saw Hogg leaning back in a chair by the fire with a glass of wine in his hand, scowling.

Shelley cleared a space and sat on the table. His long legs dangled boyishly. Outside the afternoon was fading into evening and she heard the sound of voices passing below Shelley's window.

'Love,' said Shelley, 'has many facets. The love of the sexes, however pure, still retains some taint of earthly grossness, we must not admit it within the sanctuary. It is so dangerous that even I concede it to be avoided. Earthly love corrupts.' A long

77

silence followed into which Shelley withdrew frowning. Finally
he continued, 'The love of a mother for a child is more refined;
it is more disinterested, more spiritual; but,' again he paused,
'the very existence of the child still connects it with the passion
which we have discarded.' Shelley poured himself a glass of
water. Suddenly his face brightened. 'The love a sister bears
towards a sister or a sister to a brother is, however, unimpeach-
able,' he said with an air of triumph.

'You are right to a degree. One must not give way to lust, but
surely pure love …'

A bell chimed.

'Oh well, love can wait. It's time for hall,' said Hogg, heaving
himself up. 'I'm hungry. Are you coming?'

He received no reply.

'I said it's time for hall. Are you coming?'

'No, no. I have no patience with the tyranny of bells. Let the
animals be herded to their troughs. I shan't.'

'Your absence is noticed you know.'

'When our pamphlet comes out our *presence* will be noticed to
more damaging effect. Denying food is one thing, denying God
quite another.'

9

Jennifer sat in the armchair and thought about Paul and
Shelley and Shelley and Paul until her mind was all confused.
There seemed more dead people in it than alive. There was
Shelley, Aphra, Harriet, Fanny, Rebecca and now Jane. The
people she cared for most were all corpses, except for Edward of
course. And now Paul. He was so brotherly, the brother she'd
never had, she decided. She wanted to ask Paul so many
questions. He brought so many thoughts into her head. She
wanted to know all about him. Where he was born, where he
went to school, what his parents were like, why he was
unfaithful to women, what he'd be if he weren't an architect.

What would justify living? Did he think anything does?

Jennifer paced up and down the room as both Shelley and Paul had done. What was Sarah doing with Paul? She wanted to take a taxi over to the White Elephant and join them, say she had decided to come after all. She could see the amused pleasure lifting up the corner of his mouth as she came up to their table. She could imagine her mother's frown. She could see the waiters murmuring in the dimly lit restaurant as she stood, head held high, and demanded Paul and Sarah move round to make room for her. Right now they were probably stroking hands across the table, inflaming each other with burning glances. She wondered what Paul saw in Sarah, if he saw anything in her, why they were lunching together. Of course it might just be that they were discussing plans for the restaurant, but she doubted it.

But of course she wouldn't dare. She'd get no further than the cloakroom, she knew that. How dull and muddy-mettled she was. How insufferable to be cooped up in adolescence, in this square, in cowardice. Shelley had swept Mary – a daughter of William Godwin and Mary Wollstonecraft – away from her gloomy house and off to adventure after adventure in Europe. When they eloped Mary had only been a little older than herself.

Jennifer tried to analyse the difference between her feelings for Shelley and those she had for Paul. Her affection for Shelley was less confusing. To some extent, she knew, he was a fantasy figure – a collection of all she respected and found attractive in men. He wasn't always clear in her mind. Contemporary descriptions of him varied enormously – from that of a redhead with uneven teeth to that of a golden-haired Adonis. In paintings he was shown as having dark hair. It was his charisma which made him so impressive, not any describable features of his face. She felt he was an extension of her. When she spoke to him she was speaking to some superior part of herself. That was why she loved him. Mary must have loved him for much the same reasons – for his emotional restlessness, his need and respect for women, his arrogance, the melancholy tones of his voice, the wildness of his imagination, his attachment to the bizarre and obsessive. Most attractive of all was his vulnerability – his persecution at school and at home which made him need someone to cherish him. When Jennifer imagined Shelley she saw him as a receptive, wild-eyed young man with ideas tumbling from his mind. She'd never met anyone who had his vitality.

Paul was more flurrying because he was real. The warmth and embarrassment of his presence was both pleasant and unpleasant.

But she didn't know what to do about it. She recalled the day long ago of a school harvest festival. She'd arrived at school with a brown paper bag containing a sprig of walnuts from the trees in their Wimbledon garden. The cloakroom had been spilling over with huge bunches of flowers, baskets of fruit with pretty packets of fancy tea and tins of biscuits nestled in between the grapes and the bananas and the ribbons. Nobody had explained to her that one brought baskets and cornucopias of good things to harvest festivals. She'd had to suffer the ignominy of walking up in front of the school and offering the torn brown paper bag to the jolly headmistress who had blinked in astonishment, then beamed out of politeness and pity. The paper bag had sat miserably among the bright splendour of the other girls' gifts.

It was as if she'd been forced into playing a game where everyone else knew the rules. She was always the odd one. Other people seemed so certain of where they were going and how they were getting there.

Nobody had told her what to do in a situation like this. She knew what she wanted. She wanted to know more about this Lucinda Paul had been so keen on. She crept downstairs and went into her father's study. She found the telephone directory and looked up Charles Grigson at 180 Meredith Road, N16. With a sense of disbelief at her own audacity, she dialled the number.

'Hello. Who's that?' said a rather deep female voice.

'Who's that?' echoed Jennifer.

'Lucinda.'

'Sorry, wrong number,' said Jennifer, chilled.

So she existed, this Lucinda. Jennifer wished she knew what

to do next. She didn't understand herself. She didn't understand anyone.

Jennifer sat still for a few moments then couldn't sit still for the rest of the day. She felt like a dustbin overturned by the wind. All her unsorted thoughts were blowing round her. She wandered about the house glancing at a newspaper in the dining room, eating a biscuit in the kitchen, leafing through a magazine in the drawing room. In her bedroom she collected up her keys and purse and put them in her straw bag. Still in her school uniform, she shut the door and walked along the square, past the huge tax office and towards Paul's house.

'Hello, Jennifer,' said the street cleaner. He was a gaunt man with upstanding hair and a vocation. His aim, expressed to all passing residents, was to win the prize for the cleanest square in London. As dogs got in the way of this aim, he tended to kick them. Whether or not such a prize actually existed was a mystery to the inhabitants of the square, who frequently discussed him. In autumn he always became very depressed and muttered to himself or to anyone who'd listen, 'Bloody leaves.' He knew the names of all the square's residents and was particularly fond of Sarah, especially since Edward's terrier had died.

'Hello,' she muttered.

'You looking for that young man?'

'Why?'

'No reason. Just that you're staring at his house as though you're trying to see through the bricks.'

'Oh.'

'Got a crush, have you?'

'Certainly not,' snapped Jennifer and, hearing the helpful rumble of a taxi behind her, turned and hailed it.

'180 Meredith Road, Stoke Newington, please,' she said to the driver.

'OK darling.'

'Bye, bye darling,' said the street cleaner mockingly. He watched the taxi as it drove along the square, past the dappled trunks of the plane trees on one side, houses on the other. Geoffrey and Aemilia lived in a Regency cottage with a pale pink door. On sunny days like this Aemilia was often in the front garden weeding, but not today. Jennifer was not sure why she liked Aemilia as much as she did. In many ways she was the opposite of the women she respected. For instance, she could not have been more dissimilar to Aphra. But Aemilia had a warmth and a sweetness often obscured by her own nervousness. Her front garden expressed her gentleness. It was a mass of flowers, including some wonderful white roses which seemed to exist in some other, more peaceful dimension.

As they drove out of the square, Jennifer's heart began to race. She had no idea what she'd do when she arrived at Lucinda's house.

They drove past Buckingham Palace, along the Mall's elegant sweep, past St James's Park, through Trafalgar Square, and up Charing Cross Road where there were people everywhere, bustling and gawping. Youths were buying kebabs, children ice lollies, couples ate ice creams, crowds pressed into Foyles. White skin glared from short-sleeved T-shirts. The traffic was appalling.

To Jennifer, it all looked agreeably alive. She didn't experience her usual fear and disdain when faced by a mass of humanity. She was actually excited by it. She wanted to search through the bookshops, eat a kebab (she hadn't had any lunch), overhear conversations on one of the double decker buses blocking their path.

The taxi driver was humming some tune to himself. He had a great thatch of fair hair on his head. His shirt sleeves were rolled up, showing off more golden hair all over his arms. He rested his right elbow on the ledge of the open car window.

They ploughed on up Theobald's Road, past Gray's Inn and up, past Sadler's Wells, through Islington. In Stoke Newington things began to look tattier. Houses were run down, shops less prosperous, people larger, blacker and with more children.

But 180 Meredith Road, though chipped and weary now, had certainly seen some grander days. It was a white detached house with a small front garden overgrown with laurels.

She asked the driver to wait, just a few minutes.

He interrupted his humming to say, 'OK darling.'

She walked up the crazy-paved path overshadowed by dusty

82

laurels. What would Paul say if he knew what she was doing? Would Shelley respect her courage? Is that how Aphra felt when she was spying in Antwerp? Two pillars held up the porch and beside the front door was a stone pot containing a geranium and some weeds. The door was half stripped. It had stained-glass panels. The white paint was everywhere peeling and one pane of a window to the right of the door was broken. The house had an unkempt air, a wildness, which Jennifer could not work out. It made her uneasy. She stared for a few moments at the doorbell. Would she press it? Did she dare? What would she say to Lucinda if she came to the door? 'Hello. I'm Jennifer. My father's doing a book on the trial of your brother and ...' She'd send her away at once. Or she could say she wanted to help her save Charles ... but that might involve her in no end of trouble and responsibilities. Otherwise she could claim that Paul was worried about her, Lucinda, and had sent Jennifer to see how she was. But Lucinda would soon discover that was a lie.

A crackle of leaves burst into Jennifer's thoughts. She spun round to see a cat devouring a blackbird on the path. Blood, bones and wings.

She gasped, and knew she had to leave.

She ran down the path, avoiding the cat, and out into the road where the taxi driver was still humming tunelessly.

'Sorry to keep you. Can we go to the White Elephant restaurant in Mayfair, please?'

'OK, darling,' said the man, pushing the car into gear and away.

They drove back through the streets and the people and trees and sunshine.

At the White Elephant, she stepped out of the cab into the street. The sky had clouded over. She shivered and her arms grew goosepimples. She paid off the taxi driver and walked into the dimly-lit club, willing herself to be brave. She was telling the head waiter that she'd come to see her mother when a hand fell on her shoulder. It was Saul Goodman's.

'Hello, sweetheart. You looking for your mother?'

'Yes, as a matter of fact.'

'You just missed her. She was staring into the eyes of some gigolo a few minutes ago.'

'Her architect.'

'Architect? Didn't look like that to me. I watched them for a while before joining them for a glass of wine. I came here to meet some film director chap who didn't turn up. Do you want something? Strawberries and cream?'

Jennifer remembered how hungry she was

'Well I think I'd better ...'

'Come on,' and Saul's arm was round her, guiding her to a corner table where a candle burned in the darkness. Waiters hurried by holding layers of plates. In the beguiling shadows of the room trolleys lolled luxurious with fruits, sherbets, trifles. The restaurant wasn't as harsh as Sarah's. The waiters oozed rather than rushed across the deep-pile carpet. The subdued lighting made her feel pleasantly anonymous.

Jennifer sat, back straight, eyes bright, watching. She munched through a packet of Grissini. There were one or two men dressed like Saul in white trousers and checked shirt and a tan. The atmosphere was that of a holiday, of olives, white wine and sun tan oil.

Saul ordered her strawberries and cream. Meanwhile she wolfed down some of the remaining bread and butter.

'You look sweet in your school uniform.'

'Thank you.'

'I'm fond of your mother you know.'

'Yes.'

'I think she's terrific.'

'Oh yes.'

'I don't like seeing her with gigolos.'

'I don't see that that is any of your business,' said Jennifer with a demure smile.

'Oh yes it is. Because I make it my business.'

'Is there a tiny bit of that white wine left?'

'A tiny bit, yes.'

'Have you drunk that bottle yourself?'

'As a matter of fact I have. Is that your business?'

'No. I was just curious.'

'Well, I'm curious about your mother.'

'Ooh, here are my strawberries. They do look nice.'

The waiter was spooning them out from a huge glass bowl. The smell was headily summery. 'Cream, Mademoiselle?'

'Yes please.'

'It seems this chap Paul knows everyone concerned with the trial your father's been so coy about.'

'He's going ahead with it. I don't think you should have tried to persuade him to do the book. You don't know the barrister concerned. He's very shifty. I'm worried it's all going to cause terrible trouble.'

'Trouble? Nonsense! Do you think maybe she's grilling him for Edward's book?' Saul asked.

'Who?'

'Paul.'

'No, to be honest, I don't.'

'More strawberries? Wine? Anything?'

Jennifer laughed. 'You're trying to bribe me.'

Saul was shiny cheeked and leaning towards her. There was sweat under his arms and a number of cigars stubbed out in the ashtray. He had an air of genuine anxiety.

'That's right.'

'Well I'm incorruptible.'

'You seem rather corruptible today with your bright eyes, flushed face and cream round your lips.'

'Well I'm not. I only met him today. I don't know him at all.'

'Is he very attractive?'

'I don't know.'

'Do you think your mother finds him attractive?'

'Yes.'

'Do you admire your mother?'

'No.'

'You *are* being honest. The strawberries are going to your head. Your mother is a better person than you think. She shouldn't waste herself on a little idiot like that. He was so snooty and superior I'd like to wring his neck. If she divorced Edward and married me you'd have masses of money.'

Jennifer stopped eating. 'Mummy would never divorce Edward.

85

And she is not interested in money. Neither am I. Sarah handles it well but she doesn't *care* about it. Do you see the difference?'

'You defend her when she's being criticised. *You* can say what you like but no one else can. It's a sign of love, you know.'

'Maybe.'

She continued to eat. Saul finished the wine in his glass. Jennifer scraped her plate for the last of the cream. The waiters hovered. They were the last customers except a loving couple canoodling in the corner, the man of the partnership looking old enough to be the girl's great-grandfather.

Saul wiped his mouth. Jennifer did the same. Saul picked a red rose from the small vase in the centre of the white table cloth and gave it to her.

'For your future, little one, and let it not be too school-marmish.'

She put it in her hair but it fell to the ground. She stooped down and picked it up.

'Don't tell Sarah about our chat, will you?'

Saul put Jennifer in a taxi back home. She was buoyant. Saul thought she was attractive, anyway. She hoped Paul would be there when she got back. She'd breeze into the house and explain that she'd gone to join them for coffee at the White Elephant but had just missed them. Instead she'd chatted to Saul Goodman. That would worry Sarah. Paul would be impressed by her easy command of town life. She'd look pretty curled up on the sofa, putting her red rose to her nose while her eyes watched Paul tauntingly.

She burst gaily into the house which was silent, unchanged though she felt changed. She shouted 'Hello, I'm home,' and there was no reply. Her spirits sank. She looked in every room. There was no one there.

In the living room she tried to concentrate on reading, but she couldn't.

She was in Paris, in a high-ceilinged flat panelled in oak with glittering chandeliers. She owned the flat. It had long windows overlooking the Seine and the Louvre. The wooden floor was scattered with white goatskin rugs. She was standing with him on the balcony and he said, 'I don't hear the cars when you are with me,' then he turned, and kissed her, his tongue deep in her mouth, his hands on her shoulders, her body melting. Through the window she saw, though the man with her did not see, that her mother was standing thunderstruck in the drawing room watching the kissing bodies on the balcony outside. Next, Jennifer was in the bath – a bubble bath – and he burst into the room....

10

When Sarah returned alone, she found Jennifer sitting in the armchair with her legs tucked under her, book held close to her eyes and stereo at full blast.

'You're *still* in your school uniform. It's five thirty.'

'Golly. Well, you're back late.' Jennifer's eyes narrowed. Her mother's lipstick was smeared and she had a heated, eager look.

'I wanted to see what Paul had done to his house. In fact he'd done absolutely nothing. It's in the most dreadful state with practically no furniture or carpets. Typical man.'

Jennifer closed the biography of Mary Shelley she wasn't reading.

'You haven't been wading through that tome all afternoon? God, you have no sense of fun.'

'It's brilliant and, as a matter of fact, it is fun to me.'

Sarah ran her tongue over her lips.

'Paul's quite a charmer isn't he? But his house, when I think of it ...'

'The biography is most interesting. Mary Shelley was quite remarkable. So frail and intellectual and so very brave. Giving birth to illegitimate children, writing *Frankenstein*, travelling all over Europe.'

'What are you going on about? He's adorable, didn't you think?'

'Who?'

'Paul of course.'

'Oh, him.'

'I think I'll have a drink. I know it's early but I feel quite exhausted. Won't you have one, darling, just this once?'

'No. I'm going.'

'Stay where you are. Always rushing. It was so messy, his home. Do you know he sleeps on a mattress and his room smells of old socks? Extraordinary that a butterfly like that could emerge from such a squalid chrysalis. And an architect too!'

She poured herself a whisky.

She wants me to know she's been to bed with him, thought Jennifer. She's displaying herself. How dare she? I wish she'd get on the phone to some friend of hers. If she confides in me I'll die.

'Sit down,' said Sarah. 'Relax.'

Jennifer wiped her hands, which were warm with anger, on her skirt.

'I really must change.'

'Sit down.' Sarah sank into the sofa with a sigh. She kicked off her shoes. 'Keep your mother company for once.'

'The nail varnish on your toes is chipped,' snapped Jennifer.

Sarah didn't appear to hear.

'He's a darling isn't he? So attractive and vulnerable. I saw you liked him and …' Jennifer jumped up. 'That's why I want to apologise. I want to confess. I …'

Jennifer made a lurch for the door.

'Went to bed with him.'

Jennifer stopped still.

'Why did you have to tell me that?' she said with care. 'I did not want to know. Why did you have to ruin everything quite so quickly?'

'We can't go on pretending you don't know about my affairs. I think we ought to have an honest relationship. You're practically an adult now.'

Jennifer swallowed.

'You just told me because you wanted to tell someone, anyone. Why did you tell me? Why do you always have to spoil everything?' Her voice trembled and her head drooped.

Sarah jumped up and put her arm round her daughter. Her

breath smelt of whisky. Jennifer wanted to strike out and punch her again and again with her fists.

'I'm so sorry,' said Sarah. 'I shouldn't have said anything. I'm so sorry. I just felt I had to, that I couldn't go on pretending to everyone. Come and sit by me on the sofa, please. It was selfish. I'm sorry.'

Weakly Jennifer sat down and let Sarah stroke her arm.

'Do you despise me for sleeping with Paul? You shouldn't. I like him. I really do like him, surprisingly, an awful lot. There's something so ingenuous and young about him. He makes me feel young. Do you understand?'

'I don't want to understand,' whimpered Jennifer, wishing she had the strength to go.

'Listen. Two weeks ago at a party I met friends I hadn't seen since my twenties. For a moment or two I thought it was a fancy dress. Everyone seemed dressed up and made up to appear much older than they were. I couldn't believe my former friends had become so grotesquely middle-aged. But they had. The men's necks where once I'd nestled my lips were creased ... and the women's faces sagged. There was one, Anne Marie, who'd been an actress and a sensational dresser with a figure that made men gasp. But now not even her little black dress could disguise the tyres of fat bulging above her pantie girdle. She was wearing the pointed stilettos she wore in the past but now they only made her legs look bulbous. She wore a cameo brooch and pearls. I couldn't understand why she didn't at least tint her grey hair. Probably she'd just given up, relaxed cosily into the arms of her wealthy stockbroker husband who, amusingly enough, tried to touch me up in the kitchen during the party.'

'Don't be absurd. You make yourself sound eighty. All your friends look young, or rather don't look old.'

'They're the ones we've kept up with or they're new friends. Presumably we purposely choose friends who don't remind us we're getting old. We like people who are like us, who pay attention to health and appearance, who buy fashionable clothes, who are interested in life. The old friends we met at this party were different. Some of them had given up completely. I'm determined not to give up. I'm determined to have lovers – why not? – I'm determined to be vain, to go to the hairdresser's once a week, to the Countess's once a month for a facial, to buy all the clothes I can afford the money and time to buy. But it still worries me, getting older, especially as I see no sign of living vicariously through you. It would make a difference, you know.'

'Don't you blame me for your unfaithfulness. And what about Edward? What about his happiness, his self-fulfilment? And what about that horrible Saul, won't he resent it? You *are* sleeping with him too, aren't you?'

'I was, but Saul's been boring me. He's even mentioned marriage. It'd be his fourth! And I always say to Edward he can have any affair he likes just so long as he doesn't tell me about it. As far as I know, or rather I don't know, he follows my brief.'

Jennifer snorted. 'He doesn't have affairs. Ever.'

'I wouldn't be surprised.'

'And you'd be livid if he did.'

'Maybe he does, though.' She shrugged.

'He doesn't, he doesn't,' Jennifer said in a panicky voice which seemed to belong to someone else.

'Shush, my poor lamb. Shh. Don't. But you have to face reality. You live in far too much of a never-never land, always have. Now its words and literature and history, but do you remember when you were eleven I gave you that lovely teenage doll, Matilda? I used to imagine you up in your room, playing with Matilda, rehearsing a future of romance, pretty clothes, sweet whisperings, delving kisses, elopements, mirrors and make-up. But one day, do you know what I found? I found all the silk and lace frocks I'd bought your doll thrown away in the waste paper basket and the doll on the bed with all its limbs torn apart. Around it were the legs, arms and carcasses of the beautiful, and incidentally very expensive, foreign dolls we used to buy you whenever we went abroad. But you ruined them all. Edward called your room a mortuary wrecked by a madwoman. I felt responsible, you know. You never told us why you did it. It was the teenage and well-dressed lady-like foreign dolls you destroyed as if, well, refusing to become one. It was as though you were telling me to go stuff myself, that you weren't going to grow up, let alone like me.'

'I don't know. I don't remember.'

'We thought of taking you to a psychiatrist. At school they say you're a brainbox of course. But they also say you don't fit in with the other girls. You always seem so absent.'

'I wish you wouldn't talk to me like this. You're drunk. You've been drinking all afternoon.' She pushed her mother away. 'I can smell it. Whisky.' She stood up. 'You're no better than the tramps round the Salvation Army hostel. You disgust me. You really do. You disgust me. I don't know why Daddy stays with you. He's so terribly much better than you. I wish ... oh I wish ...' and Jennifer rushed upstairs.

11

Jennifer slammed her door behind her and then the blackness descended. She was furious and hurt. She sat at the side of her bed and focused on the small flowers of the wallpaper and counted some. Sixty-three filled a small patch. And how many grains of sand on a beach, and how many people in the world?

Jennifer opened the window wide. She took a deep breath of sweet air, then she turned and hurried downstairs.

Jennifer sat on the bench beneath the horse chestnut whose leaves splayed out like hands on a piano. In the sun the air was full of heat, the sounds of birds and the sight of tiny winged insects darting through shafts of light. Fat bumble bees hummed round the lavender bushes and hollyhocks stood tall in their velvet-deep colours. She was in the shadows again.

She wanted to get out of them just once. She wanted some limelight. No sooner had Paul shone some on her than her mother was metaphorically throwing a tantrum, waving her hands, flouncing her furs, screaming she'd never appear on this show again. And as usual the spotlight returned to Sarah. For once Jennifer had trusted reality. It had let her down, as her love for Rebecca had let her down. She would not trust it again.

For two hours she sat on the bench watching the shadows lengthening.

She knew this holiday was crucial, the last of her childhood. For as she grew older she heard in her room, her sleep, her garden, the soft closing of a door. Each click shut her out of another room where her imagination had once been free. She had not murdered her dolls that day her mother had mentioned, they were already dead to her imagination. She had wrenched their limbs apart only as the worms disintegrate the buried bodies of the dead. If they'd shrieked or moved in her mind as they lay in the chest she'd have opened it up and let them live. But there were rooms still open to her, whirlpooling with movement, colour, whisperings, characters. When the doors to them closed she would die into the next stage of her life. She did not want to have to cope with uncontrollable reality.

Growing up made her frantic, as if a cancer were eating into her. She had seen the effect of cancerous maturity on her schoolmates. Her friend Stella now betrayed the games she'd once played; denied their secret garden in the derelict house where talking cats had roamed, sneered at the old lady who had lived for ever, in and out of centuries. She knew Stella was no happier in the real world, on pavements where you could walk on the lines with no fear of retribution, in deodorants, in political commentaries, in planning a career, in packaging herself into a woman, in choosing alternatives. Childhood had no alternatives, anything was possible.

And now, suddenly and strongly, she wanted to be powerful again. She clenched one hand and the veins of its back were the veins of the trees carrying sap to her body. They were the arteries of roads, pipes under the city, the veins of leaves. She released her hand and the movement thrilled her with the joy of her own power. What a piece of work is man and so why not? An idea was forming in her mind. She would hold a seance.

As the idea became clearer, it seemed she was remembering something she used to know, not creating something new. Perhaps that was what a revelation was like, a wonderful clarification, a clearing away of the fog which obscured the truth which had always been there. It made her feel marvellous, omnipotent. She couldn't stay still. She walked round and round the tree, intoxicated. She was going to rediscover the power of childhood, the ability to be anyone and summon up anyone. She would be in control. Why not?

There was such excitement racing through her she felt she was flying up, like Icarus, above everyone, above the tidy patchwork of the lives of others, above the country cottages, the theatres, the restaurants, up and up.

Jennifer didn't want to settle for the commonsense, dull, world of adults. She needed one of heroes, heroines and magic. The audacious spirits of Aphra, Shelley and Rebecca inspired her with a sense of wonder and that wonder made anything possible. She would arrange a seance. She would bring her friends back to her, play with death, avoid the world's slow stain.

But the help of the spiritualist, Mr Davidson, was essential. She decided that tomorrow, Friday, she would go and see him. She would find out for herself whether he was a charlatan or not. Everything would depend on his cooperation. She had to be sure he wasn't a phoney.

That evening she flipped through a book entitled *Spirit Raising* which she had discovered in Hampstead on a blustery day last December. While Sarah lunched with friends Jennifer wandered round the village. In a cobbled alley she stopped at a shop with secondhand books higgledy-piggledy in the window; remaindered art books, one volume of an encyclopedia, poetry by unknowns, Latin grammars galore. She entered and smelt dank and dust. Tawdry science fiction and fantasy magazines were heaped on the floor at the bottom of bookshelves whose labels bore no relation to their contents. The poetry shelves contained thrillers and the geography shelves poetry. Stacked in a chair by the central spiral staircase was an old man in a cardigan who looked at her listlessly over the rim of his glasses.

'Religion, sociology and history upstairs,' he said bleakly. The grandfather clock at the back of the shop by the tiny frosted glass window chimed three o'clock. In fact it was one thirty.

She climbed up the stairs and came to a warren of rooms with covers collapsing off paperback romantic fiction, piles of pornographic novels with their spines to the wall and rows and rows of prayer books. Cobwebs draped the corners of the room and fluffy dust shrouded the faded carpet and stone floor. Next to a black leather Bible she saw the book. She took it from the shelf and opened it.

She was so immersed she didn't hear the suede footsteps on the stairs but when a floorboard just behind her creaked she swung round, terrified. A snub-nosed young man was standing behind her, in brown corduroy jeans and tweed jacket, blinking. He had one of those scrubbed faces, all the mystery worn away by a good education and upbringing.

'Aw ... aw ... fully sorry to startle you. Just peering over your shoulder at Religion. The old man downstairs said Science was up here but, for the life of me, I can't find it. You haven't seen it anywhere have you?'

She closed the book.

'No, 'fraid not.'

His squeaky upper-class voice had blown away the black clouds that had begun to gather round her and she saw a ray of sun from the tiny window dappling the floor. She nearly put the book away but, realising the young man would then see what she had been reading, she took it downstairs and gave the old man the two pounds he demanded.

'Very old, very valuable book,' he said as she put the pound notes into his hands, their lines embedded with dirt. He stashed the money into a drawer and blew his bulbous nose vehemently. A bell jangled as Jennifer left the shop, the book in her straw bag, and the fresh-faced young man upstairs turned another page of the pornographic novel he came there to read every lunchtime.

At home Jennifer, after noting that the book was in fact dated 1965, had inserted it in a top shelf and forgotten about it. There had been something rather disturbing about the idea of raising spirits.

The next morning she washed and dressed quickly and went down to breakfast. Her parents were up early. They were going shopping at Harrods, then Edward was off to the London Library. Both seemed hungover. Her father had bags under his

94

eyes and her mother had applied more blusher than usual on her cheeks. They were drinking large quantities of orange juice.

'Don't bother with an egg. I'm not up to it; coffee and toast'll do fine,' said Edward.

'That's all you were getting,' muttered Sarah. 'And *try* not to fight that newspaper. You're bigger than it is and by the time you've finished it'll be unreadable by anyone else.'

The kitchen had every modern appliance but today the coffee was instant and the orange juice tinned.

'Look, Sarah, this corduroy suit you want me to get ...'

'No more dissent, darling. It's you, really it is. Grey corduroy. Don't you think that'd be perfect Jennifer? ... Jennifer! What on earth's the matter? You look rather happy. You're actually smiling. You haven't been for a run before breakfast or something awful like that?'

'No. Just in a good mood.'

Sarah, who was clearly not, snorted in disbelief.

'Sarah, I do wish you'd let me go to the library now,' said Edward, mournfully running his hands through his hair then pushing his glasses back on his nose. 'I have so much to do.'

'I'm sorry but last night you looked so dreadful I decided something had to be done. You always look as if you've been caught naked in the midst of an earthquake and just grabbed the first things to hand.'

Sarah looked at Jennifer as she spoke. She was wearing a red T-shirt and a tartan skirt fastened at the waist by a safety pin.

'And that Aemilia dressed like a whore.'

'Actually, I rather liked her shirt,' said Edward wistfully.

'That's because it had the four top buttons undone by the end of the evening. I saw her undoing her buttons when she thought no one was looking. Crazy little tart. I don't know why we have to see Geoffrey and Aemilia all the time.'

'They asked us to dinner.'

'That's no reason to go. I shouldn't have left the restaurant all evening. Now I'll have to stay even later tonight. Aemilia's so hopeless. She's the kind of person who joins the shortest queue at the post office and always waits the longest. You are too, come to think of it.'

'You were the one who wanted to go out and for me to do the book with Geoffrey ... oh please, darling, let's not argue, I've such a headache.'

'I feel awful too. But, you know, if I argue I forget just how awful I feel.'

Edward laughed adoringly and reached, his spirits lifted, for another piece of thick, hot toast.

'Excuse me,' said Jennifer, 'I'm going for a walk.'

She walked through Pimlico, passing stalls busy with fish, with flowers, with vegetables, or with cut-price toiletries. A girl with long hair, fringe and peasant dress was selling, or rather sitting by, a table of silver rings and bangles. Jennifer slid a bangle on to her wrist. 'How much?'

'One pound fifty.'

Jennifer bought the bracelet.

It was rather a dreary, overcast day but Jennifer didn't mind. She bought a bunch of phlox.

She passed a junk shop which hadn't yet opened, although it was ten o'clock. It was steeped high with old dresses, handbags, books, furs, chipped vases and velvet curtains all sprinkled with dust. The shop had erratic opening hours. She'd only found it open once. The old lady who owned it had sat grumpily in the midst of her muddle, demanding excessive prices which people paid because the shop looked immensely cheap.

She wandered back towards the square, buoyed up by the life of the market and the fresh perfume of the flowers in her hand.

She walked through the archway of Abbey Court and stopped for a moment by the goldfish pond, watching the fountain's spray tap-dance over the surface and the sparrows bathing. She looked up at the windows of the surrounding flats. Most were swathed in grey net curtains.

She passed through the courtyard, up the marble steps and on to the checked stone floor of the main building. A uniformed man sat on a chair opposite the lift leaning his elbow on a table spread with post and his peaked cap.

'Excuse me,' she said.

The man's head didn't move but his eyes looked up at her.

'Excuse me,' she repeated.

'Yes?'

'Could you please tell me where a Mr Davidson lives?'

'Fourth floor. Flat forty-six.'

'Thank you.' She began climbing the stone stairs.

Her heels clattered loudly as she hurried up. By the time she was at the third floor she was out of breath and wished she'd taken the lift. She hadn't because she didn't want to go through all the performance of opening and closing those lift doors in front of the caretaker, or whoever he was. Worse still, he might have helped her.

She found herself outside flat forty-six. It was odd how quiet the building was. All she had heard on the stairs and along the corridors were her own footsteps. She knocked on the door. The phlox were so fresh they almost drowned the cold, stale atmosphere of the corridor.

The door opened and the space before her was filled by the little man. She had forgotten just how tiny and just how round he was. Everything about him was rounded except for the sharpness of his blue eyes. His balding head was encircled by a few shreds of hair. Heavy bags hung in semi-circles beneath his eyes. His round inner face was surrounded by another layer of fat. Even his hands were small and pudgy. They were like a baby's fists. His arms stuck out oddly from his body. Like his legs, they were very short. He reminded Jennifer of a mole. He frowned and pushed his face forward, as if sniffing the air.

'Hello,' he said. 'And what can I do for you?'

Jennifer saw the ash from the cigarette in his hand fall to the ground. His minute feet, garbed in a pair of carpet slippers and brown socks, rubbed the ash into the faded carpet. He was shabbily dressed in a grey V-neck with enormous holes in its elbows. But his shirt was tight and prim at his neck. The trousers were of some unpleasant polyester material.

'Can I help you?' he continued, wrinkling his nose and narrowing his eyes. His voice had a rather metallic, Northern tone to it.

Ashamed at the rudeness of her wide-eyed stare, Jennifer looked down and whispered, 'How do you do?'

97

'Very well, very well. So what is it my dear? Are you selling those phlox?'

He puffed at his cigarette. It was untipped and rather untidy. He had obviously rolled it himself.

'No, no, I've come to visit you. I wanted to ask you a favour.'

'A favour! Well, and who are you?' He kept blinking, like a night-time animal unused to the day. His eyelashes were so pale they were almost invisible

'I'm Jennifer. Jennifer Hamilton. I live over the other side of the square. I'd like a private sitting please. I'll pay.' She blushed, feeling it was wrong to have mentioned money so abruptly. He wiped his free hand on his trousers and shook her hand. The touch was clammy.

'You want a sitting right now, I suppose?' he said rather crossly.

'Well, if it isn't too much trouble ...'

'Well, how do you do, how do you do? And come in I suppose, come in, make yourself at home, though this place is hardly very homely. Come along my dear, come along. But you should have phoned me. I'm in the book. I like to meditate before a sitting. Now we've my tension as well as yours to deal with.'

As he led the way, she saw his shirt collar digging up into his neck. He waddled slowly, shifting his weight from side to side.

'Sorry, I didn't think.'

The flat smelt of cigarette ends and loneliness. She saw through a door the kitchen with dirty plates piled on to an old wooden draining board.

The drawing room was dark and full of memories Jennifer had never shared but could feel, waiting, in corners, in the dust on the grandfather clock, in the wedding photograph on the mantelshelf, in the tarnished mirror above. The flower pattern on the sofa where she sat seemed made for another room, another place, a drawing room leading out to a rose garden, a place of polish and laughter and the smell of tomatoes ripening in the greenhouse. She felt that someone had died in this room.

'Can't offer you anything but sherry. Will that do?'

'Thank you but no, I ... '

'Very wise. My last guest complained that the sherry had mould in it. Mould! Imagine. Never touch the stuff myself.'

He stooped down to stub his cigarette end out in a saucer on the floor. After bending, he had difficulty straightening himself.

There were a number of dirty coffee cups and saucers littered about the room along with newspapers, bills, old magazines and books. Everything seemed covered with a veil of ash or dust, a kind of mustiness. The Turkey carpet was frayed at the edges and slightly worn in patches, where sofas or armchairs or desks had once stood, years ago. The window had not been cleaned for a long time.

Mr Davidson lowered himself carefully into his armchair.

There were some dead roses in the vase on the television set. The only life in the room was in the books incarcerated behind glass cupboard doors. Staid leather covers and gaudy paper ones jostled together.

'You like my books?'

'Very much.'

'Precious life-blood, my dear. Very precious.'

Mr Davidson had his eyes closed as he sat in his chair. His feet only just seemed to touch the ground, giving him an air of vulnerability, of a Humpty Dumpty suspended on his wall. He wiped the perspiration from his forehead with a large white handkerchief.

'Hmm,' he said, his lips closed. It was as though he was clearing his mind as others might clear their throats.

'Now shall we begin?'

'Oh yes please,' said Jennifer, sitting further forward in the sofa.

'Now I feel there is a great deal of tension in the air. Try and relax please.'

Jennifer took a deep breath to calm herself.

'Now then, let us try and clear the atmosphere a little. I believe that there is a question you particularly wish to ask me about this room.'

'Yes please. I just wanted to know ... I feel ... I wanted to know ... Someone hasn't died here, have they?'

He pursed his lips and opened his eyes narrowly.

'Correct my dear. My wife died in this room.'

'Oh dear, I'm awfully sorry. I just couldn't relax …'

'We moved here from the country when I retired. To be near good doctors. My wife had a rare kidney disease. She died a week after we arrived here. But I am in constant contact with her. You feel her presence?'

'A small, rather bird-like woman with bright eyes and very quick speech?'

'Yes. But I must remind you. It is I who am supposed to be giving this private sitting, not you.' His face was puckered into a smile. 'I don't wish us to link up with her now, please.'

'Sorry.'

He closed his eyes again. His eyebrows were bushy. 'Hmmmm,' he said thoughtfully. 'You know you're psychic don't you?'

'Well …'

'Often you have hunches which turn out to be right?'

'Yes, that's true.'

'You think of someone, then you meet him a hundred yards along the street. You are about to phone a friend, and she phones you. There seem many such coincidences in your life. But if you can see what's about to happen a hundred yards ahead, a few minutes ahead, you can extend it to hours, to months, you can extend it to years.'

'I see.'

'Hmmmm. If you wish you could develop your considerable psychic gifts.'

'And the past, could I see back as well as forward?'

'Oh yes.'

'I mean the distant past.'

'Hmmmm. The further back you go the darker it all becomes, the more unknown. But a few hundred years would not I think be much trouble to you. You obviously have very strong psychic abilities. Very strong indeed. Hmmm. You have already been experimenting on the spiritual plane I believe?'

'Yes, I suppose I have.'

'Hmmmm.' He wiped his forehead with a large white handkerchief.

After the last hmmm there was a moment or two of silence into which Jennifer felt herself relaxing.

Jennifer felt peculiar, very calm and yet very elated in the presence of this little man dangling his legs childishly and watching her with sympathy in his eyes. There was a curious stillness to the room. She didn't take her eyes off him as he spoke and yet didn't feel embarrassed. It was as though there was a circuit flowing between them which she mustn't break.

'I'm linking up here with a white-haired lady ... a grandmother perhaps. She died suddenly but didn't mind. Enjoyed cooking she says. I have an impression of her in an apron.'

'My mother's mother probably. She died a few years ago. I was upset. But I wasn't very close to her.'

'She sends you all her love. But she advises you not to do anything foolhardy. She says you should keep in your place.'

'She kept in her place. It didn't do her much good.'

'Hmmm. She says that the unknown is dangerous. She avoided it.'

'That's silly.'

'Hmmm. She is just warning you. She means well. She asks me to tell you that love matters more. Do you understand?'

'Not really.'

'She says that you will come to understand what she has said. That love matters more. Hmmm ... than what? ... She just says love matters more.'

'How funny.'

'Now I can hear an organ playing and it's in a small village church ... can you help me with this ...?'

'No.'

'It's in the past, probably some branch of your family, your maternal grandmother's family I think. They lived in the country ...?'

Jennifer shrugged. Most people had families who lived in the country. She didn't find this an especially impressive piece of clairvoyance. 'My grandmother did live in the country.'

'Did someone in the family play the organ?'

'Not that I know of.'

'If you check with your mother I'm sure you'll find that I am right. Hmmmm.' He smiled. 'I feel you don't know much about your mother's family and aren't much interested anyway.'

'That's true.'

'I'm afraid I have to pass on the messages as they come to me even though they might bore you. . . . Good, good,' he said. He made a gesture with his little arm. 'Yes, yes,' he said. He seemed to be talking to someone.

'Now I have a woman who was very old indeed when she died, very old. Ninety perhaps. She was clairvoyant too but she kept it to herself. Again a relation of yours I think?'

'My mother's grandmother was about ninety when she died but I don't know if she was clairvoyant.'

'No, well you wouldn't. Gwen her name is. Gwen ...'

'I don't remember. Maybe.'

'Dear me, she's full of messages for you.'

'Isn't there someone younger wanting to talk to me, a girl?'

'No, I'm picking up this rather plump old lady with eyes that spoke more than she spoke herself. She says I'm to tell you that your mother loves you more than you think. She echoes the other old lady in telling you that love matters more. She is very insistent on this point. Yes, Gwen dear, I know love matters.' Again Mr Davidson seemed to be talking directly to someone else. 'But there are other things apart from love which matter. I know you disagree, Gwen. But in my opinion love only keeps the world together, it doesn't push it forward. I know spirits know a great deal, but they don't always know best.' Jennifer saw that Mr Davidson was bright red and that his little feet were kicking rather crossly. He wiped his brow. 'I am not going to argue with you,' he said firmly to Gwen. 'If you feel like that, don't link up with me, I don't care.'

He looked at Jennifer, frowning. 'Your great-grandmother is being rather rude to me. She doesn't like to be contradicted.'

Jennifer laughed. Mr Davidson smiled sheepishly. 'Sorry, my dear. I don't usually quarrel with the spirits. But sometimes they get rather uppity.'

'Hmmmm.' He mopped his brow.

'There is nobody younger wanting to contact me?'

'Not at the moment.'

'Could you tell me something?'

'Yes.'

'Do the dead ever appear before the living?'

'You mean do they ever materialise?'

'Yes.'

'You have to have common sense about these things.'

'Do they ever materialise?'

'If two psychics have the same wave vibrations they might both see a spirit at the same time.'

'So they don't actually materialise?'

'I don't know. But you know perfectly well that the dead do appear before the living. You have experienced it yourself. Haven't you, my dear?'

'Yes. Mr Davidson, why were you thrown out of the spiritualist church?'

He started a little, his feet jerking slightly. 'In the opinion of the other mediums I took my curiosity about spiritual things a little too far. And I made the mistake of telling one or two of them what I had found out. If mediums take things too far, if they overreach themselves, it gives spiritualism a bad name. That's what they told me.'

'What do you mean by going too far?'

'As a matter of fact, one or two spirits materialised before me. Or I thought they did.'

'There were witnesses?'

'Oh yes, three students from my spiritual development classes. One of them denied he'd seen anything and the other two swore that they had seen spirits materialise. Both were eventually sent to see a psychiatrist and I was thrown out of the church. I refused of course to go to the doctors. All my life I had been working towards such an achievement, and when it arrived, it was denied me. My friends scoffed at me, the spiritualist newspaper refused to publish my findings. It was all very distressing. The students I had been working with were all three very receptive and very young. Such things are hard to repeat.'

'Could you repeat it with me?'

'I don't know. Perhaps. Would you dare?'

'Yes. That's why I came here. That's what I want.'

He squinted. 'Really?'

'Yes.'

He shook his head. 'I don't know. I'm building up a small reputation here. People are beginning to respect me again.'

'We would keep it secret. But *we* would know what we had achieved. I would not deny you. I would not go to a psychiatrist.'

'Hmmmm.' He mopped his brow. 'Relax please. Just relax. Make your mind empty. Let us relax. Don't fret. I feel the spirits want me to tell you about yourself. You are a solitary person. You're a virgin.'

Jennifer started.

'With a disregard, even fear, of the pleasures of the flesh?'

'Yes.'

'And this materialisation you have come to me for, you want it more than anything else, you feel it would justify your years on the earth plane.'

'Yes.'

'Hmmm. I have myself lived a quiet life, the life of a teacher of the classics. I have felt all along that there must be something more to achieve and I see you feel that too. You feel odd, uncomfortable in the world. You don't feel you quite belong here. But this – as you think of it, this "seance" – would prove to you that you mattered.'

'Yes.'

Again he mopped his brow with his large linen handkerchief.

'Hmmm. You won't achieve the seance unless you remain a virgin. Hmmm. I'm picking up someone who says her name is ... Aphra ... Aphra Behn. Dear me. She says she is looking after you.'

'Yes, go on.'

'Oh what a bad chest she has,' he wheezed. 'Very poorly. I can just see her sitting writing a poem with a quill pen. She's very sad, but quite enjoying the sadness. She's writing about the man she loves and the man she loves is ... is a homosexual who only sees her as a cover, a way of hiding his homosexual activities. She writes:

104

"His eyes are black, and do transcend
All fancy e'er can comprehend,
And yet no softness in 'em move
They kill with fierceness not with love."

Dear me, the poor lady. She's coming towards me now. She seems very fond of you. She has bulging breasts and heavy-lidded eyes with black eyebrows, and her dress trails along the ground. Does she come to you often?'

'Yes, quite often.'

'She tells me there is another spirit often with you, another poet.... Really this is quite exceptional.' He seemed very excited. He was blinking avidly. 'I once picked up a very clear impression of Charlotte Brontë in a class and ... All right, Aphra. She says she wants you to go through with your idea. She seems convinced it's a good one. She says you're a brave girl but that to find yourself you must fulfil yourself, you must follow your instincts and desires.'

'Oh *good.* And she'll help?'

'Yes, she never had much care for convention she says.'

'You did say you sometimes see the same as someone else who's psychic?'

'If we have the same wave vibrations.'

'Look behind you,' said Jennifer.

'Oh my God,' said Mr Davidson, nearly falling off his chair as Aphra stood watching them both, her hands on her ample hips and head thrown back, laughing. They both blinked as if at a bright light, and she was gone.

It took Mr Davidson a cigarette and some deep breathing to recover. Jennifer discovered she was trembling.

'Now, shall we arrange this "seance"?' he said quietly.

'Oh yes.'

'But you will have to see me once or twice before that. We must prepare ourselves properly.'

Jennifer clenched the arm of the sofa so tightly her knuckles were white.

'Where do you wish it to take place? Here?'

105

'No, at my parents' house please. Number eighteen, Abbey Square.'

'Why there?'

'I should like my father to be there. I should like him to see what happens.'

'Would he be able to cope with it? Could he believe what his eyes see?'

'Oh yes. I should so much like to have his support.'

'And admiration?'

'Yes. His admiration.'

'Would he keep it completely secret?'

'Oh yes. He's very reliable. I promise you that. He'd never mention it to anyone.'

'All right. It's up to you. You know him. And the date?'

'I thought the Saturday before I go back to school. August the thirtieth. Somehow I feel that's the last Saturday of my childhood. The next week I'll be sixteen and studying for A levels.'

'Then on no account can it be postponed. If you feel that, then it's true. The spirits have told you to trust your instincts and you should obey. You may of course cancel but you cannot postpone. So make sure you are ready, or you will have lost your chance for ever. Your innocence and youth will help us greatly. Your protectors will come to you when you call. I feel certain that they will. It will be a great achievement for both of us. I'll come to you at eight o'clock on August the thirtieth. That's about six weeks from now, isn't it?'

'About.'

'We shall see each other before then of course.'

'When?'

'We'll arrange it later. Not now.'

Jennifer stood up and scrabbled in her pocket.

He shook his head. 'No money,' he said. 'Just those flowers, they were for me, weren't they?'

The pastel flowers were lying forlorn on the sofa.

'Oh yes, I'm sorry – I forgot …'

'Thank you my dear.' He shook hands with her at the door. The hands were cooler now. 'Remember to keep your thoughts clear and spiritual. You must concentrate on your spiritual development.'

'Yes, I will, thank you,' she said.

Later that night, after some of the excitement had died down, she flipped through her book on spirit raising. It contained symbols which stirred her, reached right down to her childhood where there had been magic everywhere. Then there had been beauty and drama in her fears. Over the last years her fears had been arid, of pale-washed shoppers in the streets, of announcements of births, marriages and deaths, of being noticed and of not being noticed. In childhood there had been swirling shapes, amorphous blobs of colour in the corner of her room. Created and contained by darkness. Demons had lurked in bushes. Fluttering moths which hit her head when she read late on open-windowed summer nights were spirits of darkness, trying to escape to light, to heaven. Spiders had been enormous. Rituals such as never stepping on the third step of the staircase and always getting to her room before the phone stopped ringing had been of deadly importance. She would never even look at poisonous berries, knowing a mere glance would kill her. These fears had given significance, depth to life. Whereas the ones she had nowadays shallowed her life, prevented her from acting or saying as she wished.

She saw in spiritualism and magic a way to transcend the numbing dullness, the petty fears, of reality. Shelley himself had believed the state of terror was one of 'aweful' hypersensitivity to the world, awakening the mind to the invisible forces everywhere around which the normal mind could not apprehend.

12

The next morning, Saturday, Edward received a letter from Lucinda Brown. He read it, frowning, over breakfast. Jennifer watched him. The writing was big and childish, in black ink on thick paper.

'Well?' said Sarah, when he put down the letter, 'What does it say?'

'She's just telling me that same wild story she told Geoffrey. She says there is going to be a terrible miscarriage of justice if Charles is found guilty. She says Charles would never murder anyone and it must have been a burglar. She wants me to persuade Geoffrey he is prosecuting the wrong person. She's a bit silly, I must say. *And* she says she doesn't understand why someone as wise as Geoffrey – wise! – could bring himself to prosecute the wrong man. But she's presenting no new evidence and, as the trial's starting this Monday, I don't think she has much of a hope.'

'She must love her brother very much to be so distraught and act so wildly – calling round on Geoffrey all the time, writing crazy letters,' said Sarah. 'There's no evidence of a burglary, is there?'

'None whatsoever.'

'And Aemilia told me that Geoffrey keeps talking about the girl and she keeps calling and pestering him. I think Aemilia believes Geoffrey has a crush on the wretched female.'

'She's very attractive.'

Sarah yawned. 'I wish *you'd* not go on quite so much about this trial.'

'It bores you, does it?'

'No, as a matter of fact it doesn't. I just don't understand why you're quite so drawn into it. Are you infatuated with that Lucinda as well?'

'No.'

'Well, you seem uncommonly obsessed by this trial. You have taken very little interest in me since you began to get involved in it.'

'I don't think that's true.'

'It is, darling, I can assure you it is.'

'Come now ... I've just had to do a spot of extra work. I've had to mug up on the subject.'

'It appears to have driven out every other thought,' said Sarah meaningfully.

'I've had to read new books,' he and his mouthful of toast muttered.

'Are your publishers paying your expenses?'

'They've paid me a good advance, that's all. Quite sufficient.' Sarah yawned again.

'Do you really think he'll be found guilty?' said Jennifer.

'Well, although the judge resembles an upright cadaver he's apparently quite kindly and they've got a good chap for the defence – an Arthur Curtis. But as it is the evidence is stacked quite high against Charles Grigson. After all, he had the motive and was found on the premises – virtually with the knife in his hand. For his sake I hope the judge and the jury are charmed by his pleasant manner.'

'I don't think he did it,' said Jennifer quietly.

'What do you mean?'

'I just don't think he did.'

'You haven't met him and you haven't heard all the evidence. How can you possibly say that?'

'I don't know.'

'You think it was a burglar?'

'I don't know.'

After breakfast Edward took the letter round to Geoffrey. From there, he was going to work in the library. Sarah left for a day at the restaurant.

When Jennifer thought of the trial her mind lost its clarity and swirled with anxiety and dark colours ... like clear water suddenly polluted with oil. She remembered the cat devouring the blackbird on the path of Charles Grigson's house. She remembered her fear as she stood outside the unkempt house. She remembered the dark laurel leaves hanging heavy about the path.

And Lucinda's voice, her deep voice. Untamed Lucinda, always in need of an audience before which she could act. In a way, she felt, Lucinda was enjoying the drama of her brother's plight. Jennifer did not like Lucinda at all, but put it down partly to her knowledge of Lucinda's relationship with Paul. She detested the thought of their lying in bed together, Lucinda's long body and mane of hair entwined with Paul's. Jennifer did not mind so much Paul's relationship with Jane, and not just because in death she was no longer a threat. When she thought of Jane she did not think of sex. But when she thought of Paul with Lucinda, and with Sarah, she could think of nothing but the sharing of tongues and bodies and sweat. It made her slightly queasy. She could almost smell the bodies. She felt a hot pain in her heart, or somewhere inside her. She did not much like experiencing these new, adult feelings. They were squalid compared with her glorious plan of bringing the dead back to life.

She went for a walk in St James's Park. From the bridge in the centre of the park she watched seagulls skim down on to the water and bob there like little boats. The surface shimmered with the silver trails of ducks hurrying across the lake on some mysterious mission or another and on the banks geese pottered with their snaking, inquisitive necks and in-turned feet. Pretty little moorhens snapped at each other beneath the bridge.

'There's nice fish,' remarked a little girl looking through the railings.

'No, they're not fish, they're ducks,' said her mother.

There were a number of men prowling about the park, watching her and the other women, whispering to her as she passed.

One man's yellow shirt clashed with his ginger hair, a woman accentuated her huge breasts with a tight silver T-shirt, an Italianate male had a shirt open practically to his waist although it was not even warm. The shirt was scarlet.

How much more pleasant were the muted, reflective shades of the lake. A pair of black swans managed to look dignified even when touting for scraps of bread. Jennifer wished human beings were a little more splendid. Their bright clothes, loud voices and predatory stares littered the fairy tale park.

She crossed the bridge and walked along the path flanked on one side by the water, on the other by the dappled shades of dreaming trees, huge, dank and silent.

She sat down in one of the line of deckchairs and stared out at the weeping willows opposite. Their tips were shorn neatly off so their leaves couldn't trail in the water but still the trees were wild, their boughs misshapen limbs swathed in cloaks of green. Above them loomed the turrets of St James's.

She remembered how Shelley used to make paper boats to sail on the water. He was always drawing boats. And he died at sea. How odd it all was. She recalled Trelawny's description of his body: 'The face and hands, and parts of the body not protected by the dress, were fleshless. The tall slight figure, the jacket, the volume of Sophocles in one pocket, and Keats's poems in the other, doubled back, as if the reader, in the act of reading had hastily thrust it away, were all too familiar to me to leave a doubt on my mind that this mutilated corpse was any other than Shelley's.'

Staring out, across the water, she saw a dark, slight figure on the opposite bank. He was crouched over the water, watching something that was perhaps too small for her to see. She knew that it was Shelley there, among the weeping willows, playing with a paper boat, like Pan or some river god.

He kept leaning forward, too far forward, as if he might fall. The wind was becoming stronger, the sky suddenly darkening, the weeping willows beginning to sway angrily. A little rain began to pit the now dull, metallic water. Jennifer shivered.

She saw Shelley jump up and clap his hands with delight. Nobody else seemed to be watching the elfin figure over the other side, dancing and clapping and grinning so wildly she was sure he'd slip.

She waved at him. He waved back. The woman in the seat beside her was watching her curiously. Shelley pointed towards the water a little way over to his left, near the bridge. Then she saw it. A white speck bobbing between two mallards. She grinned, nodded her head enthusiastically and clapped her hands as if applauding. 'Do stop that,' said the woman. Suddenly Jennifer could smell the sea and, as she looked again towards the bank, she saw that Shelley had disappeared. She looked again for the boat, but it too had disappeared, or maybe sunk.

Just near Jennifer a congregation of ducks and geese and pigeons was forming in response to some crumbs. Some fell on the bank where they were grabbed by a pigeon with a gammy leg.

She closed her eyes. She heard the din of trumpeting,

quacking, screaming, splashing ducks. She heard a child shout 'Oh Mummy look', somebody chattering in French, a baby crying and a great swelling murmur of other voices and traffic in the background. Someone dragged their feet on the path behind, someone walked briskly, another ran, a few strolled. An aeroplane passed overhead.

An Arab came to sit beside her. She could feel him studying her. She walked away.

The air was moistening and the sky darkening. From the bridge Jennifer stared out across the green water. How extraordinarily black those two swans were, huge majestic launches making the smaller birds flounder in their wake.

13

Early that afternoon the doorbell rang and Jennifer hurried down to answer it. On the front porch, the square behind him, stood Paul with a ruddy tinge to his face and a hint of alcohol on his breath. He grinned. He was freckly and friendly.

'Hello,' he said and sniffed.

'Hello. I'm afraid Sarah's out.'

Paul sneezed.

'Summer cold. Think I'm getting one,' he explained. 'Can I come in and wait please?' He looked at his watch. 'I mean she should be back soon.'

'Of course. Do come in. She's expecting you, is she?' Jennifer hoped Sarah was coming soon and hoped she wasn't. In a way she wanted Paul to withdraw from her, Jennifer, and leave her alone with her thoughts of Mr Davidson and the seance. And anyway she felt so shy with Paul she wanted to hide. She hadn't really been shy with Mr Davidson, or not in the same way.

'Yup, she is,' said Paul.

They stood in the narrow hall. His jaws were moving slowly.

'I really am dreadfully thirsty. Couldn't have a glass of water could I?'

'Of course.' She walked down the corridor and into the kitchen. He followed.

'Do you get thirsty when you get colds?' he said.

'I think so.'

'One always finds it hard to remember what being ill is like if one's not actually ill, don't you find?'

'Oh yes.'

'You will excuse the gum, won't you? It's just that I'm rather attached to it at present.'

Jennifer and Paul were both standing with their arms crossed, adrift on the floor of the kitchen. It had black and white tiles like a chessboard. He sniffed, drawing his upper lip towards his nose in an apish expression. She smiled a wisp of a smile and quickly turned to the sink where she poured him a glass of water. Through the window before her she saw the still garden and would have liked to retreat out there.

'You know,' he said, 'what I'd like even better than water is a cup of tea. I mean, would that be a terrible lot of trouble? When one's got a cold, tea can be tremendously reviving, don't you find?'

'Oh yes.' She filled and put on the kettle. She leaned her back against the sink, in her mother's customary place.

'How are you enjoying your holidays?'

'Very much indeed, thank you.'

'Your mother says you work all the time. I mean, what do you work at, now you've just finished your O levels?'

Her eyes opened wider and, for a second, met his in full gaze as she realised in astonishment that she wanted to tell him all about everything. She wanted to tell him about Shelley and Mr Davidson.

She turned and swirled hot water round the tea pot.

'Nothing much,' she said.

She spooned in three teaspoons of Earl Grey and poured on the boiling water.

He was watching her intently.

'How's your work on the restaurant?' she asked.

She took out two cups and saucers of thin white china, put sugar in the bowl and milk in the jug.

'Not bad I suppose. It's silly though, really. I'm just tinkering around with the back yard, getting an outside lavatory removed, arranging for a patio to be built. Not really the kind of thing I've spent five years training for. I'd prefer to be designing something a little more imaginative, I must say.'

'Like what?'

'Oh I don't know. I'd like to revamp a Welsh castle, overlooking the sea maybe. I'd have a bedroom in a turret, and a study in another. Wouldn't that be fun? Do you want a room in my Welsh castle?'

She was staring down at the tray she held in her hands. She allowed her hair to fall forward to cover the heat of shyness which was flaring up in her face.

'I'll carry the tray upstairs for you,' he said. 'Hope I don't trip. I've just had rather a good lunch.'

She frowned, not able to see the connection.

'Plenty of drink,' he explained with his impish smile which practically made a semi-circle. His smile came out of his eyes too. 'At lunch. But my mind still feels thick as a Mars bar.'

She followed him upstairs where the sun was shafting the golden carpet and a fountain of mimosa splashed from the porcelain jug on the coffee table. She sat on Edward's button-backed velvet chair. He put the tray on the coffee table and sat on the edge of the sofa, legs wide apart and back bowed.

'I'll pour,' he said.

'Thank you,' she said. Her hands clenched the sides of the chair. He brought her over a cup of tea, very carefully, spilling not a drop. How considerate he was, she thought.

'Oh, I've forgotten to offer you sugar,' he said. He stood there, the saucer held in both hands, an engraving from a Greek monument.

'I don't take it, thank you.' She sloshed some tea into the saucer as she took it from him.

'It's funny, about my work. I can't express myself well when talking about it. I need to draw plans.'

Jennifer pressed herself against the back of her chair, drawing away while all the time her eyes gazed at him unblinking. His eyes glided towards her and she looked down. A hush of soft sunlight warmed her bare arms into the downy skin of a peach. One foot was tracing a pattern in the carpet.

'Oh yes, I, well, I understand. I don't enjoy talking about my work either.'

'Oh, I don't mind talking about it to *you*. I mean, I trust you and when I trust somebody I enjoy spreading my dreams under their feet.'

'Well, I suppose I trust you. Of course I trust you. But I really don't think I can … I really can't … say anything because I find, well, it destroys things, makes them ordinary.'

'No, if you don't want to talk about your work, I won't press you. But you ought to trust me. I mean, your mother's spoken about you and it's odd but I feel I know you perhaps because I was like you once, shy and hopeful, feeling everything I did wasn't enough. Now I'm confident because I know no one else has anything to be confident about either. I mean, you and I are alike.'

'Really? Tell me, where were you brought up?' said Jennifer, panicking.

He smiled. 'In Tunbridge Wells. My father's a GP and my mother's very matronly, a leader of good works and the local magistrate's court. I was at school at Sherborne. Very sober country middle class, you see. Highly respectable.'

'Did you have any brothers or sisters?'

'I have an elder brother but I was always the favourite. My mother adored me. I was pretty and could talk and draw very well. He's a doctor, my brother, very dull. Married and living in Swindon. You'd think with a background like that I'd be very stable and reliable.'

'And you aren't?'

'No. I change all the time – girlfriends, opinions – I'm a will o' the wisp. Somehow no woman has yet helped me to settle.'

'But you want to?'

'I don't want to settle *down*. I want to settle, I want to be happy with life, with myself.'

Paul, thought Jennifer, doesn't just talk, he confides.

'And Sarah, does she make you feel settled?'

'No. Sarah is vital. She makes life amusing. She flatters me.

115

But she doesn't understand me. She doesn't make me feel as you do, for instance. It seems that you search into my soul with those avid eyes of yours. They're like planets you know. Huge and all-seeing. Sarah takes me at face value. It is pleasant to be with her.'

'She is married, you know. Why doesn't that make any difference?'

'Whether she is married or not is not my business. She must make her own decisions and deceptions. You think that heartless and immoral of me?'

'I think it immoral because of my father. He'd be so hurt.'

'Yes ...' And Paul looked anxious, so much so that Jennifer felt guilty for having mentioned Edward in such a prissy way.

'Everything used to be so much easier when I was religious. Then I had guidelines. My parents and brother are quite devout. Are you at all religious?'

'No, I don't think I am.'

'Oh God, I'm going to ...' He gave a mammoth sneeze. 'Oh dear. I really have got a cold.' His eyes were a little red. He took a navy blue hanky out of the pocket of his jeans and blew his nose fiercely.

'Can I get you anything?'

'A brandy would be bliss.'

She went to the large shelf in the alcove where a tray of bottles hid in the shadows of an emerald fern like troops in an army manoeuvre. She poured the brandy, the colour of soft brown sugar, from the cut-glass decanter into a stocky glass. She turned and found he was standing looking out at the darkening sky. Byron had nicknamed Shelley – with his quick, noiseless movements, slim figure and bright eyes – 'the Snake' after the serpent that tempted Eve.

'The sun's gone in,' he said, 'but it's still very warm. May I open the doors?'

'Of course.'

Through the open doors seeped the hum of a radio, birds chirping and a dog barking.

He slipped back to his seat and smiled at the brandy.

'You were telling me about how you used to be religious,' said Jennifer.

'Was I? Yes, well it's true. I mean, my family's been Roman Catholic since Jacobean times. I inherited God but I also discovered him for myself in a book in father's library. It was a small, fat Victorian one with the grand title *The Universe*. How many volumes would a book like that run into today? But to me the book seemed immense and better than any fairy tale. Every time one opened it one discovered an engraving or a passage one hadn't noticed before. It told of gigantic sponges six feet high shaped like goblets ...'

Paul was leaning forward, his hands making the outline of the goblet.

'... they were called Cups of Neptune and there were also engravings of absurd nests. But all these nests were, so the book explained, perfectly suited to the lives, shape and country of the birds, or in some cases ants, who made them. It seemed obvious to me that the creatures couldn't have thought them up so it must be God. But it was the sheer beauty of all these wonders that really got me. Cuban glow worms, called lantern flies, shone so bright that women enclosed them in little cages of glass and hung them in their rooms to work by their living light. That was the book's phrase, "living light". Then there were engravings of magnificent vultures in the Andes, a crane's nest on an Egyptian monument, all sorts of strange things. And the writer documented everything meticulously and poetically, glorying in the skill of God's hand.' His voice slowed down. He was watching Jennifer closely to see how she reacted to his speech. 'So no wonder I found God impressive. What about you, were you really not impressed by him?'

'Not ever.'

The heat seemed to weigh on Jennifer's body. Outside the sky was blurring brown and the leaves twitched. Birds vanished and the dog growled.

Jennifer liked Paul for his speech. Most adults she met through her parents had an air of having seen, done and felt everything and been bored by the lot. Not like Paul at all. One moment he was languid and listening, the next he talked energetically. Shelley also had bouts of lethargy interrupted by extraordinary mental and sometimes physical activity. What's

117

more no man had ever taken the trouble to talk like this to her before, to be both intimate and respectful. As he talked so avidly his skin had seemed transparent with an inward light, just as Shelley's had been, according to Hazlitt.

'Are you still religious?' she said.

'I don't think so. You see once one starts understanding civilised people – their selfishness, wilful murders, etcetera – one stops believing in God. How, after all, could a God of anything approaching love create such murky beings and allow them to ravage and pollute His world? At school I discovered that the world of *The Universe* was dead. Most of the creatures I'd read about were extinct, murdered by man's greed, his obsession with exploitation, his machines, his power-craze. A fellow at school told me off-handedly that there weren't any crane nests on Egyptian monuments nowadays, there were too many tourists around. What's more, at public school I decided I didn't much like people anyway. I mean, everyone teased me as a cissy because I missed my Mummy and looked like a girl. It didn't take me long to realise these boys were extremely petty ...'

Schoolboys had laughed at Shelley too. How could they?

'... and the teachers oppressive and cruel. If you love people then you probably love God but if you don't it's hard to love Him. Do you see?'

'Yes.'

'Do you love people? I mean is there anyone you have really loved, man or woman?'

Jennifer thought of Rebecca. She was tempted to tell Paul about her but felt that would be a betrayal, turning her into mere conversation. Jennifer wished to keep her memory intact.

'I suppose so.'

'Who?'

'I can't think offhand.'

The distant murmur of thunder rose to a booming explosion but there was still no rain. The door creaked and the trees swayed nervously. Big blobs of water began to drop on to the concrete balcony. Suddenly the air erupted with sound and unleashed a million darting, slanting arrows of silver. They watched, shivering slightly, and the light outside was curiously bright as a dog barked angrily into the uncaring skies.

Jennifer got up and closed the french windows.

'You know,' said Paul, 'I don't think I've been happy since I lost God. It sounds melodramatic but life is rather, don't you find? Losing God is like losing a lover you're disillusioned with. I mean, you don't want to stay with her, you don't even like her, but still her absence leaves a terrible vacuum.'

He looked direct into her eyes. She returned to the pattern she was tracing with her foot on the plain gold carpet.

She pushed her hair back behind her ears.

Paul gave a huge labourer's sniff which quite undercut the seriousness of his last speech. She smiled slightly at the carpet.

'Oh dear. You make me want to confide in you and I shouldn't. I open out my soul and you just sit there with those dark round window-eyes of yours closed. I should like to see in. Won't you at least turn on the light inside, tell me something about yourself? When I'm depressed I want to lose myself in someone else.'

'I'm sorry. If you're depressed why don't you go somewhere new, do something new?'

'I don't dare. And anyway I have a good time. I enjoy life. I appreciate all the joys of life.' Suddenly Jennifer was angry, resentful.

'I just don't know … I don't believe it when you talk about the "joys of life". I don't know what you're talking about.'

'What do you mean?'

'I don't really understand the value of happiness. What's the point of it? Why do people go out trying to enjoy themselves? I just don't understand.'

'You really are a little intellectual.'

A door slammed below and they heard Sarah's quick, decisive steps coming upstairs.

'But your mother certainly isn't.'

'Isn't what?' said Sarah at the doorway standing wet and dripping like the King of the Golden River. She had a clutch of large, small, colourful and full plastic bags. When she had a new lover she always bought new clothes. 'I'm absolutely drenched

119

but I just don't care,' she announced, her skin red and glowing. Her summer dress clung to her body. She kicked off her sandals. She was wearing pink nail varnish on her toes which matched the pink flowers of her dress. With her full breasts and disordered hair she was a sea goddess. Her dark eyes sparkled as she collapsed on the sofa next to Paul.

He kissed her lightly on the lips but then his lips lingered as though they found it hard to pull away. 'An intellectual,' he said.

'Oh what an angel you are,' she said, running her finger coyly down the long sweep of his nose. Her face was, momentarily, a mush of affection. 'But I hope I'm not breaking up anything. You two looked very comfortable here.' She glanced with raised eyebrows at the brandy glass and tea cups. 'Quite a domestic scene.'

Jennifer was infuriated by Sarah's condescension, by her assumption that the idea of 'breaking up anything' between Jennifer and Paul by her dramatic entry could only ever be a joke. Jennifer wouldn't have been surprised if Sarah had gone and had a quick shower in her clothes just so she could look like an advertisement for vodka or expensive cigars. How dare Sarah treat life so breezily? How dare Paul stare at her with admiration?

'Jennifer, would you be a darling and make me some tea? Otherwise I'll catch pneumonia. I'm utterly exhausted. Paul, do you want another cup?'

'Thank you but no. I have a terrible confession to make. When I arranged to meet you here at four, and the time is incidentally four thirty now, I forgot I had to see someone the other side of town at five. So I can only stay a few minutes.'

'You're supposed to be at the restaurant at six thirty-and anyway who do you have to meet?' Sarah's eyes were sharp as a Siamese cat's.

'No one you know.'

'Male or female?'

Jennifer collected up the cups and hurried downstairs. There was an incipient storm brewing in Sarah's disappointed, down-slanting mouth.

Paul's words, his looks, his eyes kept tumbling over and over in her mind as she made the tea. It was an exhilarating sensation, a sensation which for once she made no attempt to analyse. It took her a while to make the tea because she made coffee first by mistake. There was a lightness to her body, she seemed to be floating round the kitchen like an astronaut in a space-ship, and an absent-minded astronaut at that. She heard the swish of passing cars and the drumming of pellets of rain on the misty window.

By the time she came up with the tea neither her mother nor Paul was in the drawing room. She heard them in the nearby bedroom. Her mother, once again, had got her way.

Leaving the tea on the coffee table, she hardly had the energy to walk upstairs.

She threw herself on her bed and watched the minute hand of her clock. When it clicked to four forty-seven she heard Paul yell good-bye up to her. Jennifer leapt up from the bed and rushed to the banisters. The door slammed. At least Sarah hadn't had her way for long.

Jennifer went slowly back to her room. As an observer all her life, not an experiencer, it took her a while to rationalise the heavy knot in her stomach. She came up with the conclusion that it represented fear for Paul's well-being.

Sarah was a destroyer, resolved Jennifer. What's more, if Edward found out he'd be furious. Older men were one thing, but surely a young one, particularly one as beautiful as Paul, would anger and hurt him. And he might well find out, since Paul only lived down the road.

Paul confused her. Most people took her on face value: she could see herself reflected in their eyes as just a solemn, shy girl. In a way this distressed her because it was a false image which denigrated her intelligence. On the other hand it had the advantage of allowing her a secret, remarkable self. If she laid that self open to Paul, revealing her secrets, her personality, the seance, and he didn't throw up his arms in astonishment she would be mortified, robbed of everything she most valued. She hadn't wanted astonishment from Mr Davidson, from him she'd wanted help. Paul was different. But she wished he wasn't so

121

inquisitive. He appeared to take no notice of her shyness or her apparent ordinariness, he seemed to look through them and search for her private treasures. Partly she didn't want him to find them in case he thought them mere baubles. That would be like a woman finally taking off her clothes for a man after a long courtship and his looking her up and down then asking her to please put the clothes back on at once.

Outside droplets of rain clung to spiky branches and spider webs glistened.

Edward came home from the library at about six thirty and he and Jennifer had watercress soup and a ham salad while they watched the television upstairs. Sarah sat with them, filing her nails.

At sevenish Sarah left and Edward retired to his study, drawing the yew-green curtains on the day and the branch which pressed against the window. Jennifer went back to her room.

She must go through with the seance, she must be daring: like Shelley, like Aphra and like Rebecca.

A moth fluttered through the open-windowed summer night and Jennifer fought it from her head with a squeal. She was jumpy that evening.

She undressed and stood for a moment in front of the long mirror. Her arms and legs and face were brown from sitting out in the garden. The rest of her was white. As breasts went, hers weren't too bad she thought. At least they were round and full without being big like Sarah's. She wished her hips were smaller but in fact they were neat like the rest of her tidy little body.

She pulled on her pink cotton pyjamas, pushed her feet into a pair of slippers and went to the bathroom. She cleaned her teeth briskly and splashed her face with cold water as if to splash away her fears.

But once in bed the fear descended again. It was a while before she fell asleep. Her mind was attuned to all the small creaks, plumbing noises, sounds of cars and aeroplanes which usually it cancelled out.

Suddenly she woke up. She thought she heard a footstep

outside, in the hall. Perhaps it was Shelley's. After a while she forced herself to be brave and sat up, rigid with fear. After all she had committed no crime. She had done nothing wrong yet. She'd just been studying, she told herself, and had a bad dream. She sank back into bed and brought the sheet over her head.

Eventually she got up, walked softly to the door and opened it. The hall was empty, the thick-piled carpet as unruffled as ever. She shivered as her bare toes clenched the warm ruby carpet. The Blake engraving on the wall above the stairs seemed to waver a moment and the eyes of God lean towards her, staring her out.

Was it her own mind which creaked with footsteps, bringing noise up from the underworld of fear within her? She did hope it was nothing more serious. Her mind crowded with anxieties. Was it a burglar, a cat, a trick of sound? Was it Shelley coming for her out of the past? Or Rebecca? She told herself not to be absurd when another wave of panic swamped her and she ran downstairs, past the watching eyes of pictures everywhere, into the kitchen.

She turned on the light and her heart relaxed a little as she saw the plates from dinner as she had left them, unwashed, and a packet of cornflakes on the sideboard. She drew the gingham curtains as the night pressed itself against the window and quickly poured herself out a bowl of cornflakes, swimmed them in milk, powdered them with sugar and ate them hastily. It was as if the cheery cockerel on the packet would obliterate the night, transform it to morning. When the bowl was empty save for a puddle of milk she felt a little better. She opened the cake tin and took out a fruit cake. She cut herself a large slice and solemnly began to pick out the sultanas and pop them into her mouth, like one chimpanzee grooming another for tasty fleas. She threw away the crumbly ruin of the slice and started on another. By the third slice her mind had concentrated itself away from disembodied footsteps and on to sultanas. After the fourth she boiled the kettle, put on the radio, filled her hot-water bottle, sipped at her mug of hot tea and began to go up the stairs fearless.

The front door opened and Jennifer, startled, turned round.

Her mother closed the door behind her and stood in the darkness, leaning against the door.

'Hello Sarah, I couldn't sleep,' said Jennifer, glad her mother was home.

Sarah walked slowly out of the shadows into the light and Jennifer saw that her face was sheet white and forehead covered in blood.

14

Sarah stumbled into the kitchen and Jennifer quickly followed.

'What happened?' Jennifer had her arm round Sarah. 'Shall I bathe your head? Shall I get a doctor? Shall I call Edward? Where is it, where's the first aid box, do we have one?'

'Don't tell Edward. I'll be all right in a minute. Let me sit down here, on the stool. Please get the first aid box out of the cupboard above the kettle and just wipe my forehead with cotton wool soaked in antiseptic. Then cut me a big piece of plaster. It's nothing serious. I just banged my head.'

'Where?'

'At the restaurant.'

'It's three in the morning. Why are you so late?'

The phone rang and they both jumped. Sarah picked it up quickly.

'Hello.' Silence. 'I should think you were.' Silence. 'I never want to see you again in the whole of my life.' She slammed down the phone.

'Was that Paul, did he hurt you?'

Sarah took the cotton wool from Jennifer, dabbed the blood from her forehead and carefully stuck on the plaster. Jennifer watched anxiously.

'Please, I'd love some coffee,' said Sarah.

'Did he?'

'No ...'

'All right, I'm getting the coffee. I don't believe you banged it.

It's all bruised and one of your shirt buttons is off and I've never seen you so shaken.'

'I didn't bang it then.'

'Please tell me.'

Sarah's elbow rested on the sideboard and her hand clasped her forehead. Her eyes were closed tightly.

'All right, all right, all right ... on condition you say nothing to Edward. On condition you don't deny it when I tell him I banged my head on a cupboard door left open in the restaurant kitchen.'

'Yes, of course. I won't give you away.'

'Oh Lord, you make it sound like some kind of Brownie pact ... It was Saul Goodman in fact. Until I began to get bored with him a week or so ago I used to meet him late at the restaurant, when it was empty. He's such a pig he adores picking the remains off the unwashed plates and dishes. He also adores fucking ... sorry ... making love to me. He fancied you too, you know. Don't wince, he's quite fun. But he's much more possessive than I thought and I couldn't be seeing him every other evening and I certainly couldn't marry him, which is what he wanted. For all his talk about freedom, he didn't want me to be free. He wanted to possess me and, incidentally, various other women including his three ex-wives. The Sultan mentality. Whatever he wanted he had to have.

'Anyhow, all last week I made excuses not to see him. I really couldn't cope with his jealousy. That's not my scene at all. What's more I was getting interested in Paul.

'Today I was alone with Paul in the restaurant after everyone had gone. We were both a bit drunk and happy and, well, you can imagine what happened. Can you imagine what happened next? Saul still had a key and he walked in. It was dark ...'

Red-hot memory jabbed and Jennifer saw her mother spread-eagled, nippled and scarlet-faced on the table down below. Today Sarah wore a navy skirt with a split up one side and a thin white blouse. Her heels were too high, her blouse too thin, thought Jennifer.

'He switched on the light and saw Paul and me. Paul rolled off and grabbed his clothes. I just lay there, transfixed, staring up at Saul. I said I was sorry but, standing at the top of the stairs, he looked down at me absolutely furious and huge and red.'

Sarah shut her eyes even tighter as if trying to cut out the sight of Saul.

'Paul threw my clothes at me and I started putting on my shirt. Saul came downstairs slowly. He was so angry. He grabbed at Paul, drew back his fist as if he was going to hit him. I pushed between them and somehow I got hit and Paul was trying to get away to get help. But Saul hung on to his arm. He must have been drinking. He was swearing foully. Oh it was horrible. I don't remember it clearly. You know how when awful things happen you just don't? Anyway, once he saw I was bleeding he became terrifically contrite. He begged Paul not to get the police. I did too. If the story had come out it wouldn't have done any of us much good. Eventually Saul left, and we left immediately after. I didn't want to stay in that place a second longer.

'Paul brought me home in his car. He wanted me to stop off at his place but I was too shaken. Really shaken. But he took it all quite well. Actually laughed on the way back at the thought of Saul towering up on the stairs like an ogre who finds his prisoners about to escape. He said he felt like Rupert Bear....'

'Saul was jealous?'

Sarah gazed at Jennifer with incomprehension. 'Of course he was jealous.'

'Gosh. But Paul behaved well, did he? Protected you?'

'I suppose so. No, not really. I seemed to be protecting him most of the time. Oh I do adore him, Jennifer. It's funny. I don't think I've cared about anyone so much for years, When I thought Saul was going to strike him I was absolutely horrified. I'd have done anything, *anything*, to stop him. Like a mother wolf protecting her kids or something. Ridiculous. I've only known him a few days and it seems like for ever. Oooh, this coffee makes me feel better ... you're clutching your hot water bottle like you used to hug your teddy. Why on earth do you want a hot-water bottle? It's a warm night.'

'I just do.'

126

'All right, all right ... You know, sometimes Paul has the perplexed, puzzled air of a puppy. You know what I mean about being like a puppy? He thinks he's sophisticated but he's not. There's something so vulnerable about those grey eyes of his.'

'I knew that Saul was wicked. He ought not to be allowed to go and beat people up like that. It's disgusting.'

'I hope Paul is all right. You know, it's very odd. He's an architect and yet his own house is a really dreadful mess. Not that I mind about mess. Yesterday, after we made love, I thought I was going to melt on the bed out of sheer pleasure. I told him so.'

'You ought to phone the police and tell them about Saul. I hate him. He's obviously off his head. You ought never to have had anything to do with him. I don't know why you have so many affairs and I don't know why you have to tell me about them. It's disgusting. Why do you? Do you hate Edward?'

'I love Edward but asking why I want to have affairs is like asking why anyone should want villas and yachts all over the world when they have a perfectly adequate house in London. One wants excitement, pleasure, change, my darling. One wants everything one can get.'

'Get away with, you mean. It's horrible. You should report Saul.'

'You know, it's not the calm steady content of an intimate, loving relationship nor the euphoria of success in work that makes life worthwhile – it's the bits on the side; the superficial, dramatic gropes in the dark.'

'You disgust me.'

'You're scarlet with rage, my darling. I couldn't possibly report Saul, in fact I'm rather fond of him. He was always talking about his problems with his wife and his ex-wives and I listened sympathetically so no wonder he fell for me. It was my own fault. His affection is rather flattering really. I'm sorry to ramble on so but you've met Paul and somehow I just have to talk about him. He reminds me of your father when he was younger. He's changed so, you know ...'

'I don't want to hear. I'm going to bed.'

'I think I'll sleep in the spare room again. I don't like to wake Edward and, it's a funny thing, but I don't think I *could* sleep with him tonight.'

'Is Paul coming round on Monday?'

'Yes.'

That night Jennifer did not sleep at all well. When she woke up it was seven thirty and silent. She turned on the radio and took a bath.

That morning, Sunday, the house was claustrophobic. Edward kept asking Sarah if her head felt better and she kept replying that she had a dreadful headache and would he please shut up. Sarah was enormously bored and making everyone know it: 'Being poor must be like each day being a Sunday – no cinemas, no theatres, nothing to buy, not enough food, nothing to do,' she announced, with an air of sudden revelation. 'I'm glad I can handle money.' Edward was notoriously bad with money, amiably lending to whomever asked.

Jennifer went for a walk, to shake off the darkness which had filled her head.

On Sundays people wandered without that terrifying air of assurance and London became its powerful self, not just a machine for pumping people to and from work. London had so much of its past still present.

She stopped outside Westminster Abbey and saw confusion in the faces of a middle-aged couple as they looked up at the grand building, alive with history, and saw nothing of interest. It was as though the tube had stopped between stations and they hadn't a newspaper.

As she stepped inside the Abbey, a sense of peace invaded her. A church was the religious emotion expressed in stone. The soaring height of the roof reminded her man was not really so petty. His mind could sweep to the heavens although his feet remained down here, on the grey, repetitive pavements of ordinary life.

She had entered the Abbey to find Aphra Behn's burial place, which she knew was there.

She stood over the gravestone in the main cloister. It was dark

128

grey marble, bleak as a stormy Scottish sea, and on it were the words:

Here lies the proof that wit can never be
Defence enough against mortality.

Jennifer walked on to the Little Cloister, off the main one. Two sparrows were having a shower in the central fountain and a flash of sunlight turned its water to silver glanced with gold. Lifted into a moment of timelessness, she forgot herself and became the eyes of all who had stood in that spot throughout the centuries.

She walked back by the brown-flowing waters of the Thames. Such a snippet of time since Charles II rode along the Mall, since Whitehall was his palace, since Islington was a village, since Elizabeth I drifted along the Thames. Forests decaying into coal, cities burning and being built up, the grand houses of the Strand. How huge and magnificent it all was and how terribly sad. They all thought they mattered, even the dinosaurs probably thought themselves mighty important. Oh dear, and the sweet billets-doux sent by a fop to his loved one, the scribbling of quill pens, the sighs, the gossip, and how many were even remembered out of the throng of living, dying people fretting and strutting?

But her seance, she comforted herself, would defeat time and decay and death. Aphra, Shelley and Rebecca would return to her. It would be the greatest achievement of her life. It would be the fulfilment of her dreams. It would fulfil her. 'Won't it?' she said to Shelley, who was walking beside her.

15

Monday was the first day of the trial and, late that Sunday, Jennifer had knocked on the door of Edward's study.

'Come in,' he said.

She entered and he turned his head, looking at her over the top of his spectacles.

The sturdy spines of the books lined one wall of the room in flaked brown, cedar green and russet. As a child Jennifer had been fascinated by these books with their pages rimmed in gold or mottled like oil on water. Occasionally, when her parents were out, she'd crept into the old study in their former house and lifted one of the mysterious volumes from the shelves. The bay-windows looked out on to the semi-circular drive and she'd always listened for the sound of the car on the gravel. When she'd heard it she had hurried out of the room.

On the facing wall were Hogarth prints in mahogany frames and a few Rowlandson caricatures. The brown walls set off these grotesque visions with elegance. The study smelt of cigars although Edward seldom smoked them. On the huge desk overlooking the garden were three old mugs of coffee and a cut-glass vase of bare stems surrounded by pink petals which had dropped from the roses. The desk which could be seen in glimpses beneath the piles of paper was as shiny as horse-chestnuts hidden in autumn leaves. The trees rustled through the open window.

Edward had two desk diaries and recorded appointments in each. This often caused him to miss appointments.

'Take a seat,' he said, gesturing to the chrome and leather chair which seemed out of place in this country-study where time was stilled. He swung his own maroon leather chair round. She sat down.

'I must say, you do look as though you're going to say something frightfully important.' Edward was all charm. The study was the one place which was really his in the house, where he was the host.

Jennifer's eyes drifted over the books. They looked tipsy: some leaning back, some forward, some lying horizontal on top of others. Sarah often complained about the untidy state of the shelves. The white door was studded with grey fingermarks which Sarah claimed illustrated the messiness of Edward's character. In fact they recorded that he was an avid reader of newsprint.

'Not really. It's just that I'd like to come to the trial tomorrow and I wondered if you'd take me.' She said it all in one quick breath, to get it over with.

She stared at his feet. He was wearing those tatty carpet slippers and his brown corduroy trousers dragged down at the back. He ran his fingers through his hair and grinned.

'You do look glum.'

She looked up. Her hands were firmly entrenched in the pockets of her voluminous jeans. They felt safer there.

'I'm not,' she protested with a cautious smile.

'Hmm. Why do you want to come? It's not like you to want to go out.'

'You know I've become rather interested in the case. Partly because of what you said about Jane – her being like Rebecca. And partly because of Lucinda. Will she be questioned, do you think?'

'Yes, I'm sure she will. But you know we'd have to be up in the public gallery. I want to see it all from that perspective.'

'Yes, of course, that's fine.'

'By the way, do you think your mother's all right? She keeps forgetting things and actually neglected to zip her dress right to the top which is most unlike her. I hope that bang on her head didn't do her any damage.'

He was standing up, leaning back on his heels, with his hands behind his back as he stared donnishly out at the garden.

'But I expect she'll be fine soon. Probably a little shaken,' he said.

'Yes, Edward, can I?'

'What?'

'Can I come?'

'Oh yes, of course. If you really want to. But it won't be much of a lark.'

'Oh *good*. Thank you.'

'You must be ready by nine thirty sharp. We have to be in court by ten thirty.'

They queued for the public gallery with a babble of schoolgirls, foreigners and two cockney men. The younger, in a denim jacket and jeans, kept asking her the time, as though he couldn't wait until ten thirty when the door would open.

'Friend of mine's gonna be sentenced this morning,' he explained.

The passage in which they waited was cold and concrete, a kind of limbo between the busy pavement outside and the courts within.

'No point really coming until ten thirty on the dot,' said Edward.

'Suppose not,' said Jennifer, 'but maybe we wouldn't get in otherwise.'

'There's always plenty of room,' said Edward.

At ten thirty the door opened and the young cockney rushed up, scaling the steps two at a time while the ushers shouted 'Any cameras?' in a rather friendly way, as if they knew him, and he shouted back 'No'. Edward and Jennifer proceeded more slowly up the flight of stone stairs to the wooden door of court eight.

'Is there a rape trial anywhere?' demanded a black girl, one of the tribe of schoolgirls on their day out. The others giggled and the teacher swept them forward.

The different trials showing in different courts made the Old Bailey seem like a cine centre.

A burly usher opened the door to the court eight public gallery.

'The Charles Grigson murder trial is about to start here, isn't it?' asked Edward.

'That's right, sir.'

Jennifer and Edward sat, rather cramped, along the back row of the court eight gallery. All was modern and close-carpeted and middle class. It was, thought Jennifer, almost unfair that murderers should be tried in such clean-cut surroundings. It must surely make them uncomfortable. Down below smug men in wigs whispered on the pine benches the colour of Ideal Home kitchens.

Jennifer smelt flowers, turned, and saw Aemilia had come to sit beside Edward. Over her arm was a pastel blue cardigan and she looked quite flustered beneath her powder.

'Thought I'd come to keep you company,' she whispered. 'Geoffrey advised me against taking that job so my time's my own, well, in a way.'

132

'What about house-hunting?'

'I'm trying to give it up. It's absurd,' she said firmly. She arranged her handbag on her knee and her hands on her handbag.

Every time the gallery door opened and another person entered Jennifer turned. One or two of the schoolgirls came in noisily blowing their noses and gossiping. The black girl popped her head round the door and asked if this was the rape trial. The usher shook his head.

All of a sudden the whispering and handing of papers to and from down below stopped as the red-robed judge entered and everyone stood up. He had far apart, down-slanting eyes and thin lips. He sat down, smiling at some private joke.

A bearded warder entered from a side door followed by a young man – 'that's Charles Grigson,' whispered Edward – and a second warder. Charles Grigson stood in the dock facing the judge. He swayed slightly, put his hands in the pockets of his grey suit and took them out again. He was as Edward had described, a big wholesome young man with a shiny face which looked amazingly healthy. His hair kept falling over his eyes and he kept sweeping it back. His shoulders were broad and muscular. He looked up at the public gallery and delivered a slow, rueful smile in the direction of a middle-aged couple at the front of the gallery. She presumed it must be his mother and stepfather. The man was small and dark, with round spectacles and a little moustache. The woman had youthfully long, coppery hair and a carefully made-up face which did not disguise her age. She wore a cotton suit with a T-shirt beneath, revealing small breasts.

The clerk of the court rose and said to Charles, 'Are you Charles Grigson?'

'Yes,' said Charles.

The clerk then read out the charge and asked if he pleaded guilty or not guilty. The copper-haired woman leant forward.

'Not guilty.' His voice was soft. He pushed his shock of dark hair off his face and looked up, strongly, honestly. The bright lights made him blink.

The clerk then called the names of the twelve men and

women jurors who were sworn in. None was challenged. Charles was sitting, back bowed, with his head in his hands. Jennifer's heart went out to him. He looked so alone and afraid and likeable.

Soon Geoffrey opened the case for the prosecution. He held his arms pompously behind his broad back as he spoke, referring occasionally to his notes on the lectern before him. Geoffrey's eyebrows were placed high in his face, giving him an expression of constant astonishment. His drooping moustache made his astonishment rather gloomy, as if amazed in spite of himself. He reminded the jury that it was up to the prosecution to prove the case and to satisfy the jury that Charles Grigson murdered Jane. He stressed that the jury had to make up their minds on matters of fact but had to obey the ruling of the judge on matters of law. He explained that when the police and ambulance had arrived at the deceased's flat in Bayswater on the morning of 13 February they found her immersed in a bath red with blood. The autopsy showed she had actually died by drowning – there was water in her lungs – after becoming unconscious from the stab wounds. 'The killer had actually made Jane Thomson drown in her own blood.' The knife which stabbed Jane was found shoved behind the long curtains of the bathroom. It had no fingerprints on it. Somebody who gave his name as Charles Grigson had called the police to the scene of the crime. They found Charles Grigson at the flat 'in a distraught condition, white and trembling'. He showed them to the body and did not resist when they searched him. He kept muttering about a burglar but denied having seen one.

As Geoffrey talked on and on alternatively to the judge and the jury, Jennifer could see that most of the jury were taking a keen interest in all he said. Charles had sat up and was jotting down notes and frowning at some of Geoffrey's remarks. Geoffrey's voice was as heavy as his appearance, so lumpen and drab even in his robes.

'In the search, members of the jury, what you may think was a rather important item of evidence was discovered in the accused's overcoat. It was a letter – there are copies for the jury and perhaps it might be convenient, my lord, for them to be passed round to the jury later?'

'Certainly, certainly,' said the judge.

'The letter was from the deceased to the accused demanding back all the money she had ever given him. It also said that its author was going to reveal Charles's "incestuous" relationship with his half-sister to his parents.

'Now Charles Grigson has a flamboyant and very extravagant half-sister, Lucinda, to whom he is greatly attached. The accused had admitted, and, my lord, you will hear evidence at a later stage, that for months the deceased had given him money which he had then passed on to his beloved sister. He would have naturally been worried at having to return what had already been spent. What's more the letter – which he received while up in Birmingham for a conference – threatened his relationship with his sister. The day he received the letter he rushed back – again he admits this, my lord – to try to dissuade the deceased against demanding back the money. The question you, the jury, have to decide is whether he dissuaded her by killing her or whether someone else killed her first.'

Jennifer's bottom felt sore from sitting too long on the hard seat. She was also thirsty. Aemilia kept whispering to Edward and he smiled back at her warmly.

Edward had been right about the judge, thought Jennifer, he did look like an upright cadaver, or perhaps more like a pottery head and shoulders of a strict judge that someone had placed on the desk. The judge seldom interrupted. His yellowish, wrinkled skin kept its expression of determined melancholy whatever was said. Occasionally he asked Geoffrey to clarify a point.

The sprinkling of clerks and others down below seemed to be busying themselves making notes or listening intently.

Jennifer already knew much of what Geoffrey was saying, either from Edward's notes or from conversations. What she had not appreciated before was the extraordinary charm of the defendant. He said nothing, of course, just sat in the dock with warders on either side. But there was a kind of radiance about his features.

Lucinda must be longing to hear what was going on, thought

Jennifer. As a witness, she couldn't be there until after she'd given evidence. Maybe she'd be waiting outside. Jennifer wanted to meet her and at the same time didn't want to at all.

But when they went out for lunch, there was no sign of Lucinda.

In the wine bar where Aemilia and Jennifer and Edward had cheese and wine, Jennifer saw that the couple she had thought were Charles's parents sat at the table beside them. Jennifer whispered to Edward and he turned slightly towards the woman, who was sipping at a large glass of white wine.

'Excuse me,' he said, 'but are you the mother of Charles Grigson?'

'Yes, as a matter of fact. And this is my husband, Mr Brown. Why?'

'It's just that I might be writing something on the case.'

Mr Brown leaned forward. 'Really? How very interesting. What exactly will you be writing?'

'Just a brief something in a book about a number of trials at the Old Bailey.'

'I don't think we can help. I'm afraid Charles won't talk to us about all this. He just keeps saying he isn't guilty.'

'And of course he has never had a sexual relationship with his sister,' said Mrs Brown. 'That is nonsense.'

'I see it,' said Mr Brown, 'as a fantasy of this Jane girl to explain her deep-rooted jealousy and resentment of Lucinda. A fabrication in which she herself believed.'

'Lucinda said that Jane hated her,' said Mrs Brown. 'Apparently they did meet at Harrods the day before Jane's death, as Jane's letter claims. But Jane was very rude to Lucinda and Lucinda didn't say anything about this absurd incest business. Jane made it all up.'

'Poor girl,' said Mr Brown. The psychiatrist was little and shrivelled up somehow. His face had contortions rather than expressions. There was something both ingratiating and smug about his manner.

'Lucinda is very distraught about Charles's imprisonment. She can't seem to stay still. She stayed with us a few nights, of course, but she doesn't sleep.'

'It's only natural,' said Mr Brown smugly. 'Of course she feels guilty, as we do.'

'But she doesn't, for instance, blame you at all?' said Edward.

'Oh yes,' he said. 'Of course she blames us. It's only natural. We don't mind. We allow her to express her anger. Lucinda does not sublimate her feelings.'

'Charles is such a good boy. I don't know. I'm quite stunned by it all,' said Mrs Brown. She smiled bleakly at Edward from above her brown cotton suit. She pushed her hair behind her ears. The man's nose was very shiny. It was like a rat's, decided Jennifer.

'But we mustn't spill all the beans,' said Mr Brown, his eyes turning back coldly to his wine and his cheese.

'So nice to chat,' said Mrs Brown.

Soon Jennifer, Aemilia and Edward were out again in the grey street.

'No wonder the children are strange. Poor kids.'

'Charles isn't strange,' said Jennifer.

'It's Lucinda who is strange,' said Edward.

Father and daughter looked at each other intently, for a second.

'Yes, you're both right. It is Lucinda who's strange.'

'Doesn't Geoffrey realise that?'

'Geoffrey thinks the girl is crazy. But he also thinks she's wonderful. He has told me so frequently.'

'I don't know how you put up with it,' said Edward.

'Because I have to,' said Aemilia.

At the courtroom Geoffrey continued his statement of the prosecution case. Jennifer decided she would probably not come to the trial again. It made her so uneasy. But she might allow herself to take a look at Edward's notes every now and again.

Edward appeared to be getting on very well with Aemilia. Jennifer was happy to see her so content. She was giggling and scribbling Edward little notes which made him smile.

As they left the courtroom that day they saw Lucinda waiting – as Edward had seen her before – leaning against the wall. Edward pointed her out. She was as Edward had described – tall, restless and beautiful. They walked on quickly but she ran after them, her white dress clinging to her limbs. She grabbed Aemilia's arm, who tried to push her hand off, just as a taxi came by. Aemilia summoned it with her free arm, although they were only going to wait at Geoffrey's Chambers near by.

'It's our taxi, Lucinda, we really have to go,' said Aemilia.

'What happened?' said Lucinda.

Jennifer didn't recognise the voice. It was a screech.

'It was just the prosecution giving his case.'

'Geoffrey, you mean?'

Jennifer had drawn back slightly. The pale face had red eyes as though she had been crying. Her hair was so wild it must have been unintentional. Close-up, she certainly didn't look like a tempestuous sex goddess. The white dress was virtually see-through. Jennifer was glad she was wearing knickers but wished she was wearing a bra.

'Of course it was Geoffrey,' said Edward. 'You know that. You'll do Charles more good if you pull yourself together.'

'You're Edward Hamilton, aren't you?'

'Yes.'

'I hear that your wife has been seeing Paul.'

'Who?'

'Well you can tell Paul all this is his fault. He introduced Jane to Charles. It's his fault. I'm not to blame.'

'I don't know who Paul is,' said Edward. 'But we really must go. The taxi is blocking the road.'

'Paul's the architect,' said Jennifer. 'I'll give him the message.'

'Where's he living?' Lucinda had turned on Jennifer, her eyes blazing.

'Find out yourself,' said Jennifer with a rush of spite. 'Your parents are just over there you know.'

'Oh God,' Lucinda spun round. Her parents weren't there but Jennifer understood enough of Lucinda to know she would not want to see them now.

Edward and Aemilia, led by Jennifer, jumped quickly into the taxi and slammed the door, leaving Lucinda on the pavement alone.

They took the taxi to Geoffrey's Chambers and waited for

him. He took a little time, about an hour, to come, but did not mention seeing Lucinda.

The four of them drove back to Abbey Square in Geoffrey's Rover.

She sat in the back of the car, next to Aemilia. They drove past St Paul's churchyard, veiled in golden-green summer leaves.

Geoffrey's voice was booming on and on as he drove. Aemilia stared out of the window. 'Have you been to a trial before, Jennifer?' said Geoffrey.

'No,' said Jennifer.

'Ah, well don't underestimate it, don't underestimate the law. You might think the ritual absurd. It's not. You see, man is naturally very selfish and nowadays selfishness is actually in fashion, though idiots give it different labels like "freedom", the "freedom of the individual", "women's liberation". But selfishness when it disregards possible personal injury to others is a crime.'

Geoffrey's hair was shiny with grease. Jennifer supposed that must partly be the fault of the wig.

'So you see, Jennifer, society both condones and punishes selfishness. It's confusing. You're told you have a right to happiness – but if that happiness happens to include poisoning your nagging mother-in-law or stabbing your crazy wife or robbing a bank, then it's a crime. You follow me?'

'Oh yes,' said Jennifer. She wondered why Edward was so quiet, looked over his shoulder and saw he was reading his notes.

'It's your generation who'll really pay the cost of this confusion. Glad now Aemilia couldn't have any children.'

Geoffrey glanced into his driving mirror but Aemilia's face was expressionless. She was in fact completely unmoved by this jibe which she had heard so many times. At first she had laughed, thinking he was joking, then she had been furious as she realised he was not, now she had even ceased to be surprised at the audacity with which he re-wrote the facts. It was actually Geoffrey who had been told that he was unable to have children, not she.

'In the past,' continued Geoffrey, 'society has been more

139

successful in implanting a sense of right or wrong, mostly through religion, to cure man's selfishness. But nowadays such words – right and wrong – seem as outdated as sin. If morality can't be imposed, then laws and punishment have to be. The law is here to protect people from the natural instincts of others. One man's freedom of action is another man's death. The Moors murderers thought they were free. "Sadism is the supreme pleasure," they said. "Look around, Watch the fools doing exactly what their fathers did before them. The Book, they live by the Book." Look what their freedom, unconventionality, did to those kids they tortured and slaughtered.'

Jennifer yawned and Geoffrey heard her.

'Forgive me if I'm stating the obvious but it is the obvious which we need constantly to be reminded of.'

'No, no, that's fascinating,' said Jennifer. They had driven through Fleet Street, along the proud façades of Whitehall and were now driving past Westminster Abbey, half soot-black, half buttermilk-spruce. The light that early evening was hazy, as if filtered through a yellow gauze.

'Look how clean the Abbey's getting,' murmured Aemilia to Jennifer. 'How beautiful.'

'Speak up,' said Geoffrey. 'What did you say, Aemilia?'

'Nothing of interest,' said Aemilia.

'I rather liked that chap Charles,' said Edward, putting his notes back into his briefcase. 'He had a gentle face.'

'Scoundrel!' exclaimed Geoffrey. 'I'm sure of it. And had an incestuous relationship with that pretty sister of his, sure of that too.'

That evening Jennifer sat at her desk. Her own pale face was watching her from the blackness of the window. Her hair was lost in the night. She never seemed able to see herself clearly. At school she felt rebellious against the petty restrictions and knew the boiling fluid of anger bubbled up into her face, making it seem grumpy. But she let it boil and didn't act. She couldn't see herself clearly because she didn't act as her feelings led her to act. She should have told Geoffrey to shut up. She should have put her hand on Aemilia's when Aemilia turned, bright eyed, and said how clean the Abbey was, how beautiful. But she didn't. She just waited for things to happen to her. Mr Davidson was her only rebellion, and that rebellion scared her.

Jennifer was waiting for tomorrow, to see Paul. One reason she wanted to see him badly was to find out from him what Lucinda had meant when she said everything was his fault. She hated waiting, wishing moments over like all those other women waiting, trapped, wanting to be rescued. Women waiting at the phone, waiting with meal prepared, waiting with heart ready, pregnant women waiting, tarty women waiting at street corners, adolescent women waiting for love.

She should be brave and free enough not to care for Paul, not to be kept waiting, just to be determined about the seance and nothing else. But even Aphra had given way to love. She had once written to a lover: 'How could anything, but the man who hates me, entertain me so unkindly? Witness your excellent opinion of me, of loving others; witness your passing by the end of the street where I live, and squandering away your time at any coffee-house, rather than allow me what you know in your soul is the greatest blessing of my life, your dear *dull* melancholy company; I call it dull, because you can never be gay or merry where Astrea is.'

16

When the doorbell rang at eleven in the morning Jennifer somehow knew it was Paul and it was. Sarah was out buying food for the restaurant and Maureen was in the dining room hoovering crossly in a flowery apron over blue nylon trousers. She didn't like it when Sarah was out. She missed the companionship.

Paul had obviously just washed his hair. It was all fluffy. His face had a scrubbed pinkish look about it as though he'd been languishing in a hot bath and was just about to be taken out by his parents at half-term.

'Sarah's out,' said Jennifer. Maureen switched off the hoover. She suffered from insatiable curiosity.

141

'Hello. No, I've come to see you. Sarah said she didn't think you were going to the trial today. I want to hear all about it.'

They both went upstairs and into the drawing room. Paul led the way. He seemed quite at home.

'How's your cold?'

'All gone. Had a day in bed, or most of it, on Sunday. I was exhausted.'

Pointedly Jennifer said, 'Yes, Sarah told me about Saturday night.'

'Oh, you look so severe. That Saul Goodman is absolutely repellent, isn't he? I loathe him so much I swear never to buy another of his books and, I mean, I have to admit they're actually rather readable.' He sniffed.

Jennifer knew he was glad to see her. There was a fizzy feeling in the air which made her want to grin and grin and to say stupid things and to giggle.

'Did you know there are prostitutes in this square? Last night I was walking home and a girl leaned from a top floor window and shouted hello.'

'What did you say?'

'I looked up. She was wearing a nightdress. I waved politely and walked on but I bet if I'd tried the door to the house it would have been open. Extraordinary, isn't it?'

Paul and Jennifer were standing, facing each other, in the middle of the carpet. Jennifer felt she was on a stage, perhaps because when she was with him life always seemed heightened.

'Maybe she was a patient. Are you sure she wasn't leaning out of one of those hospitals?'

'More likely to be a nurse.'

'Oh, I don't think so,' said Jennifer.

'Some funny patients around, mind you. The other day I saw a man in pyjamas hurtling along in a wheelchair with a rug over his knees. Nobody was following him. He seemed to be heading towards the police station. Most strange.'

Paul was very nervy today. He was talking quickly and smiling quickly.

'I thought you wanted to hear about the trial.'

'I do. Go on.'

142

Jennifer told him what she could remember of the proceedings and he listened, fidgeting with the gold cross in the triangle of his open-necked white shirt.

His cuffs hung loose over his hands and, combined with tatty black waistcoat and trousers, gave him an air of dissolute elegance.

'So it looks as though poor Charles is really in for it?' he murmured. Jennifer nodded. 'I must keep out of it all.'

'Why don't you want to be involved? We saw Lucinda after the trial. She collared Edward and said it was all your fault, you introduced Charles to Jane.'

'Did she? She said that?' He was stretching and clenching his hands, as if ridding them of tension. He was looking at Jennifer but not focussing. 'Well, I did I suppose. She was my girlfriend. He was a friend. Naturally I introduced them. Naturally I feel bad about it now. But I don't want to be further involved. Charles did not want to call me as a witness and I respect his wishes.'

'Why didn't he?'

'He has numerous other friends who can testify to his good character.'

'You don't want to get involved because of your relationship with Lucinda. That's it, isn't it?'

'What do you mean – my relationship with Lucinda? And why do you say it like that?'

'Like what?'

'Spit it out almost.'

'I didn't.'

'You're very suspicious, aren't you?'

'I'm suspicious of Lucinda certainly. I don't like her. She's predatory. I don't trust her. What is she up to, Paul?'

'Are you jealous of her?' he said.

'Why should I be jealous? I'm not. I just know she's untrustworthy. She's one of those people who treats her life as a public performance.'

'Like your mother?'

'Maybe. But Lucinda's unscrupulous.'

'Yes, she is.'

'But maybe Charles is too, he just covers it up better. Maybe I'm wrong, you're wrong, and he is an unscrupulous killer,' said Jennifer.

'No. Charles is a very gentle person. He once crashed his car to avoid running over a hedgehog. He couldn't kill anyone.'

'Who did it then?'

'Let's sit down, shall we?'

'Tell me, who do you think did it?'

'Probably a burglar as the defence says. Charles'll be all right. He's a nice chap, Charles, they won't convict him unfairly. There isn't the evidence.' Paul lounged back on the sofa, stretching his legs. He wore plimsolls which went well with his youthful ensemble. Did he plan his insouciant clothes with enormous care, wondered Jennifer. 'We often went out in a threesome – Charles, Lucinda and myself. Lucinda adored rest-aurants. We all had to have different dishes and she'd try bits of each. She was so greedy, don't know how she managed to keep so slim. Had a ravenous appetite. But she enjoyed having the attentions of both of us as well as having our food.'

'She keeps pestering Geoffrey.'

'How was she? Does she look well?'

'Don't you ever see her?'

'She says she can't bear to see me. She says she hates me. Did she look well?'

'She looked beautiful, if that's what you mean.'

'You don't have to compete with her you know. She's not worth it.'

'I wouldn't dream of competing with her ... except that she's so alive. She seems so positive.'

Jennifer was staring at her feet as her colour heightened.

'Nonsense ... I've just had a marvellous idea,' said Paul.

'Yes?'

'On Monday next. I should like to offer to take you to the fair on Hampstead Heath. How about that? Would you like to go with me?'

Jennifer looked up, a smile irradiating her urchin's face and her big brown eyes.

'Sarah would be cross.'

144

'No. She's a bit past fairs, isn't she?'

No remark could have warmed Jennifer more.

Paul left before Sarah returned home. Jennifer was brimful of yearning. She didn't know what for. It was a sweet pain which seemed to open out her senses. The touch of the hard chair on her body, the hum of distant traffic, the merging greens in the garden below. It was as if she were listening to beautiful music. For once she didn't want to explain, to analyse, to compress. She just wanted to let her feelings carry her off.

Her friendship with Paul was something so important. The gap in her life that Rebecca's death had made was being filled, she felt, by Paul. He was just like a brother. Although, of course, nothing could be quite the same and quite as high-minded as her relationship with Rebecca. And nothing as important as the seance.

When Jennifer went down to tell Sarah he'd called she discovered Maureen had already told her.

That afternoon Sarah went out and didn't say where. Jennifer suspected she'd gone to see Paul. She tried to ease away her confusion by sitting in the garden under the horse-chestnut tree. It was peaceful, although she wasn't. She remembered sitting there last winter and watching a blackbird pull a worm out of the hard ground. That yellow beak pecking at the slimy worm, the bird's beady eyes intent on its purpose. The cherry tree had been bare, a mass of still branches, but in a few months it was fluttering blossom. Daffodil bulbs lay beneath the dank earth, buried but living. The wall was patterned with the brittle brown branches of climbing roses, clinging but stiff, as if transfixed by death. Before long the crumbly wall was abud with flowers breathing sweet rose perfume into the still air. Everywhere was deception.

Oddly, it was spring she distrusted most. The promise of blossom and bud seemed to her a lie. Pink and clean and sweet smelling like blancmanges and party frocks of long ago. Confetti of blossom floating in the breeze. All lies. The blossom always fell and left the trees groping painfully up into stormy skies, the naked magnolia branches gesticulating wildly and the weeping willow flinging out dry stems.

Today white clouds were draped like boa stoles over the sky. A silver Siamese cat with a blue collar rippled across the lawn in front of Jennifer. Her worshipable blue eyes seemed to look back into days past. The hot leaves and grass were green and still in the humid air.

It was strange, thought Jennifer, that someone as gentle as Paul should find himself connected with incest, the murder of a girl, the jealous attack by Saul Goodman. So much violence. And Rebecca, gentle Rebecca, mutilated by a lorry. And Shelley causing the suicide of those who loved him and his own death, thrashed by waves.

On Wednesday evening Edward seemed depressed and weary. He refused to talk about the trial. Jennifer wanted to read his notes but he wouldn't let her, saying she must wait until the weekend. All he would say was that things looked bad for Charles.

On Thursday lunchtime Paul phoned up. Sarah was out at the restaurant and Jennifer answered the phone. He said he had a sudden desire to go for a walk by the Thames which was lovely in the rain and would she please come with him? Her first instinct was to look for an excuse but all morning her spirits had drizzled away with the rain. She needed cheering up. She was surprised how moody she was at the moment: one second exultant, the next gloomy. After his phone call she could hardly remember what it was like to be depressed.

They drove in his car to Chiswick and parked in a road off Chiswick Mall.

'We'll walk down to St Nicholas's churchyard,' he said. 'Whistler, Pope and Hogarth are all buried there.'

To their left as they walked the sludgy Thames was studded with raindrops. Weeping willows swayed in the cold wind and on the other side of the road whitened branches of wisteria, dripping with pale amethyst flowers, clambered up the old houses. The road was glossy and the smell of grass rich and moist. Lights were going on in the mansions and neat cottages, opening up rooms like an advent calendar. But Jennifer and Paul didn't see the men working at mahogany desks, the children staring listlessly out and the women preparing. Paul

146

was chatting about his life at university and Jennifer about school. He even stepped in a puddle and, listening to her, didn't notice. It was most flattering.

Yachts rocked restlessly on the Thames and raincoated figures hurried past, collars and umbrellas up. But the dark church at the end of the road was as steady as ever, brightened only by the cascade of golden roses by the porch. The earth in front of the church was matted with ivy and laden with huge tombs.

'That must be Hogarth's,' said Jennifer.

Within a barricade of black railings reared a pillared white tomb surmounted by a grecian urn and engraved with verses in praise of the 'great painter of Mankind'.

'Shall we stop under the sycamore until the rain stops?'

'It's beautiful here, don't you think?' Jennifer's face was moist with the rain and her eyes misty with pleasure. 'Look at the moss on that slab of tomstone. It looks as though it's creeping up, trying to take over like some science fiction monstrosity.'

'It *is* trying to take over. That's what moss does.'

'Oh let's go on, Paul, over to the big churchyard over there.'

'All right.'

They walked over the long grass sprawling with dandelions gone to grey seed and on to the tarmac path lined with gravestones leaning this way and that.

'They look weary don't they? Slouching with age,' she said.

Jennifer tripped and Paul caught her elbow. She smelt so sweet, of talcum powder and soap.

'Come on,' he said. 'Don't *you* fall all over the place.'

Blacky-green firs loomed over the path. The couple walked through the wrought-iron gates and into the main churchyard, populated only by rows and rows of gravestones, facing the church as if a congregation in prayer.

'Ugh,' said Jennifer. 'Those trees and plants look so healthy because they feed on the dead, literally.'

'You've quite a gothic imagination, haven't you?'

The noise of the drumming rain and the rustling leaves was all about them. Paul held his golfing umbrella above their heads. Near them was a freshly dug grave. The flowers of the wreaths were faded and crackly but not decayed.

147

'My feet are getting wet,' announced Paul. 'Shall we go back?'

'You're not very adventurous, are you?' Jennifer laughed happily. 'All right. But I love it here. It's such a strange place, don't you think?'

They walked huddled close under the umbrella. They talked and they talked. Below the smokey sky, the street was awash with hurrying people and in the gardens birds splashed from branch to branch. Back home, over tea, she was buoyant. He was immensely solicitous, interested and interesting but a little too inquisitive for Jennifer's liking. He asked whether she had ever written diaries, had a boyfriend, how she felt about death, could he see the diaries, what she thought of her schoolmates, what ambitions she had and what kind of person she most admired. She wanted to tell him everything but her sense of secrecy intervened and at first produced terse answers. She refused to let him see her diaries and wished she hadn't even admitted they existed. As the day went on her answers grew a little longer.

When Sarah came home and ushered her off to her room Jennifer felt a little sad. But it was a wonderful mellow sadness, not the black turmoil of despair that up to now she had thought of as sadness. He was so brotherly to her, so thoughtful and friendly, and he had said more than once how alike they were and that he felt a curious affinity with her, as if she were a younger form of himself. This affection for him, which she liked to call sisterly, was something she had never experienced before. All her definitions seemed to be changing. The simple words she had thought she understood – happiness, sadness, affection – had taken on more meaning. Life was opening up, like a flower in sunlight, and she began to feel what she had known of it up to now was only the muted underside of multicoloured petals.

She re-ran the scene with Paul at Chiswick again and again. Each time she saw it slightly differently. First she relived it with the emotions she had had at the time. This viewing interpreted it as idyllic and, in the intensity of her emotion, she was unable to believe that this sense of wonder had not been shared by Paul. Then she looked at the scene with more of a squint, more

148

drily, and saw that there were moments which her emotion had smoothed over when he had been, well, slightly irritated with her, sharper than necessary. When he said 'You've got quite a gothic imagination, haven't you?' there had, looking back, been an edge to his voice, even a trace of envy? And had he looked, for a moment, sour when she suggested he was unadventurous to complain about his wet feet? But this run-through took account of her feelings today. She was finding reasons for his still spending so much time with Sarah and his not having phoned her first thing the next morning with more things to say. If he had called round or phoned that morning she would never have thought back on the scratches on the afternoon's surface, it would all have been glossy with affection. Next she tried to draw back, be as objective as a member of a cinema audience, to see herself and him. How hard that was. How impossible, really, to see and interpret people properly when you don't know the end of their story. The fact that he snaps at you over a silly remark or sneers at your gothic imagination does not mean, necessarily, either that he is bad-tempered or is growing bored with you. It could well mean just that he has snapped at you over a silly remark because the remark is silly and that is that. In real life clues can mislead.

She thought about Paul all day, created imaginary conversations with him, stared out of the dining room window trying to recognise his face in the faces of passers-by, his Volkswagen in other cars. Twice she saw a Volkswagen coming along the road and decided Paul must have had his resprayed because the Volkswagens she saw were red and green not bright canary yellow like his.

She worried that Paul was seeing too much of Sarah. Apart from her own jealousy, which was insistent and painful, she did not think they were good for each other. Paul liked Sarah for her strength, and that encouraged his weakness. She wondered if she ought to say something to Sarah about this.

Jennifer was pretty sure Sarah did care about Paul. She was so jittery when he wasn't there, so dewy-eyed when he was. It was not good for Sarah to love Paul. It made her unpleasant to Edward.

149

Jennifer thought Sarah foolish. Love had turned Aphra into a romantic, passive fool. Jennifer had long disapproved of her silly school friends who claimed they were in love. Love, she had read somewhere, was 'a universal migraine, blotting out vision'. And love was indissolubly linked with making love, a nasty, animal activity.

It was odd but, with Paul living only a few doors away, for the first time in years Jennifer did not feel lonely.

She had often felt like a stranger but with Paul she was at home and relaxed. With Paul she felt clever. Her voice lost that repressed, somewhat pompous tone and vivacity broke through into her face. She looked quite beautiful. Paul made her someone special and in doing so, of course, he made the seance – her attempt at being the instigator, the heroine, the hostess – seem far less urgent.

On Friday Paul called round while Jennifer and Sarah were having lunch. Jennifer didn't see why Sarah had to make such a ridiculous fuss over him and open a bottle of wine to 'celebrate' when she saw him practically every day anyway. Sarah gulped down her first glass of wine urgently, as though she believed that being drunk and merry would make her more attractive to Paul. Jennifer knew she'd had a whisky or two before lunch.

Sarah was dressed smartly in a grey pleated skirt and sheer grey stockings. Her black silk shirt was carefully tailored. Jennifer had noticed that Sarah wore her best clothes even in the house nowadays. Before her affair with Paul she'd often loafed around in jeans and an old shirt or sweater. It was absurd.

Over lunch Sarah suggested that, if Edward happened to come back home when Paul was visiting, they should both pretend that Paul had come to see Jennifer. It would, she explained, stop him from becoming suspicious. Jennifer was wary of the scheme. For one thing, it meant Jennifer joining in the deception of Edward, and for another it was jolly annoying the way Sarah treated the idea of Paul coming round to see *her*, little Jennifer, as a terrific joke. But nevertheless she agreed, as if in the centre of one of Aphra Behn's comedies of intrigue.

A slow smile permeated Paul's face as they discussed the scheme.

'Well, just to establish myself, I'd better take Jennifer to the fun-fair on Hampstead Heath on my day off on Monday, will that be all right?'

'I suppose so,' said Sarah gruffly. 'You seem very odd this week.'

'It's knowing the trial's on. It makes me nervous.'

'But you don't talk about it.'

'There's nothing to say. Except that I hope Charles is not found guilty.'

That afternoon Jennifer was overcome by a sudden desire for a bar of plain chocolate. It was raining – a light, summer shower, and she ran all the way. When she got to the shop counter she found she was no longer hungry. She turned and there, in the doorway, was Mr Davidson, his face pushed forward in his customary way, as if sniffing the air. He blinked at her, then smiled vaguely. He wore a black raincoat and looked even more mole-like than usual. His little hand darted out and shook hers quickly. There was a safety pin instead of a top button on his coat. She found she was not at all surprised to see him.

'Hello,' she said.

'Why hello. How splendid. How are you?'

'Very well thank you.'

'Good, good, my dear. I was expecting you to be here. Will you wait a second while I get my tobacco? I'd like us to have a cup of tea.'

He didn't seem to be asking Jennifer back, he appeared to be commanding her. Already he knew he had power over her.

The bottom of his trousers were wet. She decided that his head was definitely too big for his body.

The assistant knew him and his brand of tobacco.

Jennifer and Mr Davidson stepped out into the street and along the pavement into the square. The bright sun cast dark shadows.

He panted as he walked. It was odd to be walking beside a man so much shorter than she was.

'I thought we might have a practice run today,' said Mr Davidson, in his matter-of-fact Bradford voice.

'Sorry?'

'I thought we might have a sitting today ... and see if we could come up with anyone.'

They passed under the arch and into the courtyard. Goldfish darted in the dank weed of the pond.

'A seance?'

'I call it a sitting.'

The porter was asleep in his chair, peeked cap over his eyes. They went up by lift. Mr Davidson leaned against the wall.

'Bad heart,' he explained, breathing heavily.

In the flat he took off his raincoat. His grey cardigan had a hole in the left elbow.

Jennifer waited in the drawing room, quietening herself, while Mr Davidson made tea. He came in with a cigarette dangling from the side of his mouth.

He put the tea things on the floor then drew the curtains a little. A large plate decorated with green water lilies and slightly chipped was piled high with biscuits.

'You *were* expecting me, weren't you?'

'Oh yes, my dear. And if you hadn't come to me, I'd have called on you. I just feel things will go well today. I'm in the mood.'

She poured out the tea and gave him his cup, containing three sugar lumps. He slurped rather than sipped his tea.

'Last time I felt we were both rather too tense,' he said.

'Yes.'

'Hmmm. But I feel a great deal has happened to you since. You must be wary of smothering your instincts in words.'

'In words?'

'In intellectual patterns rather than emotional patterns. Do you see, my dear? There is danger in too much cleverness. Success in life is based on an ability to transcribe feelings accurately and act on the transcription intelligently. Hmmm. Your psychic powers, for instance, could be rendered useless by too much cleverness. Many people's are. You must believe what you feel.'

'I see. But I find I don't necessarily know what a particular feeling is, because it's new to me. It makes it hard to interpret accurately.'

152

'Don't try and interpret too much.'

'It's hard.'

'Together we are aiming to achieve something remarkable. We can only succeed if you cease to explain and interpret. Please try to cease to think.'

Mr Davidson stubbed out his cigarette.

'Now let us relax and open ourselves up to the spirits. I want you to feel the light within you shining forth.'

Jennifer put down her tea cup.

'For the moment please don't think of anything or of any spirit in particular. I want you to make your mind blank, empty of all thoughts. Hmmmm. Now don't be impatient. I'm afraid it's your mother's mother again telling you that love matters more ... and that you should always do what you know to be right. And can you help me with a gentleman with a bad knee?'

'What do you mean?'

'There's a spirit here with a bad knee. Do you know someone in the spirit world who had a bad knee?'

'No.'

'Hmmm. He tells me that your mother is very upset at the moment. She seems calm but she isn't. You should try to help her. You shouldn't compete with her all the time.'

'Who is this spirit?'

'I don't know. He has a very bad knee.'

'You told me that.'

Mr Davidson was scratching behind his ear. 'Did either of your grandfathers have bad knees? This gentleman must have been about sixty-five when he passed on.'

'I really don't know a great deal about my relations.'

'Hmmm ...' Mr Davidson fell silent. Jennifer was disappointed. There she was sitting in front of a man who looked like Humpty Dumpty, who had no eyelashes to speak of and absurd bushy eyebrows caricaturists would love. His clothes were shabby and his flat dingy. What's more he was asking her to help him with a gentleman with a bad knee. It was ridiculous. He had probably asked her back here just out of loneliness, nothing grander. Shelley would have kept him at a distance. After leaving his flat the last time, her clothes

153

had smelt of must and cigarettes until they had been washed.

She looked up and found his eyes glaring into her.

'Hmmm,' he said, 'please try to clear your mind of unkind thoughts. It doesn't help us at all. This is not a game, or is it?'

'No, I'm quite serious. I'm sorry.' She shifted the cushions around her, to make the sofa more comfortable. And then it happened. She was jolted forwards as if in a suddenly braking car and her eyes filled with tears. She was overcome by a feeling of being near to Rebecca. Mr Davidson was jerked forward too and their gazes bumped into each other.

'Wonderful, wonderful,' cried Mr Davidson. 'What a wonderful person is with us. What goodness. Dear me, dear me, dear me. Your friend. My, my, Rebecca, Rebecca, Rebecca. It's so good of you to come to us. She says she is so pleased to see you. She misses you so much and loves you so much, loves everything so much. She died in a crash. There was pain. But she wants me to tell you that there is no pain. Only pain because she loved life. She says she loved the detail of life: oak leaves, sweet peas, autumn mornings. She says you were right to warn her about that bike. She was fond of you, you know, but says you do not love enough, you do not know how to.'

'I loved her.'

'Only after she died, she says. Hmmmm. She's a splendid girl. With lovely hair. Hmmm. Very tall with pale skin. She was always dreaming.' He stuck the lower of his thick lips out, as if suddenly moved. 'She was very unconventional, very special, a great loss.'

'What does she think of the seance idea?'

'She likes it. But she says that she understands now that one should not always be brave and wilful.'

'What does she mean?'

'That she died, that her mother grieves, that other people matter as well as oneself. She says she is very happy to see you now. She wants you to remember her.'

'I can't forget her. Especially as she's standing in front of me right now.'

Mr Davidson opened his eyes.

Rebecca was smiling at Jennifer, a peculiar, sad smile. Her

154

long, thin hands hung by her side. She wore jeans and an old sweater. She pushed her hair behind her ears. Her face was white as marble.

Jennifer had shrunk back a little. She had no desire to touch Rebecca, who looked in a way more like a statue of Rebecca than Rebecca herself. Jennifer knew the touch would be like stone. Jennifer made an effort to smile then hid her face in her hands. When she looked up Rebecca was no longer there but Jennifer was still trembling and her throat clotted with tears.

'Dear me, dear me. Did you see that?' he murmured, wiping his lips.

'See what?'

'That girl.'

'Of course I did. It was Rebecca.'

'I know, I know. But isn't it marvellous?' He sat himself up. 'In jeans too! No gothic white dresses or any such nonsense. Marvellous.'

Later, as she walked home, she found she wanted to run, that a rush of life suddenly burst through her, that she was incredibly happy, that she was capable of anything.

From the window of the drawing room she saw the leaves were shadow puppets, dragons against the sky. The magic was back again.

17

Over the weekend Edward let Jennifer see some of his notes on the trial which he'd typed out on Saturday morning.

On the second day, after the first day's narrative of the prosecution evidence, the trial started in earnest. Aemilia turned up, looking well. We both felt oddly nervous for Charles Grigson. Backstage – in the judges' dining room – there are portraits, splendid silver, deferential waiters. And out here a young man is having to sit and listen to an account of a horrifying murder which will probably send him to prison for a good part of his life. He was wearing his dove-grey suit again. This time his face was paler. The skin had dulled to a greyish yellow. I saw he held a white handkerchief in his hand. He kept kneading it.

First of all evidence was read which established the carving knife as the murder weapon and ruled out the possibility of suicide. The pathologist's report showed she had been stabbed in the back four times while she was in the bath. She had died, however, not from the wounds but by drowning. Her lungs were full of water, therefore she had still been breathing – been capable of drawing breath – when she slumped down into the bath. The stab wounds were not all that deep and had not necessarily been made by someone with strength. She had died some time in the hour before the doctor reached her. The evidence for all this was rather technical and I shall have to rely on the shorthand notes for the details.

I took better notes once the detective who'd first arrived at the scene of the murder was examined and cross-examined at length. Detective Sergeant Williams was a square-jawed, square-spectacled, smug chap, obviously rather pleased at 'catching' Charles. He leaned forward ingratiatingly as he spoke. I found his heavy black glasses irritating.

'I want to take you back to the day of the alleged murder, February the thirteenth of this year. Were you on duty?'

'Yes.'

'Can you tell us what happened?'

'I received a phone call.'

'Did the caller give you any name?'

'Yes. Charles Grigson. Could I refer to my notes, sir?'

Geoffrey looked at the judge who nodded.

'Certainly, Sergeant Williams. Could you please tell the jury what the caller said?'

'He said, "There's a girl badly hurt here at 25 Parkhurst Mansions just by Harrods. You must come quickly. I think she's dead. Please come quickly. I'll wait. I've called an ambulance but I don't think they'll be able to do anything. She's in the bath. I haven't moved her." '

156

The detective had a rather dowdy voice which he kept to a monotone, as if to enhance his impression of steadiness.

'What time was this?'

'Ten fifteen in the morning.'

'How quickly did you get round there?'

'In ten minutes.'

'How did you enter the flat?'

'I rang the bell and he opened the door.'

'Who opened the door?'

'Charles Grigson.'

'Did you form any impression of his condition?'

'He was very pale and seemed in a state of shock. There was blood on his hands.'

'What was he wearing?'

'A leather jacket – as they wear on motor bikes. That had blood on it too.'

The words 'they' and 'motor bikes' were pronounced coldly.

'And did he have anything else to go with this jacket?'

'Yes sir, a pair of leather gloves. Soft leather ones. We found them lying by the phone.'

'Was there anything special about these gloves?'

'Yes sir, they had blood on them and they were flexible gloves, not gauntlets.'

'May I see exhibit A1?'

Geoffrey was handed a pair of gloves in a cellophane bag.

'Do you recognise these?'

'Yes, these are the gloves I took off the accused.'

'What happened after you were let into the flat?'

'He took us into the bathroom and we saw a girl lying in a bath red with blood. "Who is she?" I said.

' "My girlfriend," he replied. "Her name's Jane Thomson." Then he said, almost under his breath, "We had an argument."

'I couldn't stop myself saying, "So you killed her?" "No," he said.

'Then I cautioned him. The doctor was examining her and announced that she was dead. Mr Grigson sort of stumbled into the sitting room and sat on the sofa with his head in his hands. I asked him what had happened. He said, "Please don't question me now. I can't bear it. She's dead."

157

'Police Constable Edwards came out of the bathroom and said he thought he'd found the murder weapon. I followed him into the bathroom while another constable watched over Mr Grigson. Police Constable Edwards showed me a large, blood-stained carving knife hidden behind the long curtain in the bathroom. I called in Mr Grigson and pointed out the knife. "Have you seen this knife before?"

' "Yes", he said. "It's her carving knife. It's usually in the drawer under the sink."

' "It's sharp is it?" I asked him.

' "I suppose so," he said. He returned to the sofa and put his head in his hands again. He said, "I must think this out."

' "Did you kill this girl?"

' "No", he said. "It must have been ... Oh, a burglar. Or suicide."

' "She has been stabbed in the back. Does that sound like suicide?"

' "No," he said.

' "Do you see anything stolen?" I said.

' "No."

' "I mean can you see signs of a burglary?"

' "No," he said, "I can't." We searched the flat for any evidence of a break-in but could find nothing.

' "You had a key to the flat?" I said.

' "Yes. Of course. She was my girlfriend."

' "But you had an argument."

' "Yes, we'd had an argument." We searched him and found a letter from the deceased in the left pocket of his jacket. "That's partly why she wrote me the letter, because of our argument," he said. "She wanted me to marry her. I'd said I wouldn't, or not yet."

'Later, at Knightsbridge police station, we questioned him about the letter. I said to him, "She was finishing your affair?"

' "That's what the letter says. I came back to try to persuade her not to finish with me."

' "Did you have an argument while she was in the bath?"

' "No, she was dead when I came to the flat. We had argued before, that is what I meant when I said we had had an argument." '

The judge was watching the detective with disapproval in his half-closed eyes and down-turned mouth. He really is a most unnerving man. Oddly enough, after a glass or so of wine he's flushed and cheerful. He obviously doesn't like his job much. I met his wife at lunch on Thursday. She's a taller version of him with greyer hair and slanting instead of round spectacles. They make a very spooky couple.

The self-satisfied Detective Sergeant Williams was puffing himself up as the eyes of the court watched him. He was clearly a man who enjoyed attention.

'I asked him to tell me what his story was. He replied, "I received the letter over breakfast this morning while I was in Birmingham. At the Royal Arms Hotel. I speeded back on my motor bike to reach her before she said anything to my parents – about my having an affair with my sister, which was nonsense – and to persuade her not to cut off relations with me."

' "What about the money she says in the letter that she wanted returned?"

' "I was going to try and talk her out of it, persuade her to let me owe it to her a little longer.".

' "What time did you receive the letter?"

' "At about eight."

' "And you were in London by ten?"

' "Yes, just before ten. I drove fast."

' "Because you were angry?"

' "Because I wanted to reach her quickly."

' "You opened the door with your key?"

' "Yes."

' "And where was she?"

' "I didn't know. But the radio was on in the bathroom. I shouted her name and there was no reply so I went into the bathroom. I found her submerged in the water. I dragged her head up but I knew she was dead. I pressed at her chest but I knew it was hopeless. I thought I'd better ring the ambulance. Then I spoke to the police. While I waited I just kept pushing at her chest hard, hoping to squeeze out the water. I didn't know what to do."

' "How did you know she was dead? Was it because you had held her down until she stopped struggling?"

' "No," he said. He seemed angry. "Why don't you listen? I did not kill her. I shan't answer any more questions. I want to see my lawyer."

' "One more question," I said. "Had you been borrowing regularly from Jane Thomson?"

' "Yes I had." He refused to talk any further.'

Geoffrey asked the detective a few more questions before the defence counsel – Arthur Curtis – cross-examined. I've met Arthur a few times and always found him a relaxed and pleasant person. He's in his late forties but looks younger. He has curly ginger hair, sideboards and a rather debonair manner.

It wasn't until Thursday that Geoffrey started to examine Jane's parents and friends.

Jane's mother looked more like her elder sister. She's a pretty woman with mousy hair piled into a bun. She wore a Laura Ashley-style smock over a green sweater and matching tights. Her few wrinkles ran gracefully through brown skin. She stared fixedly ahead of her and spoke in a mechanical voice. She told Geoffrey that Jane had first mentioned Charles about a year ago.

'She said she had fallen in love with an architect called Charles Grigson, that's all. I wanted to meet him but she's always so secretive about her boyfriends I knew it wasn't worth asking. She mentioned him sometimes when she rang. We had lunch at Fortnum's about a month before her death and it was then that she admitted she would like to marry him but that he had never asked her. I remember she said, "He's devoted to his sister." It seemed to me that she idealised Charles Grigson. She told me how good he was, what a good person I mean. Apparently he became excited about music and the colours of flowers and old churches just like she did. She felt they were very similar, "made for each other" I think she said.'

Jennifer stopped reading and thought of Rebecca. She could almost feel her beside her, watching. Jane sounded so like Rebecca: the naivity, the sweetness. Even her mother reminded

160

Jennifer of Rebecca's mother. She knew Charles wouldn't have killed Jane – or Rebecca. She wondered what she should do with this certainty of hers. What would Aphra have done? Or Shelley? Jennifer knew she herself would do nothing.

'Was your daughter given a regular income by you?'

'Yes. We paid her rent and gave her sixty pounds a week to live on.'

'That seems a great deal.'

'Not to us. That's how much she asked for. She's our only daughter – was our only daughter – and a very good girl. We were very pleased she won a place at the Royal Academy, we knew London was expensive, and we could afford to give her that much.'

'Did you know she was lending it to her boyfriend?'

'I had no idea.'

'Would you have been angry if you had known?'

'I suppose so.'

Eventually Geoffrey steered his way round to an important point. He leant back on his heels self-importantly. His abundant pomposity is, I'm happy to say, undercut by the absurdity of his shooting eyebrows.

'Could Jane be firm? Once she had made up her mind about something was she determined?'

'Oh yes, surprisingly so. Takes after me. Always kept her threats.'

'Mr Robertson,' said the judge, 'I don't think we should permit leading questions in this courtroom.'

'Sorry sir. I wanted to establish …'

'The jury are in this court to hear evidence not opinion, thank you, Mr Robertson.'

But Geoffrey had already succeeded in suggesting that Charles, knowing her well, would have taken Jane's threats seriously.

Another witness was a skinny friend of Jane's – a pianist at the Royal Academy who talked about Jane's relationship with Charles. She had bulging eyes and stick arms, like an insect. As far as her friend knew, Jane had been out with no other men for the last year.

161

'When was the last time you saw Jane?' he said.

'The night before her death. She phoned me up because she was upset. I went round to her flat and she made me spaghetti.'

'And what did she say to you?'

'She said she'd been shopping in Harrods that morning and had met Lucinda Brown – the sister of Charles.'

'Half-sister I believe.'

'That's right, half-sister. And Lucinda insisted they have coffee together. Over coffee she told Jane that she had been having an affair with her brother – with Charles – for years and that ...'

'Is this admissible Mr Robertson? I don't think we should allow any hearsay in this court,' said the judge. He blew his nose crossly, then scratched it....

Jennifer stopped reading. She had a headache which kept running from one side of her forehead to the other as if something was trapped beneath her skin.

18

On Monday evening Paul came round at six and, at the bottom of the outside steps, met Edward returning from the Old Bailey.

'Hello,' said Edward 'Are you coming in here?'

'How do you do sir? My name is Paul Hughes and you must be Mr Hamilton.'

An old leather briefcase in his hand, pin-stripes on his body (he'd lunched with the Old Bailey judges) and sweat glistening on his forehead, Edward looked rather out of place before a background of summery saunters-by. Paul was dressed more suitably: jeans and a well-ironed blue and white striped shirt.

'I am indeed,' he said, shaking Paul's dry hand firmly. 'How do you do?'

'Very well thank you. And you?'

'Oh, the trial I'm attending is stressful and getting more so and hot weather and work don't agree with me anyway. Can take one at a time but not both together. Mind you, they do have air conditioning where I'm working at the Old Bailey, but it makes a blasted noise.'

They walked up the steps and at the top Edward turned to Paul and said, 'Who are you, by the way?'

'I'm sorry, sir. I didn't explain. I've just moved in to number twenty-five down the road.'

Illumination swept over Edward's face.

'Of course, of course. The architect.' Edward seized Paul's hand enthusiastically and shook it even more vehemently than he had the first time. 'How very nice to see you. Did we ask you round for a drink? I know we meant to.'

'No. I've come to take your daughter to the fair on Hampstead Heath. I hope that'll be all right, sir?'

'Good grief. Why certainly. Of course. I remember Sarah saying something about you and Jenny. Dear me.'

The intensity of Edward's stare slightly discomfited Paul as they stood at the doorway.

'Do you have a key, sir, or shall I ring?'

'No, no, I've a key.' Edward searched through all his pockets and his briefcase without success.

'Better ring,' he said eventually.

Sarah opened the door. Her face looked tired and its features sagged still more at the sight of Paul standing before her with Edward.

'You're late,' she snapped at Paul before she could stop herself.

'Oh, you've been keeping my little daughter waiting, have you, Paul?' he said with a genial smile. Paul observed that Edward's sickle-shaped eyebrows gave him an air of amusement. His golliwog grey hair was, Paul imagined, rather as his would be when he grew older. Paul liked Edward.

'Jennifer,' roared Edward. 'It's Paul.'

'Go up and have a drink, you two. I'll be with you in a moment,' said Sarah. She left them while she went to the bathroom to renovate her face and recover her poise. Sarah dabbed perfume behind her ears, on her wrists and on her hair.

She reminded herself once more of what she had told herself every day since that Friday when they first made love: she must take care.

Paul was just a little too young, a little too good-looking, a little too much like Edward had been when he'd first courted her. Paul had seemed so vulnerable and sincere that Sarah had allowed herself to open a little gap for love. The waters had come rushing in and she found herself floundering in a passion she hadn't experienced for years. It was a bloody nuisance.

She'd avoided danger for so long. She'd had plenty of affairs but they hadn't meant anything. She prided herself that she was one of the very few women who could keep their hearts to themselves while offering their bodies generously. And generosity was one reason she had affairs. Sarah liked to give other people pleasure. She also was curious about other people's bodies and homes. Lying in a strange bed was as good as spending a night at a strange hotel: great fun, a tame adventure. What's more she adored men becoming infatuated with her. It was so flattering. She remembered Saul Goodman swearing he loved her and her pert reply (read in some women's magazine), 'Love is just prolonged infatuation.' She never felt guilty about her affairs because they weren't serious. The men were usually sexually inept and always boring or fat, or dreadfully middle-aged or otherwise unsuitable. It was as though she deliberately chose men who did not endanger her heart. Up to now her heart had stayed safely with lovable, kind, perplexed Edward who brought out all her maternal instincts, entertained her, worshipped her and was also a perfectly adequate, if irregular, lover. But now ...

But now when Paul was late she imagined that he would never come, that he had gone off with someone else, been killed in a car accident or just couldn't be bothered with her any more. She suffered agonies. This afternoon he'd come an hour late and during that long hour she'd phoned his house six times, filed and varnished her toenails, plucked her eyebrows although they didn't need it, broken a glass by mistake, viciously punched the cushions in the drawing room and drunk one cup of tea and two whiskies. Every time a car went by or the phone rang she jumped. It was as if she were a girl again waiting and waiting for a call from her latest boyfriend.

The pain he caused her brought back the many pains of youth: the man who'd taken her to bed then had a quick bath and said he must return to his wife, the boy who after a two-month relationship with her poured out his love for another girl, the one who'd gone on holiday and never come back. All these pains were jagged peaks in her past, ineradicable parts of her. She thought she had learnt to go round the dangerous peaks when they loomed ahead. She thought she had become strong.

This love of hers was such a *foolish* indulgence. She must have wanted it, her heart must have been ripe or he would not have been able to pick it with such ease. She supposed she must have become bored with safety. Usually she didn't take gambles.

Some years back she'd visited Las Vegas and loathed it. She claimed she had detested the vulgarity of the white polo-necked men and guinea-fowl women wobbling on high heels but really it was something else. The weird city in the desert was dangerous, unpredictable. Here man had turned day and night into one long night. The gambling rooms were benighted by ruby lights, heavy curtains, coarse shows and buxom hostesses even when the sun was at its height. Shirt-sleeved and intense, the gamblers were oblivious to time. Man appeared to be in control but he wasn't. It was the long, long, spin of the wheel which broke and made men.

Since marrying Edward or, to put it another way, since growing up, she had made a point of never gambling with emotions, never laying them down and waiting, with palpitating heart, for the wheel to stop spinning. But now she didn't know what was happening and would happen between her and Paul. She had to wait and see. Practical and efficient as she was, Sarah found mooning around an infuriating waste of time. But there was very little she could do about it.

Helplessness did not become her, she decided, as she stared at the worn face in the mirror. She must pull herself together. Edward needed her to be competent and active. The trial was draining him emotionally and he needed her support. Sarah could see that Jennifer despised her when she showed weakness

165

even more than when she was blithely capable. Jennifer made Sarah feel miserably guilty. She seemed to find living so difficult. But she would grow out of it. Sarah herself had gone through a brief stage of hating her mother and adoring her ghastly father when she was Jennifer's age. More important, Sarah feared that if she showed weakness, if she lost her briskness and strength, she might lose Paul.

Paul must not know that inside she was as gooey as a lovesick sixteen year old. Sarah understood that in love, as in everything, what you have is nothing. It's what you haven't got that counts. If he knew he had her he might not want her. Already she had paid him far too much attention.

She smeared gloss on her full lips and pouted into the mirror. Her eyes were so tired she felt as though the surrounding skin were covered in glue. How she wished her crow's-feet didn't exist. Perhaps she ought to have a face-lift.

Upstairs she found Jennifer, Edward and Paul earnestly discussing epic poetry. Before she could stop herself she said, 'I wish I knew more literature so I could make witty in-jokes about fusty old books no one else ever reads.' Three faces stared at her in surprise.

Sarah's education had been sketchy. Maths and cookery were her best subjects at school. The nearest she got to university was her secretarial course at Oxford. Common sense, ambition, hard work and of course her marriage to the ever-encouraging Edward had propelled her where she was, owner of a fashionable restaurant with a well-justified reputation for a high standard of cuisine and service. Previously she ran a Sarah's Restaurant in Wimbledon village, near where they used to live. The profits had helped to buy this house as well as the Pimlico restaurant. But in spite of all this the name Milton still had the power to make her extremely angry.

'Come and have a drink, darling,' said Edward. 'Don't stand there looking so bleak. We'll stop being pretentious at once.'

Sarah immediately felt better. Pretentiousness, that's all it is. Showing off knowledge. Who cares about Milton anyway? Jennifer only learnt about literature to side with Edward against her, but Edward wouldn't play games like that. Edward was straightforward. She was glad he was in the room looking after her, giving her a warming whisky and smiling gently on this day on which, for some reason, she felt more insecure than she had for years. But, oh God, Paul looked so beautiful. She wished he wasn't going to the fair with Jennifer. His suggestion about pretending to be Jennifer's boyfriend had seemed amusingly ingenious at the time. Now it seemed obscene and she felt so far away from him. He was over the other side of the room, on the sofa. He was not looking at her. He was talking to Jennifer. How could he be talking so intimately to Jennifer when he was part of Sarah and Sarah wasn't over there talking to Jennifer? She couldn't understand it. She wanted to possess Paul completely. She didn't want him walking out of the house. She wanted to bar him up in a room, squeeze out all his secrets until she knew everything about him and she was him and he was her and they were one. But now there was such a distance between this middle-aged but attractive woman sitting here on her elegant chair and that handsome young man with the curly hair who was staring so intently into the eyes of the pretty young girl beside him.

Jennifer was pushing her hair shyly from her face and looking up at Paul through those long lashes of hers. Luscious mouth, deep liquid eyes, sweet cheeks, pert nose, the gooseberry fuzz of her arms, why hadn't she realised? Of course, he found Jennifer attractive. Saul had found her attractive, why not Paul? Damn her. Jealousy wrenched at her stomach.

Edward was watching her watching them. She saw him and was angry. She bet he was misinterpreting everything. She bet he thought she was upset that Jennifer was growing up, making the first tentative thrusts to leave the cosy womb of family life. What a fool he was. How could he misread her so? For a moment Sarah hated Edward because it was Edward who had forced her into this silly deception and prevented her seeing Paul this evening.

'Ed, you've completely drowned this whisky,' she said harshly.

'Sorry,' said Edward.

'Is yours drinkable, Paul?' she said in a different, caressing tone.

'Oh yes. It's terrific, thank you.'

'Very good, very good. So when will your plans for the restaurant be finished?' said Edward.

'Well, sir, I don't exactly know. In a few days, I think.'

'Oh good. I hear you know Charles Grigson and his sister Lucinda. And that you used to know Jane.'

'Yes. As a matter of fact I used to go out with Jane. I left Lucinda for her. It's one of the reasons they disliked each other so much.'

'Really? This hasn't come up in the trial.'

'I hope it doesn't, sir. It wouldn't help anyone.'

'What do you mean?'

'Just that it won't help anyone. Charles will get off, I suppose? There seems no proof from what Jennifer says.'

'Not necessarily. Yesterday there was evidence from friends and work mates saying what a good chap he is, how impossible it would be for him to kill. But the evidence on the other side is much more weighty. Being found on the scene of the crime, for instance. With blood, literally, on his hands. And Lucinda didn't help much. She gave evidence today. She's been surprisingly quiet all week. And when she gave evidence for the defence today she was white and trembly. The judge kept on telling her to speak up.'

'That doesn't sound like Lucinda. She's not usually nervous,' said Paul.

'She looked ill to me. Shadows under her eyes. Rather shabby dress. Not the grand performance I'd been expecting.'

'What did she say? How did it go?' said Jennifer.

'Not too good.'

'Have you got your notes? Please read them to us.'

'Please, sir,' said Paul.

'Oh all right. They're rather approximate.'

Edward scrabbled in his briefcase and took out a shorthand note book. He flipped through. 'Here we are.'

'What was she wearing?' said Jennifer.

'A rather dull blue shirt dress with no belt, though it was obviously supposed to have one, ordinary stockings and a pair of court shoes. Not very special at all. Her hair was a mess but not, somehow, the exotic mess it usually is. It just looked rather unkempt.'

'Is she ill do you think?' said Paul.

'Maybe. She seemed to be swaying rather as she spoke. Could be drugs, I suppose.'

'She didn't take them as far as I know …' said Paul.

'Go on,' urged Jennifer. 'Tell me what happened when she was cross-examined.'

'Well, she was scowling at Geoffrey and answered his questions in a very surly way. He asked her whether she'd borrowed money from her brother.'

'Yes,' she said, 'About a thousand pounds.'

'What did you spend the money on?'

'Clothes mostly.'

'And what did you tell your brother you spent it on?'

'I told him I was lending it to a friend who needed the money because of a gambling debt.'

'He believed you?'

'Yes.'

'He is very fond of you?'

'Yes.'

'Looked after you?'

'Yes.'

'How long had you lived together in your house in Stoke Newington?'

'Three years.'

'Your father is your brother's stepfather?'

'That is correct.'

'Speak up, please,' said the judge.

'I said that is correct.'

'Have you ever had sexual relations with your brother?'

'Do I have to answer that question?'

'Please.'

'Never as a matter of fact.'

'Then why did you tell Jane Thomson you were having an affair with your brother?'

'I didn't.'

'You are saying she was a liar?'

'It must have been a fantasy of hers that I said that, to explain to herself why my brother wouldn't marry her. She was very jealous of me, I think.'

'Why should she be jealous of you?'

'Because I lived with the man she loved. And because she was shy and dull.'

'While you?'

'While I am not shy and dull.'

'This is very curious. You are saying she made up the story about your affair. Are you denying she met you in Harrods?'

'No, Mr Robertson I am not.'

'Do you deny you told her about the money your brother was giving you?'

'No, I told her.'

'Why?'

'Because she was looking so smug when I met her, mincing round Harrods with that goody-goody look on her angelic face. I felt I wanted to wipe the smirk off her face.'

'Why deny you mentioned your affair with your brother?'

Lucinda shrugged. 'I didn't mention it.'

'I put it to you that you did.'

'No, Geoffrey, I didn't.'

'I should be grateful,' said the judge, 'if the witness would address crown counsel by his full name.'

'Sorry,' said Lucinda. 'No, Mr Robertson, I didn't.'

'You did. Because it was true and you wanted to break up the relationship between Jane Thomson and your brother.'

'You are mistaken, Mr Robertson. I have not committed incest with my brother nor did I tell Jane Thomson that I had.' For a second Lucinda met Charles's eyes, she reddened, and dropped her glance.

'Are you in love with your brother?'

'No, and it's none of your business.'

'He would do anything to protect you?'

'He wouldn't. He loved her.'

'But loved you more, was willing to kill to protect you?'

'He loved her. He'd never have hurt her.'

170

Her eyes were bright and the whole court was watching her.

'My brother, Charles Grigson, is a gentle, kind person. Too gentle, in my opinion. He spends too much time looking after others and not enough fulfilling himself. He believes in the sanctity of life. He rides a motor bike, but that doesn't make him violent.'

It looked as though Lucinda would cry if she went on. Her head was bowed and she was staring at her hands.

'Can I go now, please?' she said very softly. 'I'll come back tomorrow.'

'The judge let her go.'

'Oh dear,' said Paul. 'So she wasn't very impressive?'

'But Charles's sure to get off. He's so obviously innocent. Just because he might have cuddled his sister once or twice doesn't make him a murderer.'

'It gives him strong, dark passions, and that's what the jury are after.'

'I don't want to hear about it any more,' said Paul, standing up. It's too distressing. What a fool Lucinda is. Why couldn't she behave better?'

'She wasn't in a condition to behave better.'

'We must go, Jennifer,' said Paul.

Sarah found she was pressing her nails into the palms of her hands.

'Oh yes,' said Edward, cheerfully rising. 'Don't let us oldens keep you young things from your pleasure. Off you go to the fair.'

Jennifer and Paul drove off in Paul's battered Volkswagen. She sat bolt upright staring out of the window.

'Sarah was cross,' said Jennifer.

'Very. But she has no right to be.'

'Hasn't she?'

'No. She agreed to the arrangement.'

'I suppose so.' Jennifer was not really too grieved by her mother's irritation.

Paul drove fast but well. Jennifer clutched her seat tightly.

As they approached the fair the noise and bright lights stirred Jennifer with excitement.

171

'Shelley used to visit Leigh Hunt at the Vale of Health,' she said. 'But I don't think Hunt's house is still standing. Otherwise we could have gone and had a look.'

'Yup,' he said.

It was a warm evening and the smell of hamburgers saturated the air. Emerald trees loomed above the gaudy lightbulbs luring customers to hoopla stalls, dart boards, rifle ranges, dodgem cars. A stocky little girl carried in one hand candyfloss which gave a beard to her round face and in the other a goldfish in a plastic bag. There was no one with her. Engrossed in the sticky pleasure of candyfloss, red from her lick, she seemed untroubled. Old-time music rang out cheerfully from a little train circling round and round with no one on it. Even the children favoured the more raucous sounds of the dodgems – the screams, the pop music, the clash of cars. They stood around, entranced by future pleasures. Waiting their turn. The ground was tipsy with coke cans, chewing-gum wrappers, cigarette ends. As Jennifer stood by Paul at the rifle range she saw on the earth a tiny green plastic comb and, she didn't know why, felt sad.

Paul's gun shot one, two, three tanks and at least ten soldiers. They lit up when he hit them.

'Not bad,' he said to her as he accepted a coconut as a prize. 'Shall I give it to your father to win his approval?'

'No, he doesn't like coconuts. But I'd like a toffee apple.'

'I never thought you'd be tempted by such worldly things as toffee apples.'

'I've always liked toffee apples.'

Paul bought the apples and they ate them solemnly. Paul had assumed an air of boyish merriment which was infectious. Jennifer found Paul's look of concentration as his teeth chipped away at the toffee, leaving the apple, very funny. She grinned at him from over her half-eaten feast and he laughed.

'Come on,' he said, chucking his mangled apple on the ground. 'Let's have a go on the dodgems.'

Paul resolutely banged their blue dodgem car against the others. Knocked about and pleasantly scared, a wonderful senselessness overcame her. She was free of care. 'Go on, hit it,' she screamed.

Staggering out of the car and down the steps, she hardly recognised herself. That astronaut lightness had returned.

'Are you all right?' he asked, holding her elbow for a second.

'Fine.'

'And I thought you were so timid. "Go on, hit it," you screamed.' He grinned. She pushed her hair back and smiled that lovely wide smile.

She was standing at the side of a hoopla stall and its circle of coloured bulbs softly lit her face. It was curious, thought Paul, that even here in the tawdriness of the fair she still looked so innocent. The sleepy innocence of a child he had once seen at a friend's house. She had been lying with the light of the night-lamp on her, curled up in her nightdress. A group of adults came to see her in the middle of a party and she didn't waken, she was lost in her dreams, murmuring softly, wiping the hair from her face but still asleep.

'Let's go on something dangerous. The big wheel. As it spins round it twirls each car from side to side and gets faster and faster. You'll scream. You'll love it.'

In the big wheel he put his arm round her when she began to scream. The world was below her as they rose up, above the tall trees, the lake, the houses, above everything. Then down, plummeting down again, seeing the uplifted faces below become bigger and bigger then, whoops they were soaring again.

The ride didn't last long and when the bristle-chinned fairground man released the metal bar which had kept them safe Jennifer stumbled out and again she could hardly walk she was so dizzy.

Paul put his arm around her to support her and suddenly they were one of dozens of couples holding on to each other as they staggered round the hurly-burly of the fair. Surprisingly, the feeling of being normal, one of a crowd, pleased Jennifer.

'I liked your father,' said Paul, as though nothing out of the ordinary was happening, as though his arm wasn't round her shoulder, as though her skin hadn't suddenly come alive.

'Oh, so do I,' said Jennifer.

'He seems to adore Sarah.'

173

'Of course. He's her husband.' And suddenly she was irritated.

'Do you disapprove of my relationship with your mother?' He sniffed again that absurd, lovable labourer's sniff. It wasn't a sniff of sadness, or a reaction to the cold, or a signal of a cold, it was just a habit of his. He opened his eyes wide, questioningly.

'I suppose so,' she said, dragging her glance away from the dancing caverns of his bright eyes. Sometimes he was so bewitching she thought he was doing it on purpose.

Jennifer made an unconvincing attempt to push him away with her shoulder but the gesture was a shrug not a push. She was actually perfectly comfortable where she was.

'Please, don't be cross,' he said.

'Well, I'm sorry, but I do find it upsetting. For one thing, I'm sure she doesn't care about your career at all. It's a waste of your time messing around with that back yard. You should be designing wonderful houses or hotels or castles.'

'Remember I've got to work in an office for two years before I'm fully qualified. I shouldn't be earning money at all now. Anyway, I plan out more ambitious schemes at home.'

'Do you?'

'Oh yes.'

'I bet she stops you working though. She's always wanting to see you.'

'Yes,' he said. 'But what can one do?'

'I don't know,' she said, staring at the ground. She knew what he could do. He could stop his affair with Sarah.

'You see, one needs encouragement and love from someone.' Shelley had needed it too. Vapid little Harriet had been no help but Mary, with her great tablet of a forehead and undying love, had been a source of inspiration.

'Yes. But don't you see, Sarah's so practical. She'd never encourage you to create anything more imaginative than a patio or an efficiently fitted kitchen. She's so down-to-earth.'

'You're quite right, of course.' His hand was moving infinitesimally slowly, cautiously up and down her arm. That part of her arm was curiously hot, as though it might just melt. What

174

was that her mother had said: melt on the bed from sheer pleasure?

The smell of onions was heavy in the air, and the throbbing music seemed suddenly far too loud. A woman with blonde hair, green nail varnish and a face like a crumpled map knocked against Jennifer and a whiff of cheap perfume assaulted her. They passed a fortune teller's tent and Jennifer remembered how, in her childhood imagination, she too had been a gypsy, but one with real power to foresee and change the future. But here, with Paul's arm round her she was powerless, clamped down, an ordinary silly girl screaming on the big wheel.

'Shall we go home soon?' said Jennifer.

'We've only just come,' said Paul.

He stopped. His right arm encircling her shoulders held her still and his left stroked back the wild hair from her forehead. She flinched.

'What's the matter?'

Jennifer shrugged.

'I don't know. It's just that the fair's suddenly depressing. Corrupt.'

Paul knew she was right. Although it appeared childish and innocuous, the fair was actually rife with sex, screams, gambling, greed, all the gaudy pleasures of life. Tempting, robust but, finally, depressingly ephemeral. The fair would be moving on in a few days, leaving only litter behind. The stalls would be dismantled, the hooplas and fluorescent pink teddy bears carried to another green space where another group of identical people would amuse themselves throwing ping pong balls into goldfish bowls. He didn't like it either.

A group of yobs were scuffling by the caravans.

'Too frivolous for you?' he said.

'I just don't like it.' She walked on ahead. He followed, his face pale and frowning through the gloom.

'Have you ever really let yourself go, let rip, thoroughly enjoyed yourself?'

'Why do you ask me that?'

'Shall I tell you what you should be when you grow up? A

nun. Your reclusiveness, secrecy and repression are excellent ingredients for a life of religious confinement.'

She swivelled round. Her lips narrowed dangerously.

'What do you mean?'

'What I say.'

'That's nonsense. I'm not religious at all.'

He smiled innocuously. 'Oh yes you are, but you don't know it. From what you've told me you have a profound worship of man and his capabilities.'

'But worship of man, not God. And don't you say I'm a prude.'

He sniffed. 'I didn't. Hey, do you want another toffee apple?'

But the carefree tone of the evening had been irrevocably lost and a serious, passionate one had taken over which was out of keeping with the lights and giggles of the fair.

'No, thank you. Shall we go back to the car?'

'Or we could go down and see if we could find that cottage of Leigh Hunt's. Keats visited it too, didn't he? I've always loved Keats.'

Jennifer was a little appeased. 'I'm sure it isn't there but we could look all the same.'

As they walked Paul continued the argument more gently. He hadn't realised how quick-tempered little Jennifer could be. Beneath that urchin face was a determined will. Was it in its own way, a will far more determined than Sarah's?

'Worship of man and God are really the same thing, you know,' said Paul. 'The unconquerable human spirit so much greater, freer, than any living, copulating, feeding animal. It's worshipping God through man. Man in God's image. But the problem is that that particular way of thinking can take much of the fun out of life. It means you're always striving for something out of reach, something to prove one's so much greater than any beast, something to, in effect, glorify God. Nuns, for instance, are crazy to renounce the grubby pleasures of life for the future glory of heaven. It's most unlikely they'll ever get it. Take my advice, don't take risks, don't strive for something out of reach. Grab the concrete pleasures every time. Go on the dodgems, the rides and don't bother with the hoopla

176

stalls. Nobody ever wins the champagne.'

'That sounds clever but I don't believe it. It's worth daring. Nothing grand has ever been achieved without a little daring.'

'Maybe, but it's a shame to miss out on life while you're doing the daring. Sarah says you're always working away up in your room at something. What is it? What are you so determined *about*?'

'Nothing. But you, you must be tremendously dedicated to be an architect. I mean, you don't earn much at first, do you? But you don't care about that sort of thing....'

'I don't know what I care about,' he said in a shuddering small voice as they passed through the shadow of a large horse-chestnut.

'You care about your work. You're ambitious, you said you were.'

'I didn't say that.'

'You are ambitious,' repeated Jennifer shrilly. 'I know you are.'

'Shh,' he said. All his life Paul had suffered from other people knowing things about him which he didn't know himself. His parents had always been quite sure he'd become, of all things, a heart surgeon although he had never shown the least aptitude in any kind of science. His master at his public school had presumed he'd get into Oxford. He didn't. His driving instructor had been certain he'd pass his test first time. He hadn't. Women, for some reason, tended to see him in whatever form their long-awaited saviour happened to be. It was as though he was just a blank canvas on which people painted their hopes and dreams and then, when they found these hopes and dreams weren't real, were sorely disappointed. People were always accusing him of deceiving them when in fact, of course, they deceived themselves. It still astonished Paul a little. It also frightened him. It was almost as though he didn't exist. Usually he believed the opinions of others about himself because he had no firm view of his personality and capabilities. This meant that his view of himself was constantly changing, blurring, shifting until sometimes he thought he was going completely crazy.

And now, suddenly, with Jennifer's shrill cry, the familiar

177

and terrible abyss of emptiness opened before him. He had to talk quickly to stop himself falling.

'You know, Jenny, I feel this terrible sense that at the centre there is nothing. Someone says ... my parents' friends say – you look *exactly* like your mother, another you look *amazingly* like your father or *uncannily* like your uncle. The ambivalence. I feel how unreal everything is. At parties people standing around – I mean, it's so funny, you know? On the outside looking out all the time. People say I'm amusing, find me attractive – yet those things are exterior to me.

'I find it impossible to care, to be committed to anything, anyone, don't want to be. Yet one wants some kind of permanence – your mother and me, for instance, or anyone really – I know she's got Edward but still I wonder, you know, if anyone could actually love one enough all the time, to be always there. I talk to the front of people not their insides. I never reach anyone's insides. Oh, I make love to women, but never reach them somehow, you know?' It was beginning to get better: the emptiness was moving away as it always eventually moved away.

'No, I don't know at all.'

'I'm just a performing animal who goes through the tricks and doesn't know why he does them. All my life. I say all the right things in public but really I'm just a shoddy imitation of myself. And nobody seems to notice, that's the funny thing.

'Socially, I'm a success. I listen and agree and flirt while people pour out their preoccupations. They boast about their achievements, affairs, odd opinions. They lay it all down, yet presumably they don't leave it all behind. But I seem to have left myself somewhere. I'm just a gaudy wrapper announcing non-existent goods.'

'Don't be silly. You're terrifically intelligent and kind and sensitive.' Jennifer was quite afraid. Paul's eyes had gone glacial and he was walking quickly looking neither to one side nor the other, just straight ahead. She had to run to keep up with him and she didn't think he'd notice if she stopped. It was as though something were pursuing him.

'I'm whatever anyone wants me to be,' he said in a cold voice

178

unlike his own. 'That's why when I'm alone I don't seem to exist. You know, I'm ripe for conversion to anything.'

'Good grief,' panted Jennifer, hurrying. 'Everyone finds being alone difficult sometimes. Why, even Shelley wrote that he often found it dreadfully worrying. I can't remember the exact words but ...'

'I can't stand it, the emptiness, the rattling awfulness. Sometimes I feel I just cannot stand it. In the past everything was so alive and breathing. I wanted to paint the shadows of curtains, the smell of summer, the movement of prowling cats. But then I grew up and the colours seemed to fade. I can design now, I can't paint. In a way, it's because I've lived too much, I think. I've had a bordello of women. The fuck in the back of the car, in a plush flat, after a meal. But there is only emptiness, watching but not feeling anything more than physical desire and release. Thinking each time it will be different, special, will bring back ... and I don't know, I blame women in a way. They've taken me from innocence to experience and dumped me there.

'But I hope I'll be able to build something really wonderful one day. Something special. Something I'll be remembered by. That's probably just a dream.' Paul was talking more quietly now. 'I suppose everyone has to have their dream, their private escape clause. For some it resides in the past, for others in the present and for others it's out of time. Immersing themselves in a hobby, a book they write, an invention, even a language, they escape from trivia. It's man's constant desire to lose time. In sex, that moment when you know neither present, past or future. The moment in the rose garden that Eliot speaks of, the moment in church when eternity and you are all one. And, finally, death. But real escape is seldom found. Do you understand?'

Jennifer swallowed. Paul was behaving in an extraordinary manner. He was even more Shelleyean than usual. She was impressed by what he was saying but didn't know how to reply. He seemed so hectic. She loved him. She wanted to look after him. But she didn't know how to explain. How had Mary Shelley explained?

'Sort of,' she said.

'Oh, I don't know myself. I just feel so confused and worthless. And I've missed so many opportunities to make myself less worthless. I don't want to be responsible, to take hold of my own destiny, and yet I do.'

'I don't think you're worthless at all. You're just ... vulnerable.'

'You don't know, sweetheart, you don't know.'

19

Sarah was waiting for Jennifer and Paul to come home. She sat lonely in the drawing room curled up on the sofa with her feet under her and a pile of old *Vogues* on the coffee table beside a whisky bottle, a glass and a jug of water. Edward had retired to his study after she had repeatedly snapped at him. If only Edward would have the gumption to arrange something for Monday evenings when the restaurant was closed. He always left everything up to her. It was most tiresome.

For the umpteenth time, she wished she had not suggested that Paul should pretend to be Jennifer's boyfriend. So much for plans laid in jolly, effervescent moods. She remembered a midnight feast she'd arranged with her next door neighbour when she was twelve or thirteen. It had seemed a terrific idea. When she knocked on the friend's window at midnight there had been no reply. She had knocked again. It had started to drizzle. The dog had begun to bark. Still her friend had not woken up. Eventually Sarah had gone home disappointed and soaking wet. She was met by her father, in his pyjamas, furious because the dog's barking had woken him up.

Sarah could smile now at the memory. But the smile faded as she thought of Jennifer. How confusing it all was. She loved Jennifer and wanted her to be happy. Since Paul had started coming round there had been an added glow to Jennifer's cheeks and a confidence in the way she walked and talked. For a long time Sarah had very much wanted Jennifer to have a boyfriend, to go to parties, to wear pretty clothes. She would have been overjoyed that Paul liked Jennifer if only ... well, if only Paul hadn't been Paul, if only Paul hadn't been the first man she herself had cared about for years.

But she was sure Jennifer thought of Paul as just a friend. Sarah's mind slipped back to her first boyfriend. Surely Jennifer couldn't feel as she had felt? Sarah had only been seventeen, or perhaps eighteen, at the time. She remembered the kiss in the deserted street at night-time, his body next to hers, and the stillness lapping perfect peace into her mind. The smell of jasmine in the garden as they touched lips. The hard push of his tongue as she lay on the sofa at home, stirring her body into the fullness of painful yet inexpressibly sweet desire. But when the desire had been fulfilled everything had changed. She lay with him in bed. He was asleep and his body gave out no heat. Cool, the death of a relationship. His back was marble in her memory.

He'd left her, leaving the world flat and empty. But only for a while. The next lover followed on soon, and the same pattern was repeated. It was as though her emotional make-up manufactured an endless production line of similar situations. In youth everything had seemed so significant. She'd thought her first grief would last for ever, as she had her first love. As she learnt this was not so, life became shallower but more bearable.

She wondered if Jennifer was suffering now. She was such a difficult child. But for all her flinching, her shyness, her habit of plunging her hands into her pockets, Sarah believed Jennifer was not as vulnerable as she seemed. Her secretiveness gave her an inner strength which was almost frightening.

Paul had mentioned Jennifer's secrecy. He'd appeared quite fascinated by it. Sarah wished she'd been more mysterious herself instead of opening herself out as though she knew nothing at all about the wiles of love. Damn this pain, damn him, damn her. Jennifer was even looking older, more like Sarah. In a way it was pleasing. But a younger version of oneself could hurt if one's lover preferred the younger one. But this, thought Sarah, was mere foolishness. Paul needed her support and strength. His uncertain grey eyes drew her to him. He was vulnerable. He needed her.

Sitting, waiting, thinking about him, the agony had a poignancy, a memory of a time when everything was difficult because everything was important.

Edward went to bed early.

At eleven a car drew up with a screech of brakes and Sarah went to the window. She fluffed up her hair in the mirror and smeared on glossy lipstick for the fifth time, each time after a glass of whisky had taken it off. Sarah positioned herself on the sofa with her legs elegantly crossed and slippers from Afghanistan elegantly dangling. But when she heard the steps on the stairs her heart was shivery and tender and she leapt up and greeted Paul with a kiss.

'Hello there, where's Edward?' he said.

'In bed. I wish we were,' she whispered.

Over his shoulder she saw Jennifer arctic-eyed.

'Did you enjoy yourself, Jenny?'

'Yes,' said Jennifer. 'Quite.'

'You'd better go to bed now, don't you think?'

' 'Fraid I must too,' said Paul. 'I don't want a scene with Edward and I have to get up early as Jennifer's been admonishing me for not working.'

'You can't possibly go now. You must have a drink,' said Sarah, very softly.

'Couldn't touch the stuff. I'm queasy from Thrills Machines and Big Wheels. But I've a present for Edward. A coconut.'

He drew it out with a flourish from behind his back.

'Nothing for me?'

'You're a little old for teddy bears and cheap dolls, aren't you? And I can't imagine you keeping a goldfish.'

'Did you win anything for Jennifer?'

'No,' he said. 'But I bought her a toffee apple.'

His false cheeriness upset Jennifer nearly as much as his open misery a while back, outside, in the night. He was playing a part, making quick gestures to keep his persona alive. She wished Sarah would leave him alone. She couldn't bear it.

'Goodnight,' said Jennifer and ran upstairs. He made a movement as if to follow her but Sarah took his hand and dragged him into the drawing room, closing the door.

'Paul. You mustn't play on the girl's feelings. It's just not fair. Jennifer is extremely sensitive and is growing far too fond of you.'

'Oh, do you really think so?' said Paul in a pleased voice.

'Yes, I bloody well do.'

'I think you must be wrong. She treats me as an elder brother, that's all.'

'The way she looks at you isn't the way of a sister. And that sparkle in her eyes, that's ...'

'Don't you want me to take her out of herself? I thought you were worried that she was too withdrawn and socially retarded for her age.'

'Your job is not to transform Jennifer from Eliza Doolittle to My Fair Lady.'

'What is it then?'

'To pay me just a bit of attention. And anyway she's probably safer within herself. I am too, I expect.'

'What do you mean?'

'Only that I missed you this evening.'

'Look, Edward was there. I think Edward's awfully nice.'

'Edward's not as lovely as you,' said Sarah, running her fingers over the soft down of his face then pressing herself to him.

'You look tired,' he said.

'Old you mean?' She drew back slightly. She knew about the crow's-feet, she knew about the invasion of wrinkles along her forehead. She did not want to be told of them.

'No, just a little weary.'

'Come and sit down ...'

'No, I must go.'

'This morning I arranged a party for Wednesday night. To celebrate Edward's birthday. You aren't doing anything else are you? Will you come?' she said.

'Of course. How wonderful.'

'White wine, strawberries ...'

'Very nice,' he glanced at his watch, 'but I really should go now.'

'Please ...' and she knew she was playing her cards all wrong.

'All right, you go now. But come tomorrow ... at three. Edward will be at the trial.'

'All right.'

They kissed.

'Your mouth tastes sweet.'

'Of toffee apples.'

'What a child you are.'

Up in her room Jennifer heard the door slam as Paul left. She thought her mother was behaving in an absurdly possessive way.

She thought back on the evening. He'd said she ought to be a nun. Was she really so dull?

She looked down at her hand and suddenly felt sad. Pink and yellow and lined with paths. So many paths. But all leading nowhere. Her life in her hands. Staring at the helter skelter of dead ends and deep scars, she wondered. In mid-air, the hand was surrounded by empty space. Were there no goals, was there only the moment of ecstasy which cut deep but only arrived at itself? The moment in the Abbey's Little Cloister, before Rebecca's yellow roses, up in the big dipper? Is that what Paul had been trying to tell her? That she should cease to strive, to dare, that she should enjoy the moment?

After all, she admired Aphra and Shelley for their lives as well as their work but she herself renounced life. Until she'd met Paul her life had been, by and large, secondhand – either she had watched herself pretending to be a gypsy, a card-sharper, a thief, or she had watched her heroes living their lives. Maybe she ought to do as Paul advised, go for the rides. But was that enough? Her mother had gone for the rides and now she had nothing. She had about her the taint of the darkening fair, a sort of emptiness.

She wanted to see Mr Davidson just once more before the seance. She needed his support. She wanted to see Shelley again. He made her feel so much better.

20

Paul phoned at eleven o'clock the following morning.

'Jennifer. I've got to talk to you. Something terrible has happened. Will you come round now?'

'Of course. See you in a moment.'

A minute later he phoned back.

'Look, it's Paul. Forget what I just said. It was nothing. Nothing at all. Don't come round. Please. No point. OK?'

'But Paul ...'

He had rung off.

Paul's panic of the previous night came back to her. She ran downstairs, out into the square and up to the door of Paul's shabby house. She rang the bell.

She rang the bell again, impatiently moving from foot to foot. She could smell bacon on the air and that made her slightly queasy.

Jennifer hammered at the door with her clenched fist.

'All right, all right,' she heard shouted from inside, 'I'm coming.' And Paul opened the door.

He stood before her in bare feet, jeans and an open-necked shirt.

'What the hell are you doing here? I told you not to come.'

'I was worried.' Her lower lip protruded sulkily. Standing there with her hands in her pockets she looked so thin and frail, so very much a child, that he softened.

'Come in, then.'

She grinned, said 'Oh good,' and hurried in before he changed his mind.

'Was that your bacon?'

'Bacon? No.'

'Horrible smell.'

'It's the man next door. He seems to love it.'

The house was cold. There were no pictures on the walls, only discoloured rectangles where they had once hung. The floorboards were all bare. He took her into the front room which faced the square. A sofa with stuffing bulging out was the only

185

furniture in the room. He drew back the curtains but didn't let in much light as the windows were filthy.

'What's happened?'

'I told you. Nothing.'

'Oh, come on. It must have been something. You sounded in a terrible state. And you look awful. Green.'

'Don't be silly. Do you want coffee?'

'No, thank you. It doesn't look as though anyone's living here. Why's it so empty?'

'Everything was sold to pay off my aunt's debts. I could of course have painted it all tangerine and put up jaunty posters but I've been busy. And anyway, I quite like it as it is. Down-and-out chic.'

She shrugged and sat down. 'Come on. Please. What's happened?'

There was a quarter-full mug of coffee on the floor by the sofa. It was growing mould and it smelt. Through the dusty grey window at the back of the long room – once obviously two rooms, now divided only by an arch – Jennifer could see faint leaves brush against the window.

Paul was sitting on the floorboards with his knees up in front of him and forehead on the knees.

'What is it, Paul?'

He muttered something.

'Sorry?'

He looked up. 'I said it was nothing.'

'Paul. Please,' she insisted.

'No.'

'Paul ...'

'You really are a very determined little thing, aren't you? OK. I'll show you.' He jumped up and sat beside her. She flinched slightly. He put his hand behind her bottom, which she moved forward quickly, and down the back of the sofa. Her bottom was hovering right at the edge but she didn't like actually to stand up in case that looked rude. He took out a sheaf of thick blue paper, and waved it in front of her.

'It's the letter I had this morning. From Lucinda. That's why I'm in a state, this letter here.' He was waving it at her as if not quite sure whether to show it to her or not.

'Will you read it to me?' said Jennifer quietly.

'No. I won't.'

'Can I read it, then?'

'No, you can't.'

'Oh Paul. Please. Why are you being like this?'

'That's none of your business.'

They were glowering at each other on the sofa, both facing inwards, knees nearly touching.

His hand went out to her neck and pulled her lips towards his. It was a chaste, brief kiss but she looked shocked. For a moment he hated her and that impregnable innocence which made him tawdry.

In Jennifer he saw an earlier form of himself, someone full of hope and determination, someone capable of being alone, someone who didn't vanish when the party ended. All the doors were open to her but as the years had gone by the doors to his rooms of hope, of imagination, of bright colours and shapes had slowly closed one by one and he was left screaming in the bleak room of himself.

Her eyes were staring at him, wide and startled. He could see through the windows of most women's eyes into silky bedrooms, waiting negligees, bathrooms of bubble bath and perfume. Languid and longing for him to burgle their secrets. But Jennifer, her eyes were dark. The curtains drawn, the windows locked. Until, suddenly, now, when he knew she wanted him to kiss her again.

His hand caressed the nape of her neck and drew her to him. Again the smell of soap and talcum powder and innocence. He folded her in his arms and she softened into them, making him almost forget the anger he felt. He blew in her ear, ran his tongue over her lips, covered her neck with little kisses until she was almost laughing with pleasure. 'Oh Paul,' she said. 'You mustn't.' But it all seemed so innocent, so gentle, she didn't want to stop him. His kisses became more insistent and she leant back and found soon she was lying back with his body over hers, exploring hers, his hands squeezing her breasts, his kisses hard, penetrating her mouth, deep and persistent and angry. Her

187

whole body was alive and burning. She forced her eyes open and saw Paul's face had changed. It was like a mask over the face she knew. It scared her. The face was red and eyes narrow with desire. The mask pressed down again, enveloping her face in bristles and in a mouth which was everywhere, all over her body, absorbing her, leaving her incapable of revolt. 'Paul,' she said in protest which sounded like a moan of desire as he slowly unzipped her trousers and slid his hand down into the moist curls between her legs.

The phone rang.

Paul took no notice but it startled Jennifer out of her entrancement. She began to struggle as the phone rang on and on. 'Stop it,' she murmured, pulling away his hand and tugging her lips away. 'Stop pulling at my hand,' he replied crossly. The phone was still ringing. 'No. You must stop it,' she said. 'Who the fuck is that on the phone?' said Paul, sitting up straight on the sofa. 'Answer it,' said Jennifer.

'OK, I will.' He sped off, stubbing his toe on the staircase and letting out a yell of rage. The phone stopped ringing and she heard his voice talking upstairs.

He had left the letter on the floor by the sofa. She resisted the temptation to read it. She zipped up her trousers and pulled down her T-shirt. She felt utterly miserable. What had she done? She couldn't make sense of all these new feelings.

Paul returned, hopping slightly.

'It was your mother, of course. Who else would have such timing and such persistence?'

She saw, beyond Paul, the shadowy forms of trees through the dusty windows. It was as though just this room existed, outside there were only grey shadows.

'She wanted to know where you were.'

'What did you say?'

'I said you were with me, of course.'

'She was furious?'

'Yes. You better go and splash your face with cold water. It's beetroot.'

He was standing above her, staring down with a look she thought was contempt. She scurried past him and into the bathroom where she splashed her face.

Paul stood looking out of the window. A tall woman with a mass of beigey hair and a long nose passed by with her Afghan hound, also with beigey hair and a long nose. The dog lifted his leg and peed against the black railings which barricaded the front garden from the pavement.

The street cleaner scowled at the woman and the dog as they crossed the road. Paul watched the man as he worked. He swept with such ferocity, such single-mindedness, clearing space after space in the wilderness of sweet wrappers, cigarette packets, fag ends, leaves, twigs and bus tickets. His peaked cap sat proudly on his head. Even his aluminium truck carrying filth and leaves glimmered. Briskly his brush beat chaos to one side from where he picked it up and flung it into his aluminium inferno. It must be pleasant, thought Paul, to be in the grip of such a simple obsession, to be protected from the outside world, to be indifferent to everything but a pile of dirt turning into a patch of clean pavement.

'Good-bye.' He turned. Jennifer was hovering at the door of the room. 'I think it's best if we don't see each other again,' she said.

'That'll be difficult. I'm coming to your father's birthday party tomorrow and so are you.' Paul had an amused smile on his face. She hated him.

'We can meet but that doesn't mean we're friends.'

'Don't be silly, Jenny,' he said softly and tears darted into her eyes.

She swivelled round and hurried down the sour-smelling corridor. She slammed the door after her and walked, head in the air, back home, knowing he was watching her.

Jennifer locked her door and wouldn't come out for the rest of the day. Paul knew her better than anyone and he treated her with contempt so how could she be worth anything? He didn't think of her as a sister. She wasn't spiritual, she wasn't pure. Shelley wouldn't come to her seance now. He had spoken of the 'earthy grossness' of love between the sexes. He would despise her. She despised herself.

She sobbed, cried, howled, whimpered and wailed as wave

after wave of misery and anger swept over her. She tore up newspapers. She beat her legs up and down on the bed like a child. Her eyes were puffy and her nose red and that brought on another attack of self-disgust. For the first time, she really could see how people commit suicide. She was so angry she needed to be violent and throw herself on a knife, shoot off a gun, jump out of a window. Not for the sake of a gesture. Her grief seemed enormous and eternal. There was nothing she could do, wanted to do, this wailing would just have to go on and on because it was grief which was real, everything else temporary and lying. Thoughts kept bombing into her mind and exploding into howls of rage: Rebecca's death, her own passivity, Paul defiling her, laughing at her, her father's remoteness, the seance unprepared for, Paul and Sarah deceiving Edward, their betraying her with their disgusting lust. The thought of Paul and Sarah in bed gave Jennifer the most extraordinary physical discomfort. It was as though her stomach and heart had come loose and were hurtling round her insides like clothes in a washing machine.

When her orchestra of grief had finally quietened down into soft sobs she was still utterly desolate, as hot and empty as the desert.

How, Jennifer wondered, could she ever have thought Paul similar to Shelley? Paul was obviously base while, as Mary Shelley wrote after her husband's death, 'We have lost him – not, I fondly hope, for ever; his unearthly and elevated nature is a pledge of the continuation of his being, although in an altered form.' Paul didn't have an unearthly and elevated nature after all. And did Shelley? Was that an illusion too? Had Mary Shelley been wrong, as Jennifer had been wrong about Paul?

21

It was the evening of Edward's birthday party. Jennifer lay in the bath wondering how Paul would react to her that evening. She hadn't seen him since yesterday morning. She compiled a few cutting phrases to deliver. She would be looking ravishing, would brush past him while his mouth hung open in wonder at her beauty. When he spoke she would raise her eyebows and say, 'Haven't you caused enough damage?'

'I'm so sorry but you will forgive me, please?'

'Never.'

Jennifer's toes, pink and crinkly, played with the tap. The foaming green was hot. She was melty, soft and feminine. Then her toes gripped the cold tap and turned it on. How could she be so weak? How could she revert to foolish fantasies? She hated Paul. She must see things as they were, not as she'd like them to be. It was the real curse of women, this mindless, uncreative, time-wasting fantasising. Her hair floated round her, loose and soft. She bet she looked pretty … stop it, stop it, she told herself, stop treating yourself like an advertisement for bath essence.

She pulled out the plug. Her hair subsided into wet straggles. She thought of Jane immersed in her own blood and of Harriet, her face white and bloated and her clothes, billowing, lying on the edge of the Serpentine, dead. The trees casting shadows on to the dank water. A cold wind ruffling the lake and Harriet's hair swaying like reeds. The evening muffling the colours, illumining only the awful pallor of the girl's open-eyed face. Poor Harriet, destroyed by fantasies, committing suicide when her idealised version of Shelley proved false.

> Why dost thou pass away and leave our state,
> This dim, vast vale of tears, vacant and desolate?

As she dried her hair with a white fluffy towel she heard the imperious shouts of her mother below.

'Put the Chablis in the fridge!'

'Whip the cream!'

'Lay out the glasses!'

When her hair was dry and shiny, Jennifer went downstairs. The scent of flowers and furniture polish warmed the house. In her mother's bedroom were two eyes peering into the mirror from a face concreted white. On the dressing table frilled with pink flowery damask sprawled a film-star array of foundations, scents, lipsticks, powders, rouge, eye shadows of every hue, wrinkle cream and an empty tube of face pack. In kimono and white mask, her mother was a character from a Japanese play. On the huge double bed lay a heap of clothes, flouncy, lacy, demure, sexy, in a jumble of colours clashing and merging.

'I'd like to wear something nice. Have you any advice?' said Jennifer.

Sarah watched Jennifer through the mirror.

'What are your options?' she said in a tight voice which cracked the mask slightly.

For once the problem of what to wear really did seem important but, keeping up the appearance of nonchalance, she shrugged.

'Jeans and a pretty top?'

Her mother's forehead creased into a frown.

'Far too casual for ...' her voice trailed away into a whisper as she realised wrinkles were radiating from her mouth.

'That long coppery one?'

'Too formal.'

'The just below the knee chiffon, pink and black?'

'With the low neck?'

'It has a high neck.'

The corners of Sarah's mouth perked up.

'Lovely, darling.'

'Can I borrow some make-up?'

'Yes.'

Jennifer gazed at the magic pots and tubes. Tempting as Woolworth's wrapped sweets used to be. The dressing table was an alchemist's laboratory of strange, transmuting liquids and powders.

Her mother was removing her mask and her face looked softer and younger and her eyes were bright.

'Will you help me put it on?' said Jennifer.

Sarah smiled sadly into the mirror. This is what she thought she'd wanted for so long, a younger version of herself to dress up, but now that she saw Jennifer hankering after the secret arts of women it was faintly distasteful and, because of Paul, threatening.

192

She smoothed Jennifer's face with biscuit beige foundation, highlighted her cheekbones, put rouge on her cheeks, mascara on her long eyelashes and silver glitter on her eyelids.

'What about some lipstick?' said Jennifer.

Upstairs Jennifer ransacked her sock drawer for a pair of tights. Her hair flowed over her shoulders. From the stripped pine wardrobe she took out the pink and black dress which had never been worn. She held the dress up against her in front of the long mirror. The little pink flowers brought out the colour in her round cheeks. How pretty she looked. What fun it was dressing up again, turning herself into someone else. She knew the dress would give her the confidence to spurn Paul. She put it on and twirled round, then slipped on a pair of black shoes with heels. The patent was a little cracked.

Music seeped up from below and she felt part of this world as she had for a while at the fair.

The bell rang. First guest? The bell rang again and later again. Was Paul here yet? She walked slowly downstairs, past her parents' bedroom, past the watching pictures, more and more nervous. At the top of the stairs her butter-flies stopped dead, pinned in a cold glass case. Paul and Sarah were at the bottom and his eyes were piercing up at Jennifer.

Sarah swung round and raised her eyebrows. Sarah's shiny orange lipstick matched the huge gold earrings which swung from her earlobes beneath ebony hair piled into a large bun. Little tendrils strayed down and framed her face softly. Her skin was animated.

'Hello,' said Paul. 'You look lovely.'

Jennifer's eyes roamed over his head, as if eager to see someone about to enter through the front door. She walked demurely down.

'I must go and see to the other guests. Edward is still in the bedroom. He finds it impossible to be on time for anything,' said Sarah.

She hurried off, head held high, to the back door which led out into the garden.

'Excuse me,' said Jennifer, pushing past Paul, her bones and muscle turning to water as she brushed his shoulder. 'I must get a drink.'

'Oh Jenny, I'm sorry if I upset you but I was in a dreadful state. Over the letter,' he said, as he followed her into the kitchen where a hired waiter was pouring out wine.

'I keep falling asleep on the floor all over the house. It's as though I'm drunk. I mean, do you ever have a sudden, overwhelming desire to lie down just where you are and fall into a deep sleep? It would be quite comical if someone else lived with me ... they'd have to keep stepping over a prostrate body....' His attempt to be cheerful collapsed lamely. Jennifer was not smiling. 'Oh dear,' said Paul.

'What would you like, madam?' said the waiter.

'Chablis, please.'

'I didn't know you drank alcohol,' said Paul.

'Well I do.'

'I like your dress,' said Paul.

'Thank you,' said Jennifer primly.

'Did Sarah put on your make-up for you?'

'Yes, why?'

'Nothing, I just thought it looked very professional.'

'I'm going outside.'

She was caught on the way by a treble-chinned man in a pink shirt and purple necktie who slipped an arm round her waist and declared, 'Who's this? Whose nymphette?' His voice was slurred and he breathed whisky over her.

'My name is Jennifer. I'm Sarah and Edward's daughter.'

'Oh,' he lurched his glass towards the waiter and his bottle of wine. 'You are a pretty little thing, aren't you?' Jennifer slid a triumphant sidelong glance at Paul who was standing with his arms crossed, his forehead low and drawn. She wished this man with the haystack of yellow hair was more impressive. It would be enjoyable to make Paul jealous. Serve him right.

'Come into the garden with me,' said the man.

Outside the lamp on the wall shone on the brown backs of women.

'My name is John, by the way. I am a dear friend of your parents.'

Jennifer remembered him from a previous party of her parents. He looked like a cross between David Hockney and an ageing wrestler.

Paul was standing near the door, watching her.

She smiled up at the man, attempting to look vivacious.

'Are you an art dealer?'

'How did you know? Do I look like one? What do art dealers look like – sensitive?'

'I don't know. I only thought you were because you were when I last met you.'

The man's piggy eyes roamed round the garden, bored.

Jennifer noticed her mother talking to a dark-eyed young man in a Hamlet-style cream shirt and black velvet trousers which looked too hot for summer. She too was attempting to sparkle.

Edward joined Jennifer and John. He had on his new corduroy suit, or rather it had him in it. New clothes were always in command when Edward was wearing them.

'Hello, John, you're looking well.'

'I was hoping someone would say that. I've just come back from a health farm. It was bloody torture. Sauna, ruthless massages and cold baths. I'll tell you, it was like being back at public school, all rules and regulations.'

'What were the people like?'

'The women? Huge bloated figures like jellyfish mostly. Some were less odious but a health farm isn't conducive to romance. You feel like a farmyard animal, only difference is you're being thinned down instead of fattened up. And the lectures! Bowel movements, constipation ... ghastly. Anyway, I was so enfeebled by starvation I don't think I'd have looked twice at Ursula Andress if she'd lain naked on my bed with her legs apart, pleading. Can't say you look well. You've got that hunted look.'

'Too much work. I've been following a longish trial at the Old Bailey. Interesting, though.' Edward's eyes had drifted over, and were now resting on Sarah and the Hamlet-style young man who had been joined by Paul. The young man was looking left

195

out while Paul and Sarah talked in a close-packed, intimate manner. Jennifer thought she had better get into her room before her body exploded from emotion. She made a move to go. Her eyes were still on Sarah and Paul. She saw Sarah touch Paul on the arm, say something, then come over to her. In her hand was a bottle of wine. She filled up the glasses, including Jennifer's.

'Jennifer, let me introduce you to someone.'

Sarah introduced her to the young man in the cream shirt. His name was Rob.

As he talked he gesticulated with his glass, chucking wine on the grass. Jennifer watched his swaying glass and remembered being seasick on the way back from Paris as a child.

He was heavy-featured but reasonably pleasant, thought Jennifer vaguely as her eyes kept drifting back to Paul. Why wasn't he looking at her? Why wasn't he jealous?

'... You see, I'm a novelist,' continued Rob.

'Gosh ... how many have you written? She was craning her neck but Rob didn't seem to mind.

He stared into his glass and moved his weight from his left to his right side.

'I'm gathering up experience. Making mental notes. Haven't written anything yet. You see, a friend of mine wrote a whole novel then his house burnt down with the novel in it. He scrambled round the ruins and could only find the charred remains of his great work. So it's much safer to keep it in your head. Anyway, it's impossible to write in London.'

'Why?'

'It's so claustrophobic and anyway the television's always on.'

'You ought to tell them to switch it off,' she said.

'I can't.'

'Why?'

'I don't live with anyone.'

'Oh,' said Jennifer, confused.

He brushed his hair back from his face and grinned.

She was beginning to like him.

Paul came up to Jennifer and grabbed her arm tightly and, once more, she melted inside. In a throttled voice he said, 'Come on,' and, to Rob, 'Excuse me.' Rob was left looking long-faced.

She walked a little way then said grimly, 'I was busy, talking. You have no right ...'

'Shut up,' he said. The cold anger in his eyes silenced her and she let him lead her through the swaying glasses, the earrings, the flirting. She saw the women's faces watching him, their heads turning like sharks' fins.

He took her through the greenhouse and out into the secret garden where the huge chestnut tree cast its shadow. Roses hung heavy and luminous in the half-light.

He seized her shoulders.

'Stop it,' he said. 'Stop behaving like this.'

'Like what?'

'Like your mother.'

'Why, you seem to like her enough.'

'It's disgusting, you're only young.'

'I'm nearly sixteen.'

'Why are you behaving like this?'

'It's your fault. You know it is.'

She looked straight into his eyes and his face went out of focus and her mind and body blurred, like a mistimed photograph. He drew her close to him. His body was hard and hers so soft, all chiffon and flowers. His lips touched hers lightly. Then he sucked her tongue into his mouth and with it her whole body. In the small space of those melting mouths was a smithy of fire, of red tongues melting together in an ecstasy of heat. She collapsed into him, all anger forgotten, and his squeezing, kneading, burning hands moulded her body into pure desire. She was clutching at his hips, pulling him towards her. Beneath her chiffon dress her thighs tingled as if shot through by an electric current. It was exquisite torture, this struggle of yearning, burning flesh to meet through the ever-melting armour of chiffon and velvet. She was crushing her breasts against his chest, wanting to be crushed and annihilated and destroyed. There was a moist pain between her legs and his hand was there, making her body twitch and sigh, opening her out, making her gape with longing for the hardness pressed against her soft stomach. She was moaning softly, clutching, wanting.

197

Her legs were apart as she stood and his hand slipped into her pants and pressed and moved and caressed and he moaned too as he felt the slippery awakened texture of her young unentered body. . . . She clutched at him, her mind centred on the feverish pleasure of his moving fingers, her voice whimpering and murmuring and what was happening? He was taking his hand away, pushing her away, severing their bodies, ripping his mouth from hers ... oh, she couldn't bear it. She pushed herself towards him but he held her shoulders and kept her away from him. 'Stop it,' she said, like a spoilt child. 'Let me go.'

'Your face is flushed,' he said. His lips were quivering. 'You little whore.' He spat out the word.

She brushed her hair, ruffled by his caresses, back from her face.

'What?'

'I said you were a little whore.'

A car roared past on the other side of the high wall.

His face was odd, drained and harsh. It was so separate while a minute ago it had been hers. About a yard away, he seemed to have retreated miles. It was dark in the shadow of the chestnut where he stood tall and accusing. How cruel his thin nose was, the beautiful nose of a Greek statue-boy who has weathered the ages and sneers at mortals made of flesh. Paul was inhuman. His heart was marble. She hated him. She wanted to break him into little marble chips.

'You ... you ... beast,' she said and, overcome by the inadequacy of her schoolgirl words, she turned from his sneering face and stumbled away, leaving him in darkness. Everything was foggy from the hot tears in her eyes and in her mind.

In a fever of shame and hate she walked through the lawn and the people, hearing the sound of laughter and high-pitched talk.

Her father caught her arm as she passed. 'Are you all right? You look funny.' Aemilia was standing by his side. Jennifer brushed at her tears with the back of her hand.

'I'm all right.'

'Go and get yourself some food. It'll do you good. You're not used to drink.'

198

Mechanically she obeyed her father.

The dining room had the quality of a nightmare. It was piled high with food and people. The women with their brown, polished skins, the collapsed men. Faces opening and shutting like goldfish. A man with lank ginger strands of hair swept back to cover his balding head. Bits of coleslaw on a beard. The lights were too bright, the voices battling with each other. Men pretending to discuss when really they were boasting. I, I, I, and the women listening, flaunting their eyes and their breasts silently. A young man on the floor bloated and bloodless. Slouching rancid with food, backgammon and laziness, his stomach under his buttons bursting into the room and his pretty vapid girlfriend shaped exquisitely by him, curled like a foetus. His face was a white puff ball wearing glasses and fair hair.

She piled food on a plate. Nobody spoke to her. Excluded again. She heard snatches of conversation 'She was very nice, but no oil painting' ... 'I only like people who impress me' ... 'Wasn't it Balzac who said "The desire to conquer is as quickly aroused by the easiness of a triumph as by its difficulty"?' ... 'Oh darling, do stop spilling your drink on my dress. Put it in your mouth' ... 'Put what in my mouth?' ... 'You think you're clever, don't you?' ... 'Only comparatively.'

Salmon mousse, creamed chicken, salads galore, cheese in variety and quantity, wonderful cakes. The food disgusted her and made her retch slightly.

What would Rebecca think of her now? What would she say? Rebecca would have despised her. Jennifer felt she had betrayed Rebecca's memory, become like other girls, lascivious, hurrying to be normal.

She took a gulp of wine.

A low-fronted girl stood by her with a mouth slashed red. She was with a bald man in jeans.

'I do not, as a rule, sleep with men,' she said. 'I'm a good girl.' Her tone said the opposite.

'Like you were good with me last night?'

The girl started. It was as if she had mislaid the episode from her mind and had by mistake intoned a flirtatious formula.

'I'll forget all about it, though,' he said. 'Or is that rude?'

'Yes, it is.'

He pulled her to him and kissed her for a long time. Jennifer noticed his hand was caressing the girl's bottom. Jennifer was sure these must be all Sarah's friends. They couldn't be Edward's.

She went to the kitchen for a glass of water. She encountered Anita, the divorcee with the cropped ginger hair and cockney accent whose conversation had so shocked Jennifer,

'Hello, Jennifer, how are you? I meant to talk to you before, but you always seemed so tied up.' To her astonishment, Jennifer realised there was a trace of envy in Anita's voice.

'Oh, I'm very well, thank you.' Aware of her red eyes she said, wildly, 'Except for a touch of hay fever.'

'I was thinking how well you look. You seem grown-up all of a sudden.'

'It's illusionary. Dress and make-up, that's all.'

'Good. Don't grow up too quickly.'

Anita had pale skin and freckles on her face and round her plunging neckline.

As Rob – the Hamlet boy – passed, nodding at them shyly, she said to Jennifer in that cohesive, feminine way that men fear, 'I'm going home now, alone for once. Hot-water bottle, a read maybe and a drunken stupor all by myself. I am.' She laughed a wonderful schoolgirl laugh which descended into a giggle. 'A hot-water bottle,' she repeated and sought support from the wall.

Jennifer blinked, unable to see the humour. But as Anita continued to giggle, back against the wall, Jennifer began to laugh with her. Suddenly everything seemed funny. The couples, Anita's tartiness, the sexual throb of the conversation everywhere, the self-important men – all seemed absurd, nullified by the wonderful, ultimate, security of a hot-water bottle.

Still giggling, Anita stumbled up the stairs to the bedroom where the coats had been left.

Jennifer watched the skinny figure swaying happily up the stairs and decided she liked her after all.

After being violently sick, Jennifer went to bed and, in spite of the noise downstairs, fell into a thirsty, dream-tossed sleep.

200

22

After Jennifer had gone to bed, and the party had dwindled to a few couples and the debris of two am, Paul took Edward and Sarah into the kitchen. Edward switched on the light but its brightness made all three squint. Paul said, 'My eyes. Unaccustomed. Do you think we could have it off?' So they sat in the semi-darkness surrounded by lipstick-smudged wine glasses. The room smelt of ash and alcohol. Outside the roses spread themselves, pale and lavish, under the full moon.

'Look here, I need some advice from you both.' He took a wad of pale blue writing paper from his jacket pocket. 'I was going to chuck this away but I couldn't. It's been worrying me sick ever since it arrived. Yesterday morning, in the post.' He paused. Paul's eyes seemed to have receded back into his head and the lids bulged out. Edward wiped his glasses with a red handkerchief.

Sarah sat wearily on the kitchen stool. She kicked off her shoes and coughed. Ash from the saucer beside her fountained into the air.

'Ugh,' said Sarah.

'I mean, I want to discuss it with you both. It's rather important. I need some advice.'

'So you said,' drawled Sarah.

'Now what is it?' said Edward. 'It's two o'clock in the morning and you look rather ill. It's not anything to do with Jennifer, is it? She's been in a state this evening.'

Edward's voice sounded agreeably schoolmasterly to Paul, who couldn't see the coolness in Edward's clear eyes.

'I'm afraid I was rather unpleasant to her. I do apologise, sir. I was just very overwrought.'

'I see.'

'Don't be tetchy,' said Sarah. 'Give him time to speak.'

'Sarah ... I really ...' and Edward's speech subsided into a sigh.

'The thing is that, well, I've had a letter.'

'Yes, go on,' said Sarah. 'It's not from Jennifer, is it?' Her voice rose and brow fell.

'No.'

'What is it then?'

'The letter is from Lucinda Brown. And in this letter she says some extraordinary things which I probably ought to tell you. I don't think they're true.' He was leaning uneasily against the closed door which led into the dining room. His eyes were closed.

'Oh God,' he said. 'I feel so ill I think I really should go home.'

'Don't tell us anything you're going to regret,' said Edward.

'Don't be absurd, Ed. You tell us what's troubling you,' said Sarah, her body animated and sympathetic as, imperceptibly, she leant towards Paul.

'Can I have a drink of water?' asked Paul.

'Don't stall,' said Sarah gently.

'I'm going,' said Edward, opening the door into the hall.

'*Don't,*' said Paul. 'I want you to read the letter.'

He gave it to Edward, who closed the door and switched on the light. Sarah slid off her seat and read the letter with Edward. Every now and then she let out a little gasp.

It was written in black ink with many a flourishing loop and line. It read:

Dearest Paul,

When I was going out with you I felt I was living my life for someone. I saw what I was doing through your eyes. When you withdrew, I was an actress on a stage with no audience. I had a sense of performing to an empty hall. Charles was all I had. It was so unfair. Those who perform quietly, for their own pleasure, can continue when a love leaves them. But your interest and applause was essential to me. Charles's was too. Remember how we all three used to go out together? And I was always the centre of attraction. You left me, then Charles left me. I thought about slitting my wrists. I decided I'd rather slit hers.

I hated her ever since she took you away from me. I wanted to remove her from life. I wanted her to no longer exist. As you know, I believe in obeying my feelings. My father has always encouraged me to fulfil myself, not to repress myself. And now look what has happened.

But I blame you, Paul. You started it all by introducing Jane to Charles and now you must end it. This is a confession and it's up to you to do with it what you like. You must decide. Charles might get off. But I won't. Because I'm guilty. You suspected it, I bet. But you kept quiet because you thought Charles would not be found guilty. You didn't want to get involved, did you, Paul?

Why did I love you? I don't know. You seemed to need me so. But I gave you myself and suddenly you didn't need it any longer. You rejected me. Finally you finished with her, or drifted from her, and for a while I quite liked her because I knew how she felt. But then she latched on to Charles. He was always seeing her. He used to stay overnight in her smart flat and leave me all alone in our house. The last straw was when he told me he was going to ask her to marry him. He told me on the phone from Birmingham. They'd argued about marriage before he left. He'd said he didn't want to marry her yet. But after the argument, when he was away from her, thinking back on what he'd said, he changed his mind. That's one reason why he rushed back so quick.

I didn't tell the police anything because I thought as Charles isn't guilty he'd get off scot free anyway. Now I'm not so sure. Charles isn't defending himself properly. He knows I did it. He guessed, he said, as he sat on the sofa with the police after the murder. He suddenly knew it was me.

When I stabbed I wasn't angry, just very certain this was what I wanted to do, that this expressed all my frustration, all my hatred, all my long nights alone. Because I only ever cared for you and Charles and she tried to steal you both. I've been jealous of her for so long. I doubt if you've ever cared for anyone enough actually to feel jealousy. It blots you out so you can't think or feel anything except hatred. The first time I saw you laughing into her eyes I was amazed by the pain I felt in my stomach. Acute physical pain. But I got used to it.

Her mouth had blood in it. Curious how red blood is. In a way, I actually enjoyed it. The power, the completeness, the finality. Like suicide, I suppose.

I bet you don't want to know all this. But you daren't throw the letter away.

I 'borrowed' Charles's key to her flat and had a copy made sometime before. At this stage I had planned the murder in my mind but had not intended to carry it out. It was only when Charles mentioned his marriage idea that I thought about it seriously. Seeing her so smug in Harrods clinched it.

Charles was at the conference in Birmingham and I knew Jane would be alone. She always had a bath at nine-thirty in the morning while listening to something arty on the radio. At nine-forty, about, I just opened the door and walked in with the knife in my handbag (the crocodile handbag you used to admire). But I saw a carving knife on the table and decided to use that instead, because it would be less traceable. I heard the radio on and tiptoed into the bathroom where she was sitting facing away from the door. I came up behind her and stabbed. She struggled and screamed but I'm very strong and the radio was very loud and she sank down into the bath, unconscious or dead. It was a white bath and her body was brown but suddenly everything was red.

I was going to steal a few things, rough the place up, make it look as though it'd been a burglar. But I was just in the hall when I heard a key in the lock, I ducked down behind an armchair. It was Charles. I let him go to the bathroom, heard him gasp, and then I crept out of the front door, closing it softly behind me. I ought to have called to him then and explained and we could perhaps have escaped but all I could think of was that I was discovered and had to get out.

But do you understand why I killed her and why I've let Charles take the rap? He always took the rap when we were kids. He doesn't mind. You must come and see me. You've got my address. I keep thinking of the sliced skin and Charles in court with that fixed expression, and her mother weeping outside the court. It closes in on me. I'm so alone suddenly. I seem to have stepped outside humanity. I thought I was flying high above it but I wasn't.

Lucinda.

'My God,' said Sarah. She was sheet white. 'Have you been to see her?'

'No, I didn't dare.'

'She must be lying. She couldn't have done that. She's upset because of it all. It's nothing to do with you.'

'You're right. It is nothing to do with me. How was I supposed to know? I mean she said she was keen on me but I didn't believe it. I didn't *want* to believe it, of course, because it was inconvenient, I suppose. I mean, why, though? Why kill poor Jane? I didn't even care much about Lucinda really, I mean I wasn't in love with her. I was fond of her but didn't *feel* anything for her.

'She was strong, though, physically very strong, very frightening physically. She bruised my arm just from gripping it. And her rages … fearsome. I mean, I told you about that car chase? And once I'd been talking to another girl at a party for a long time and Lucinda admitted she'd wanted, very badly, to rip open the girl's face with her nails. Horrible. She slapped me, of course, frequently.'

'I'm afraid,' said Edward firmly, 'you have no choice. You must give the police that letter, or let me. Charles will probably be acquitted and the girl, well, if she's lucky and everyone's feeling kindly, she'll be allowed a plea of diminished responsibility.'

'No,' said Sarah with burning eyes. 'He mustn't do that. His name will be caught up in the whole sordid business. It'll be a disaster for him, and very distressing for everyone. I won't have it.'

'You won't have it?' exclaimed Edward, raising his eyebrows slowly. 'It's not up to you. You have no jurisdiction over this young man.'

'I ...' and Sarah stalked out of the room slamming the door so that the whole house shook.

'Well?' said Edward.

'I'll do as you say, sir.'

23

At breakfast Edward told Jennifer what had happened last night. Sarah sat, lips pursed tightly, savagely grinding a cigarette out on her mother-of-pearl ashtray.

'You mean he wasn't going to tell anyone about the letter?' said Jennifer. 'That's awful.'

'I don't really think he's behaved well. Rather cowardly. Irresponsible,' said Edward. 'I wouldn't bother with him if I were you. Don't you agree, Sarah?'

Sarah's diamond wedding ring glared from her hand which clenched tightly the handle of her coffee cup. 'I wish you would just go to hell,' she said, slowly and deliberately. Then she put down her cup, stood up and walked out of the room.

'I don't think Sarah wants me to hand the letter over,' said Edward, running his fingers through his hair. 'But of course I must.'

'Yes, of course,' said Jennifer.

'Ought to have done it last night but Sarah insisted I didn't.'

Jennifer went up to her room. How could Paul have even considered not showing the police the letter? She felt exhausted and lay down on her unmade bed. She fell into a light doze. When she awoke she was just as exhausted and her hangover just as bad. Her eyes felt small and prominent.

It was a sultry day. An air of stagnation filled the house. Her clothes stuck to her skin. She noted her room was a mess. In the last few weeks she'd been so scatty – absorbed in Paul and her work – she hadn't bothered to tidy. She began putting away the puddles of clothes from the floor and chair, the shoes which were strewn like cars in a scrap yard, the skyscrapers of books piled up by the wall. But she couldn't stay interested for more than a few minutes. Life stretched before her like a desert. It was eleven thirty in the morning and not only did she have to get through the day, she had to get through the rest of her life.

She wandered from room to room picking up stray glasses and cigarette ends which she found in some odd places: behind clocks, in vases, between books.

In the drawing room she sat down and picked up a green onyx egg from the coffee table. Someone had given it to Edward for his birthday. In slow motion she juggled the egg from hand to hand. How cold it was, how hard. Nothing but itself. As if, like, as if, like. Why did everything have to be like something else? Why did she have to relate the past to the present and so confuse both? A fly started to compete with Maureen's hoover.

The fly was getting on her nerves. She picked up a magazine from the coffee table. The fly landed on top of the hessian table-lamp. It started to have a wash. Up went its back legs round its bottom, then its front legs round its face. Washing its sweet face with its paws. Jennifer swotted it.

As day dawdled into evening Jennifer jumped at the least sound or thought. But it was foolish to be frightened.

She was at her desk and the pictures on the wall of Shelley and Aphra seemed to be watching her. She knew she ought to rip down the dead but she didn't dare. She feared that something, she didn't know what, would happen if she did. The strange, senseless fear was a fear she did not want. It was the fear which, in childhood, had made it essential she reach her room or the bottom of the stairs before the lavatory stopped flushing. It was the fear which had lurked at the corner of her bedroom at night, in the shed at the end of the garden even in day. The fear was not something one had been able to do anything about. It was not possible to mention it. It was controlling, it couldn't be controlled. Perhaps childhood hadn't been so great after all. Perhaps her memory had edited out the bad parts. At least the fears of adolescence were known ones: ageing, making a fool of oneself, being crushed in a car crash, having babies, doing badly in an exam. Fears you could tell people, though she seldom had. They had seemed awful, engulfing fears but now they seemed minor. They were just a slippery ice rink while the fear she experienced now was the swirling drowning water beneath.

Was this how Lucinda had felt afterwards? Had she thought herself free, in control, then all of a sudden found she wasn't?

Jennifer heard, or thought she heard, the creak of a footstep outside in the corridor. She sat still. She sat for two minutes which were longer than hours. She stood up very slowly, very carefully and on her toes, watching her toes, walked to the door and opened it. The corridor was dark. She closed the door. She stood staring at the door. She opened it again and made a lurch for the light switch. The corridor was empty and silent.

She wondered if she'd gone too far with the seance, as Lucinda had gone too far with her plan. Was she defying the rules? Perhaps Lucinda hadn't even been aware of her potential for savagery. But once she'd crossed the borderline between desire to kill and fulfilment of that desire, once she had crossed into lawlessness, the darkness within her had risen up and taken control. In her selfishness she had even been willing to let her own brother suffer for her sins. What was it her mother had repeated from the letter? – 'I seem to have stepped outside humanity. I thought I was flying high above it but I wasn't.'

In 1814 Shelley's first wife wrote, '... here I am, my dear friend, waiting to bring another infant into this woeful world. Next month I shall be confined. He will not be near me. No, he cares not for me now. He never asks after me or sends me word how he is getting on. In short, the man I once loved is dead, this is a vampire!'

A vampire. What a fool she'd been, understanding neither herself nor others.

People said that the same book was a different book at different stages in one's life. She understood what they meant now. Personal experience must constantly re-interpret words, clichés, history, famous quotations, friends, relations, acquaintances, novels. The inexperienced must therefore be incapable of arriving at the truth. No wonder people treated adolescents with such contempt.

Before now her mother had said, 'You'll think differently

when you're older' and, as it promised, this once empty and irritating cliché had now filled with meaning.

The knowledge she'd so prided herself on – facts, dates, documents – and which she'd been sure would help her discover the truth about her heroes – now seemed as pointless as a crossword puzzle. The accumulation of information was merely an intellectual exercise. Only the wise, the experienced, could see what were lies and what was the truth. The rest, herself included, could only distort history, interpret it in terms of their own limited personal experience or leave it as dry fact. She decided that all the words she'd read, the poetry, the history, had remained mere words, unfuelled by understanding.

Knowing nothing but literature, she had confused literature with life. She had transformed Paul into Shelley, Shelley into Paul. Paul was not what she had thought him to be. He was no Shelley. He wasn't brave, he was a coward. He'd shattered her dreams, the Romantic literary notions culled from poems and biographies which she'd superimposed over him. She'd seen him as she wished to see him, not as he was. There had been an undertow of anxiety which her mind had refused to acknowledge. Her emotions had been severed from her thoughts, her instincts smothered in words, words, words and silly dreams. He'd tried to drag her into maturity, she saw that now. He was a coward, a deceiver, a destroyer. She felt confused. She felt a fool. She felt as though the ice of experience was covering the cool stream where the faces of her heroes had once flitted. Now she could see only herself. And could she even see that? How did she know she was not still deceiving herself? That the next experience wouldn't reshuffle events, make her see them, her and her heroes anew?

She had no confidence. She couldn't know what Mr Davidson was really like, whether he was good or evil, whether her plan was splendid or wicked. She couldn't know Shelley well enough to summon him up from the dead when she didn't even know herself or the young man down her own street.

Shelley was a trick postcard. She had only looked at him in one light. Paul's behaviour had jolted her arm, made her see the selfish features lurking behind that vulnerable, beautiful face.

Paul didn't care for her, he cared only for her admiration of him. When he knew he had it, when her legs as well as her heart were open, he was no longer interested in her.

But could she give up her plan? She was still drawn to Paul. Perhaps the darkness within her – the lust, the desire to be abased, and the pride which, in the guise of a high-minded plan, had first inspired her – was also still drawn to Shelley. Drawn and drawing. And it was Shelley she wanted to see. There was now, she noted, very little pull towards darling, innocent Rebecca.

She read again the letter Shelley had written to Mary after Harriet's suicide. She found herself pitying poor sweet Harriet, victim of Shelley's oh so plausible charms. Harriet with the love-beaming glance had been betrayed. She'd been promised so much, as Paul with his looks and concern had seemed to promise so much to her. Paul had hurt her, made Lucinda Brown's life miserable, in effect killed Jane. He had caused havoc.

Previously she'd thought Shelley's letter to Mary truthful but a trifle overblown: the letter of a grief-stricken man. Now she no longer trusted Shelley she saw it differently. It typified the self-satisfied callousness which had driven Harriet to suicide. He had left Harriet for Mary but would take no blame for her death, as it appeared Paul at first refused to take blame for the death of Jane. Shelley wrote:

'It seems that this poor woman (Harriet) – the most innocent of her abhorred and unnatural family – was driven from her father's house (in fact she ran from it with Shelley, thought Jennifer), and descended the steps of prostitution (unfounded accusation) until she lived with a groom by the name of Smith (snobbish fabrication), who deserting her, she killed herself (it was Shelley she loved, Shelley who deserted her). – There can be no question that the beastly viper her sister (Eliza who looked after and loved Harriet), unable to gain profit from her connection with me – has secured to herself the fortune of the old man – who is now dying – by the murder of this poor creature (one moment it's suicide, the next murder). Everything tends to prove, however, that beyond the mere (mere!) shock of so hideous a catastrophe having fallen on a human being once so nearly connected with me (once! She was his wife and had been for five years when she died), there would, in any case, have been little to regret (How could anyone be so self-centred as that? How could anyone write such beautiful poetry and have such a wicked soul? How could she – Harriet and herself – have been blind for so long?) Hookham, Longdill – everyone does *me* full justice; – bears witness to the uprightness and liberality of my conduct to her.' (How dare he?)

Perhaps she had unconsciously distrusted and feared Paul, otherwise she would have been more open, but she had stupidly refused to believe her feelings.

She had thought of Aphra's love for the unconventional John Hoyle illustrative of her independent spirit. She'd let him live off her money at a time when women were all kept, men the keepers. The description of him as 'an atheist, a sodomite professed, a corrupter of youth, and a blasphemer of Christ' had seemed to her a description of the prejudices of the period against which he'd rebelled. As for his indictment at the Old Bailey on a charge of misconduct with a poulterer and his death in a tavern brawl, the first seemed comical and the second romantic. But now she knew from experience that Aphra, far from being independent, had been his victim. The steadfast love expressed in her letters to him was mere slavery. It was as unheroic as Jennifer's own desire, under the chestnut, to give way to Paul.

Aphra's was a nicely expressed affection but irredeemably normal. She wrote:

'If you are destined (destined – a passive, female way of thinking like trusting in God, or parents or the safety of the underground system) to be he, the Lord have mercy on me, for I'm sure you'll have none. I was born to ill-luck (no mistress of her own destiny here) ... You are so unreasonable (ah ha, a spark of fire!), you would have me pay, where I have contracted no debt; you would have me give, and yet, like a miser, would distribute nothing.... 'Tis I was first in friendship and shall be last in constancy (constancy, patience – unrebellious, female virtues) ... Though it be very late, I cannot go to bed, but I must tell thee I have been very good (it's as though she's making a confessional to a father-priest) ever since I saw thee, and have been a-writing, and have seen no face of man, or other body, save my own people ... I love you more and more every moment of my life. Know it, and good night.'

And yet, and yet, Jennifer couldn't help but be moved by that last, guileless shred of Aphra's heart and love herself a little more. Aphra wrote of a lover:

> His eyes are black and do transcend
> All fancy e'er can comprehend,
> And yet no softness in 'em move,
> They kill with fierceness not with love.

Killing eyes. Ought she perhaps to write a note to Mr Davidson explaining that she had changed her mind, she no longer trusted even her own feelings? She could not summon Shelley or Rebecca from the dead because she would not know who she was summoning.

She scribbled a note, then remembered Mr Davidson's words when the seance was first discussed: 'On no account can it be postponed. You may of course cancel but you cannot postpone. So make sure you are ready, or you will have lost your chance for ever.' For ever. The seance still meant a great deal to her: her independence, her ability to revolt against the pattern of things, her chance to become her own heroine. She did not want to settle for reality.

She put the note quickly into the drawer of her desk.

24

'What happened?' said Jennifer to Edward when he returned home. She followed him to his room and stood over him as he sat on the bed and took off his shoes.

'I showed the letter to Arthur Curtis, the defence counsel, who showed it to the police. The police went immediately to Lucinda's house and interviewed her. She said everything in the letter was true. She said the young man who said she'd been with him that morning had not been lying. He'd been asleep and thought she had been too. The police arrested Lucinda. Before the jury entered the court this morning Arthur discussed the letter with the judge. There's been an adjournment. Geoffrey's looking very sour.'

'So rather than looking the hero in your book, he might look rather foolish?'

Edward shrugged.

'What will happen next?'

Edward was unloosening his tie and unbuttoning his shirt.

'Geoffrey will have to declare that as a result of new evidence come to light the prosecution no longer wishes to continue with the case. The judge will direct the jury to enter a verdict of not guilty. The jury will naturally give that verdict. And Charles will be asked to stand down from the dock, a free man.'

'And will Paul have to give evidence at Lucinda's trial?'

'No, not if she's admitted to everything. He might have to have his written and signed statement read out in court, but that's all.'

'Will she be allowed a plea of diminished responsibility?'

'I certainly hope not,' said Edward. 'She killed Jane in cold blood.'

That night Jennifer dreamt that Aphra stood in a courtroom with her hair tangled, breasts naked and huge, eyes bulging right out. She was screaming that she had behaved irresponsibly. She hadn't meant to kill her boyfriend but he'd been late for a meal she'd cooked. He'd been in the coffee house. She quietened down and related every item of the meal – fricassee of rabbit and chicken, leg of mutton boiled in claret, roasted pigeons, lobsters, tarts, anchovies, cheese and prawns. All lovingly prepared. But he hadn't arrived. No wonder she'd gone mad. 'Wouldn't you?' she asked the jury of women, all characters from Coronation Street with hats on. They nodded their heads fervently and smiled at her chummily.

Sarah sat with her elbows on the breakfast table and her head resting morosely in her hands.

Edward's plate was left on the table coated with the greasy remains of fried egg and tomato. Sarah was staring into her mug of black coffee.

'You going to have some breakfast?' she muttered listlessly.

'No, thank you. I'm going to have some coffee, that's all. I'm not hungry.'

'Paul phoned earlier.'

'I heard the phone,' said Jennifer. 'What did he want?'

'He just wanted to talk to me. Clearly he needed some comfort, poor boy. It must have all been so distressing for him,' she said, in a deadpan voice.

'Distressing for *him*? What about poor Charles?' said Jennifer.

'He should have taken that letter to the police at once,' said Edward.

'He thought Charles would get off.'

'He wanted to think that,' said Edward. 'Because it was the easiest thing to think.'

'Oh stop being so self-righteous,' snapped Sarah.

'You didn't see Charles in the dock,' said Jennifer. 'You didn't see him sitting there.' She pushed away her plate. 'It was dreadful of Paul to leave him there.'

Jennifer went for a walk in St James's Park to calm herself down. She amused herself thinking up things to say to Paul the next time they met: 'I saw you through the distorted window of love, that lay in my heart, now your cruelty has smashed the window and the splinters hurt me still' ... 'For you our relationship was a mere dalliance. You deceived me. Why did or do you want to destroy me? God knows, I'm not really so proud. Are women allowed no dignity, must they always grovel?' She knew, of course, that she would say nothing of the kind.

Sarah was still at the breakfast table when Jennifer returned.

'You OK?' said Jennifer.

'Fine,' said Sarah, who wasn't. There were so many things Sarah couldn't understand now. She seemed to have lost control of things. When Paul had phoned earlier that morning he in fact hadn't wanted to speak to her at all. He had just told her he wasn't going to continue wasting his time mucking around with her absurd patio. He said that he wanted to speak to Jennifer. Sarah had told him that she was out.

'She must be in. It's nine in the morning. Is she asleep?'

'No. She's out. Went for a walk.'

'You're lying. Let me speak to her.'

'No. She's out.'

He had slammed down the phone. She phoned him back but there was no reply.

All that week Paul had been broody and moody with Sarah. Sometimes his words came out harsh and disconnected like a mynah bird who says hello or good-bye without meaning it. He had heard that he had passed his exams moderately well but had not seemed especially pleased. He had even refused to accept the bottle of champagne she had bought him as a celebratory present.

Jennifer wandered outside. The weedless earth of the main garden beds gave her pleasure. The smoothness of the grass comforted her. It was so sane, so ordered, so cultivated. A well-kept English lawn kept savagery at bay. So many tall military flowers: lupins, irises, a few carnations for the vases inside, some delphiniums. Flowers on their way up, not looking round.

There was a sweet smell in the air, a smell of gardens not of flowers.

Edward had once remarked that he liked weeding because it had a soothing monotony. The garden did too. She remembered looking down on the garden recently and thinking how ridiculous Edward looked in his floppy old white hat, bending down over a rose bush. But now the clouds had parted and the sun was hot and she could see why he needed the hat. To keep the sun off his head. One needed protection.

Jennifer decided against sending off the note to Mr Davidson just yet. Perhaps tomorrow.

Sarah stubbed her sixth cigarette that morning on to Edward's empty plate smeared with ash and egg. She had dropped some ash down the front of her dress but didn't care, she just rubbed it in.

Sarah couldn't understand why her desire for Paul seemed to be increasing rather than, as was normal with her relationships, decreasing as the days went by. When he pecked her on the cheek, or slid his arm round her waist, these actions were as erotic as an orgasm to her. He had brushed fallen ash from her bare leg once last week and her whole body shuddered with desire. Sex with Paul was so delicious. His body was agile and controlled. The mere sight of it excited her. He built up her desire with caresses hard then soft, achingly slow then rapid with urgency.

He had been so distracted he hadn't made love to her that week. She presumed distraction was the reason. Secretly she wondered if it was really because her foundation wasn't blended at the chin, her wrinkles too deeply etched, she was too fat, she was uneducated.... He had started being offhand with her after Monday, when he took Jennifer to the fair. On Tuesday she had made sure her make-up was immaculate. She wore a low-cut shirt and buttoned-up-the-front skirt sliding over satin underwear. When they were alone he was not aroused. There was a barrier between them. He said some odd things, things she couldn't really understand, in a disjointed way. He said he'd been putting his feet carefully into his own footsteps in the snow. He said he was like a swan gliding gracefully through peaceful water and paddling frantically beneath. He said it was hard to keep afloat. He sat in the middle of his drawing-room floor all huddled up as he rambled:

'It's so hard to keep going – I look all right but I can't go on preserving the pretence ... this life here, this life of acquiring, it's like climbing a huge flight of spiral stairs, you keep thinking you're nearly getting to your goal, the achievement which would really fulfil you but each time you see more stairs until you finally understand there is no summit, there is no goal, there is only the climbing ... terrifying ... makes me panic and grab ... and no one helps because they don't see it all going on ... and I have to continue with the women – with you, with Jennifer – because I see myself reflected so flatteringly in their

216

eyes ... and I'm dangerous ... poor Lucinda, poor Jane ... and yet how much do I really care? ... how much can someone who doesn't exist care?'

His talk distressed her. It didn't link up with any part of her practical, concise world and she found herself blaming her world, not his.

That evening Edward was too exhausted to tell them much about the trial, except that it had gone as expected. Charles had been found not guilty.

Sarah rang Paul up and got no reply. All evening she rang him, from home and from the restaurant. Eventually she called Edward at home.

'Hello, darling, it's me. Paul hasn't phoned, has he?'

'What?'

'I'm sorry, darling. I've woken you up.'

'Yes. Never mind. What's happened?'

'Nothing, nothing at all. I just wanted to know if Paul has phoned.'

'Is that all you were phoning for?'

'I didn't realise it was so late. Did he phone?'

'No.'

'Perhaps the defence counsel – that man Arthur Curtis – might know where he is. Do you have his number?'

'It is past twelve at night. I have no intention of giving you any phone numbers whatsoever. Good-night.' Edward slammed down the phone, rolled over in bed bringing the bedclothes with him, and fell asleep.

Sarah lay in the spare room that night, not sleeping, feeling hot and mistreated.

25

Before Sarah went out that Saturday morning, the three of them – Edward, Sarah and Jennifer – sat with the french windows open to the sounds of summer: the breeze through the plane trees whose leaves danced outside, voices of gossip in the street, the faint chatter of birds.

Sarah's bun was loosely, even messily, pinned up. Her carelessly applied lipstick made her lips look dead and she had not fully pulled up the zip at the back of her dress. The arch of her eyebrows was overgrown with dark hairs.

Edward was worried about Sarah. The old cat-like elegance had been missing these last few days. There was a softening about her eyes and a slowness to her speech. While before she slid from place to place with undulating yet deliberate movements, now there was a sense of effort in everything she did or said. He'd have done anything to cheer her up. He couldn't bear to see his darling, capable girl all defeated and thoughtful, wearing that new oatmeal dress as though it didn't belong to her, as though she were just trying it on. But Edward didn't know what to say or do. He felt helpless and angry at himself for being helpless.

'That girl Lucinda might be allowed to plead diminished responsibility,' he said. 'It's outrageous but actually can't be helped, I suppose.'

'Oh, Ed, don't let's have a law lecture. I really am far too exhausted.'

'Go on,' said Jennifer. '*I'm* interested.'

'Well, actually, it's just that ... Sarah, darling, are you all right?'

Sarah's hands were trembling as she lit her snow-white cigarette with the gold band. She had not been able to contact Paul. He seemed to have disappeared. There was an awful darkness and emptiness inside her. The fairground of amusements had stopped and she was left with only the ghost tunnel of her own mind. Last night again she had hardly slept and when she had she had fallen into panicky dreams. A sense of panic, accompanied by fluttering heart, kept returning to her but she couldn't ask anyone for help because she never had. She was someone others needed. She was not someone who needed others. Her pride would not allow her to pour out her sorrows. She did not want to be pitied.

But, in a curious way, it was good to feel again. For too long she had been a robot moving efficiently through the days, being indispensable. She had never before allowed her emotions to get out of control.

And anyway, Paul would soon realise his mistake, sort himself out, surely?

'Of course, I'm all right,' snapped Sarah.

'Good, very good.'

'What were you going to say?' said Jennifer.

'Oh yes. Well, just that Geoffrey's right to some extent about psychiatrists. They can be a liability. For instance, they'll make out that it was Lucinda's instability, her abnormally close relationship with her brother, her parents' divorce during her childhood, and the ardency of her love for Paul which all caused her to act irresponsibly.' Edward was watching Sarah anxiously as he spoke.

'Modern psychiatry is so damned understanding nobody's considered sinful any more. Nobody's depraved any more, they're all deprived. Nowadays it seems society actually glorifies the passions, the subconscious, the outsiders who rebel against society, and the law reflects this Romantic glorification. What do you think, Sarah?' he pleaded.

'I think you talk pretentious nonsense,' said Sarah, insolently blowing smoke from her mouth and nostrils like some stallion in the cold dawn air.

'No I'm not, as a matter of fact. What I'm saying is important.' Edward put on his glasses to give extra weight to his words. 'You see the law exists to keep the passions at bay. That's why this diminished responsibility plea makes a mockery of the law. It's practically saying that because a chap's passionate then he's excused. If everyone let their passions rip life would be absolute hell. Unleashed egos battling, uncontrolled, for sex, money, power, revenge ...'

'If you don't shut up I shall scream,' said Sarah. She stood up. 'You sound like Geoffrey. You just go on and on and on, don't you? I just can't bear it.' She stubbed out her cigarette viciously. 'I just fucking well can't bear your going on and on and on. I just can't.'

She walked out of the room, with her head held high, and Edward followed, fumbling in his pocket for his glasses' case. Like her lackey, thought Jennifer. She was relieved when they both went out and she was left alone in the house.

219

After a few minutes the doorbell rang. It was Paul. He was looking pale. He was wearing a tie, a light grey suit and battered cream suede lace-up shoes. The suit made him look younger, just out of public school, and the trousers were a little too short. Trelawny's first impression of Shelley came into her mind: 'was it possible this mild-looking, beardless boy, could be the veritable monster at war with all the world ... I could not believe it; it must be a hoax. He was habited like a boy, in black jacket and trowsers, which he seemed to have outgrown....'

There were beads of sweat on his brow, beneath his tangle of hair.

'I wanted to talk to you about something.'

'I can't think how anything to do with you relates to me. And Sarah's out,' she said disdainfully. He'd already come in and closed the door. Oh good, she thought, I don't feel anything for him. 'And I'd like you just to say what you've got to say then go.' He was leaning on the back of the door and he wiped his forehead with his hand. It was dark where he stood, in the shadows.

'Oh stop it, Jennifer,' he said. 'Please. This is very difficult for me.'

'You, you, you.'

'Let's go outside. The house seems dark today,' he said. He came towards her and she realised, oh God, she did still feel for him.

They walked solemnly, heel to toe, round the lawn. She watched his scuffed shoes with their big round toes, she noticed the daisies, she felt the grass cold on her bare feet and the sun hot on her head.

He stopped walking. Jennifer stopped. He turned to her.

'Hey, Jennifer ... '

'Yes?' Her face was upturned and curious.

'Let's go in and have some coffee.'

As she made the coffee, they talked about the weather. He said he'd seen numerous butterflies recently and wanted to know whether it was a good or bad omen. She said how magnificent the secret garden was looking and, overcome by the memory of their last encounter, immediately blushed. Her

220

hands shook as she poured the boiling water into the mugs. She spilt some. She mopped it up.

Upstairs they stood on the balcony. Both of them stared across the square, four hands clenching the rail.

A bald-headed man was walking along the street below with his labrador dog.

'As a kid at the cinema, up in the gallery, I used to aim bits of chewing gum at the bald heads in the stalls,' remarked Paul.

'Did you ever get caught?'

'No.'

'That was lucky.'

'Not really. I always missed. Probably intended to miss.'

Jennifer was dismayed by herself. She found she hadn't the guts to be rude to Paul. She couldn't say what she meant to say. It was a seemingly normal social situation and violent, angry words refused to rise up to her mouth. She couldn't say anything. She was too aware of the normality of the afternoon, the coffee, the square, the passing man. The desire to conform was more powerful than her anger.

Jennifer was disappointed. She'd been building up to a passionate drama of vows and accusations and rebutals but he was behaving as he had before sex had intervened, before he'd stopped his play-acting and become his true, ravenous self. He was making a mockery of everything that had happened, pretending it hadn't, rewriting it.

'Wish you'd stop glowering and let me talk.'

'I haven't been stopping you.' At least if he had thrown her down on the ground or hit her it would have been something. Something positive. But the smile on his lips was turning his former desire for her, and his cruelty, into a farce instead of a tragedy. It made her insignificant, a victim instead of a tragic heroine.

'Sorry. I mean, I'm just very relieved.'

'That you finally did the right thing over the letter?'

'Partly.'

'Well good, but I jolly well think ... ' she said and her politeness cracked under the sudden weight of acute self-pity. 'You're laughing at me.'

'Shh.' He put his arm round her and she unfurled it at once. The back of her hand pushed away her tears. She sniffed. The wind rustled the trees and out of the plane trees whispering before them flew a blackbird. The playing field was dotted with seagulls as if they thought it was a green lake.

'Go away,' she said peevishly.

'Look, I apologise for hurting your feelings. I mean, recently I've realised how much damage one can do out of sheer carelessness. I've been so busy thinking about myself, trying to work myself out, that I've forgotten about others. About their feelings. Do you understand?' Bleakly, he kicked at the rails with his right foot.

'I suppose so. But that doesn't mean I forgive you.'

A cloud was drifting indolently across the sky and below them on the pavement walked a woman with a multi-coloured cardigan and a child on each hand.

Elbows resting on the rail, he stared out. The cry of the seagulls cracked into the air like shrapnel.

'Well, Jennifer, I mean, I've been so weak for so long, vacillating from one mood to another, one aim to another, having only my self-absorption and the respect of others to stop me falling apart. Then came all this. My relationship with you, with your mother, the trial ... It must all stop. Everyone should do something really dramatic at least once in their lives and I'm going to do that something soon.'

'What do you mean?'

He sniffed emphatically, as if clearing his throat in the wrong place.

'I'm going to end this life of mine.'

He spoke with a firmness which alarmed Jennifer. He was grinning dementedly, a new lop-sided grin, and his eyes were looking at her intently. Wild, Rasputin eyes.

'Don't worry. I shall start another.'

He said that he had been so obsessed with himself, with defining his own ego, with making people approve of him, that he had been unable to look beyond himself. He had barged into other people while he wasn't looking and had hurt them badly. But until recently he hadn't much cared because secretly he knew that, like him, other people did not really exist. Until he met Jennifer. In her he recognised himself as he had once been before he lost himself in smiles. Jennifer took life so seriously, as if it actually mattered.

'Our coffee must be getting cold,' said Jennifer.

'Jennifer,' he said earnestly. 'Please listen. I'm sorry if I treated you badly. I was, I suppose, jealous of that almost religious look in your eyes. I mean, you seemed to be above everything and one wanted to destroy that secrecy, bring you down to earth. Listen. Or, more simply,' his voice rose as her face remained indifferent, 'I wanted to fuck the living daylights out of you.' Her eyebrows shot up like a jack-in-the-box and she turned to him, amazed. 'But remember I didn't ... And that's what counts.'

'I don't know about that.'

'I do. Don't look so sulky, it only makes you more lovely.' He spoke softly, caressingly and she held the rail tighter. 'I didn't mean what I said outside at the party. It was me I was calling those names, not you. You do see that, don't you?'

'Suppose so,' she said churlishly. 'So what's happened, what are you going to do?'

'I'm going to leave England.'

She shrugged, as if that was of no consequence.

'For a long time.'

She looked at him sideways.

'Maybe for ever.'

She turned, frowning, forgetting the impression she was making.

'But why? Where are you going?'

'To help design a hospital in India. I'm joining a religious order – the Order of the Knights of St John. They set up hospitals.'

'Why? You don't know anything about hospitals.'

'Don't need to. I know about architecture. I'll be working with a firm of English architects out there.'

'You're not religious ...'

'I am now. A bit.' He grinned self-deprecatingly. 'I've got to do something positive, Jennifer. It's all right for you. You're so determined, so full of hope ... I've got to *find* all that. I've found some in you, little one, you know.'

He leant forward and kissed her gently on the lips, touching her with only his mouth.

'But I don't want you to go,' she said shakily.

'Yes you do. I'll only hurt you if I stay. Don't worry, I won't be existing on fried locusts in the desert.'

'Have you told Sarah?'

'No, and you mustn't either. Please. It'll cause trouble.'

'How did you know she wasn't here?'

'I was watching from my window. I saw her go by. But I want to give you my address. I want you to write to me.' He pushed a piece of paper with an address written in block capitals into her hand.

'Sarah might be back soon. I'd better go now,' said Paul. 'And I have to get ready. The plane's leaving this afternoon.'

Jennifer looked up the street in the direction Sarah usually returned from the shops. She saw Mr Davidson hurrying along beside the black wire fence of the playing field. He looked up at the balcony as he passed and smiled a quick, questioning smile.

'You look quite pale,' said Paul. 'Don't worry.'

'Don't go.'

She went downstairs with him and, as he left he undid the gold cross and chain from round his neck and put it into her hand.

'Good-bye, little one.'

'Good-bye, Paul.'

The golden puddle lay in her hand for some time before she turned around and walked slowly upstairs to her bedroom.

After a few minutes alone, thinking, she hurried down the steps, out into the square and round to Abbey Court. She rang the bell of Mr Davidson's flat.

He opened it almost immediately and took the dangling cigarette from his mouth.

'You look astounded,' said Mr Davidson.

'I'm so excited. I just came to tell you how excited I am.'

'Come in, my dear, come in, sit down, relax.'

'I know it's all going to work. We're going to see them all in

224

the flesh and blood. And they'll eat the food I prepare, I just know it. And they'll talk to each other. I believe in it all again. I know. We'll have Aphra talking to Shelley and Rebecca talking to me. I'll be entertaining the dead ... we'll be entertaining the dead! Oh Mr Davidson. They'll talk to each other. We'll find out so much. It'll make everything worthwhile. My life, your life. It'll be such a fulfilment. It's what I want more than anything and I know we can do it.'

Mr Davidson wiped his head with his huge handkerchief.

'Yes, yes, my dear. You're right. We can do it. I know, I know.'

He turned and stood looking out of the window. 'But you must remember. Hmmm. There are no second chances. Hmmm. The evening of August the thirtieth is your chance to make the impossible possible, to celebrate your ability to step beyond the normal. It is the last day of your childhood, perhaps of your special powers.'

Jennifer's mind was racing, she was hardly listening.

'It's what people have schemed for, aspired to and been willing to sell their souls for. And we ... little Jennifer Hamilton and you, Mr Davidson ... are going to achieve it. And my father will be there to see me playing the hostess. I'm so happy Mr Davidson, I am, really.'

Mr Davidson turned and smiled.

'Your eyes are so big and shiny they look as though they're about to float out of your head and become planets. Would you like some tea?'

'No, no. I must ... yes. Please. I would like some tea.'

He waddled off to the kitchen, his shirt collar sticking up into the flesh of his neck.

26

All that day and Sunday Jennifer had difficulty restraining herself from telling Sarah the news of Paul's departure. After the shock had worn off, she was inspired by his act of daring. It seemed so unlike him, or so unlike what she had thought was him. It made life suddenly remarkable again. It made him a hero, and gave her the possibility of becoming her own heroine.

It was, she thought, the mature and cynical who made life and people unremarkable. It was people like Sarah's mother. She had been given a rotten life by her husband and therefore thought it impossible to acquire a life which wasn't rotten. Not so. She was apparently an attractive woman. She could have walked out on him any time. But she'd learnt that life was rotten, learnt to put up with it, to be mature, and that was that. Jennifer saw that this process of 'maturing' had started to happen to her over the past weeks. Experience, especially painful experience, was liable to narrow people. It made them see everything in terms of their painfully acquired wisdom. It made them put barbed wire round their heads to protect them from more painful change. Like Geoffrey and his cynicism, they had a world-view and were jolly well going to stick to it, they'd learnt it the hard way, after all. Jennifer was determined to discover no more truths, only questions. She must be open to change always. She would be naive like Rebecca had been, would judge everyone and everything separately. She would not confuse the past with the present or one person with another.

The next morning, Monday, Jennifer bought herself a bunch of yellow roses to celebrate. There was a month to go before the seance. She knew she would be ready. Her determination and daring would bring the dead souls she loved to her for that one, glorious, evening. For once, she would be the hostess.

She arranged the flowers in a white porcelain vase, placed them on a table in the hall and gazed. They were Indian dancers, their leaves expressive hands darting out of slender bodies. Rebecca had been right. They were yellow and gold and pink all at once ... they were sunsets ... and yet they were all those things yet only themselves. And they were moving, dancing, but absolutely still. They were erupting within her and yet she felt tranquil.

She was standing before the table as if it were an altar when the door opened and her mother came in. The love she had for

226

the flowers shifted to her mother. She had a grease mark on her denim skirt.

'There's something I want to tell you,' said Jennifer.

'Let me put these things away, come and talk while I do it.'

Jennifer followed her mother into the kitchen.

'Or perhaps you know?' said Jennifer.

'What?'

'About Paul.'

'What about Paul?'

'He's gone to India.'

'I don't understand what you're saying.'

. 'Paul has gone to India. He's left England.'

'Why?'

'To design a hospital. For at least a year.'

'What?' said Sarah. In one hand was a tin of soup, in the other a packet of mixed herbs. Colour had drained from her face.

'He's left.'

'You're lying.'

'I'm not.'

'Of course you are. He hasn't gone.'

'He has gone. I promise you he has gone.'

'You've made a mistake.'

'I have not. I'm absolutely certain. He left on Saturday evening.'

'For how long?'

'I told you. At least a year.'

To Sarah, it seemed the world had come to a sudden halt. She sank down on to the stool. Jennifer's face gazed anxiously at her from under a fluster of reddish hair like some minor devil. In slow motion Sarah seemed to be reeling back and forth from the blow.

Her face in her mind spidered into a network of lines, a window suddenly smashed. And her body was a lump of lard.

'But why?' she murmured.

'I don't know,' said Jennifer.

'What?'

'I said I don't know why.'

227

'And he told you?' she said.

'Yes. On Saturday.'

Sarah had been hovering on the brink of middle-age for many years and to Jennifer she suddenly seemed to have fallen. Jennifer was oddly detached from the spectacle, half enjoying her victory, half upset by her mother's grief.

Suddenly a realisation brightened Sarah's face.

'So why the fuck didn't you say anything to me then?'

'He told me not to tell you.'

'You always were a deceitful little brat,' said Sarah.

'Thanks for the compliment.'

'Don't be so *stupid*. This is my life we're talking about, not a child's silly game.'

Sarah's eyes were roasting into Jennifer's flesh and she couldn't stand it.

'Stop looking at me like that,' said Jennifer. 'I'm fed up with being treated as though I don't exist. I do.'

'Couldn't miss you, could I?'

'Oh shut up,' said Jennifer, her eyes blazing back.

Sarah lost her temper. She stood up and lifted the can of soup as if about to throw it at Jennifer. Sarah's furious face loomed above Jennifer and she cowered back. Sarah swivelled round and smashed the can through the kitchen window. Sarah looked round for something else to throw. Her hair was strewn all over her face. She was beetroot-red, trembling all over. She swept all the herbs, the potted plants, the packets of coffee, the tea-caddy, everything, off the sideboard. Then she kicked the sideboard, hurt her foot and burst into tears.

The sight of her capable mother in tears was too much for Jennifer. Sarah's face was all deformed and red like a blubbering baby.

'I'm sorry, Sarah, I am, I ...'

'I'm sorry, too,' whimpered Sarah. 'Everything's gone so wrong, so suddenly. I can't bear it. Really, I don't think I can bear it.'

'You'll have to.'

'No. I don't have to. I'll do something about it. I will.'

Sarah stayed in her room for the rest of the day, refusing food

228

and phone calls. Occasionally, coming past, Jennifer heard her crying. She noticed the whisky bottle had gone from the drawing room. Jennifer felt miserably guilty.

Sarah came out to watch the early news.

'Do you have his address?' Sarah asked Jennifer.

'No.'

'Really?'

'Yes.'

'Really?'

'Well ...'

'Give it to me.'

Jennifer went to get the address.

Soon Sarah had a quiet smile on her face.

They heard the slam of the door downstairs and Edward shout 'Hello, Sarah.'

'Hello,' she yelled back.

In a minute he was up the stairs and in the drawing room. 'Oh, darling,' he said, eager and loving as ever, 'We've got an invitation ...'

Sarah was standing with her back to him, pouring herself yet another drink. She turned round.

'What is it, baby? You don't look well. You don't look at all well.' Concern spread over his face as he darted towards her and then stopped, a magnetic wall of rejection erected between them by Sarah. 'What is it, baby?' he repeated.

'What's happened?' he asked Jennifer.

Jennifer shrugged.

'It's your fault,' said Sarah coolly. 'You kept us apart.'

He looked from Jennifer to Sarah.

'Come now,' he said soothingly. 'I haven't done that ... mothers and adolescent daughters are not known for their friendliness. It's just a stage ...'

'Not Jennifer and me, you buffoon. You kept me apart from Paul.' Her shoulders were up, belligerent.

'From Paul?'

'Yes. From Paul. I loved Paul ... I love Paul.'

'Should we discuss this with Jennifer in the room?'

'Yes.' she snapped. 'Why not? She knows. She knows it all.'

229

'Would you please pour me a whisky?'

Sarah poured one and shoved it into his hand. He opened the french windows and stepped out on to the balcony. He leant on the balcony, took deep breaths and sipped the whisky.

'Don't *escape* out there,' screamed Sarah suddenly, gripping her glass tightly and standing, belligerent, in the middle of the room, her face snarling. *'Face me.* You heard what I said and I don't care if the whole bloody square hears it too. I love Paul.' And, a little softer, she said, 'And I don't love you any more.'

After a moment Edward moved back into the room. With his free hand he ran his fingers through his grey hair.

Jennifer made for the door.

'Stay,' said Sarah. 'You've *both* got to face things for once. You can't turn away any more. I'm not going to let you.'

'Actually, I have never ...' Edward's voice was shaky and he had to level it with an effort. 'Actually, I have never kept you apart from anyone, quite the contrary I would have said. I must say I thought you thought me, and I've always thought myself, remarkably tolerant.'

'I agree,' said Jennifer.

'Be quiet,' roared Sarah. 'You never knew anything, Ed. You've been blinkered, not tolerant. You're a buffoon. A kindly buffoon.'

'Am I allowed to sit down? My legs feel rather tired.'

'Of course.'

He sat down, closing his eyes for a moment then opening them.

'Actually, it's not true. I did know you were having an affair with Paul. I'm afraid I also knew about the others.'

'The other affairs?'

'Yes. Saul for instance.'

'You're lying.'

'When have I ever lied to you?'

'You're an idiot then. You should have said something. Weren't you jealous?'

'Yes, but remember I had your love. And I wasn't an idiot. Actually I thought, or rather I knew, that without freedom you'd have been miserable. You wouldn't have been you. But all these years, since that affair with – what was his name? – that solicitor …?'

'The one who looked like a goblin? Richard Strong.'

'Yes. Since him. Since him I've known. Remember we are quite close. I do know you well. I've loved you for – how many is it? – for more than twenty years. Of course I know when you're having an affair. But this is the first time one has become a problem. What is so special about this fellow?'

'He's gone away to India,' said Jennifer.

'Well I must say …'

'That's not the reason,' said Sarah. 'I don't know the reasons. Who cares? I know I love him.'

'But he doesn't love you,' said Jennifer.

'How do you know? I believe he does, you see. In fact I know he does.'

'Then you're just believing what you want to believe.'

'Maybe. Why not?'

'Look, I want you to be happy more than anything else …' said Edward.

Sarah cut in with a short derisive laugh. 'Good! Then you won't mind what I've decided to do.'

'And what's that?'

'I'm going to leave you.'

'Don't be silly.'

'I'm completely serious. I have the address of the hospital he's gone to and I shall follow him there. I've already booked my flight. It leaves tomorrow evening. I'm not going to repress my desires. I must fulfil myself. Women have a right to freedom. I will not sacrifice myself to husband and family. I have a right to happiness.'

Jennifer could hardly breathe the humid air. She slipped out of the room and walked down the stairs and out into the darkening garden. She sat under the horse-chestnut until she was cool.

Why couldn't she leave him alone? Why couldn't Sarah leave Paul alone?

Passing the drawing room on the way up to her room Jennifer looked in. Edward sat on the sofa with his back curved wearily and his head resting in his hands.

'Are you all right?' said Jennifer.

'No. Not really. I've just hit Sarah and she's locked herself in the bedroom.'

'You what?' Jennifer crouched down before her father whose face, she saw, was ashen.

'I hit her. Quite justifiably in my opinion. She has a responsibility to you and to me, not just to herself. But she can't see that. I hope she's all right. I hope I didn't really hurt her.'

'I'm sure you didn't.'

He looked through Jennifer and said, 'Did she think I haven't known and been hurt by her other men? I have, blow her. But I let her, I let her have her own private arena.'

That evening Jennifer nursed them both, giving them whisky and coffee and sympathy. She made up a bed for Edward in the spare room that night, smoothing down the sheets lovingly and bringing him up chocolate so hot he scalded his tongue. He wore striped pyjamas. Usually, in bed with Sarah, he wore nothing.

The next day, after appointing a manager for her restaurant, Sarah left for India. Before she left, she kissed Jennifer gently on both cheeks.

'Bye, bye, little one. I'm sorry. I don't mean to hurt you. I don't want to hurt Edward. But in life one only has one chance.'

'Will you be back, Mummy?'

'Oh darling. Oh yes, I will be back. Look after Edward, will you?'

Edward was standing behind Jennifer, watching, with vacancy in his eyes.

'I wish you wouldn't go,' said Edward. 'I didn't mean to hit you.'

'You did. I don't blame you. But I must go. There's no question about it. I must go.'

'Please don't,' said Jennifer. 'Please.'

'I'm sorry, darling.'

Jennifer was surprised at how very upset she was to see her mother climb into the taxi – struggling with her suitcase, refusing to accept help – and drive away.

27

The day after Sarah had left, father and daughter wandered down the garden, towards the wild part. The air smelt of summer, of roses and breezes and orange blossom. White cumulus clouds floated, as in a child's drawing, across a blue sky.

'Do you know I suddenly feel an adolescent again? So alone,' he said.

'What do you mean?'

'I was so lonely. Of course I had girlfriends. Or rather had crushes and cuddles and kisses with girls. But none of them lasted. Because actually they don't. Not when you're young.'

'I wouldn't know about that,' muttered Jennifer. There were daisies on the grass and butterflies in the sky and she again felt suddenly, recklessly, happy.

'You ought to. It's good to glut yourself, meet plenty of partners, so when you meet the right one, you know it. You see how different she is from the girls with giggles or gum-stinking mouths or dreadful friends. Also you're fed up with the back rows of cinemas. No, that's not what you're fed up with. You're weary of rejections and pain and emptiness and fear of death.'

She looked up at the tall shabby figure marching by her side, his head flung back and chin forward like some don taking his Sunday morning walk across weatherbeaten cliffs. His old checked shirt had a button missing on one cuff and the brown corduroy trousers were worn at the knee. They walked through the greenhouse and felt for a moment the sudden, musty heat of mouldering earth and warm plants. The tomatoes were doing well.

'And what's more each time an adolescent love caved in I became more certain that I was, in fact, unlovable. That there was something fundamentally wrong with me. But of course that wasn't it. It was just that everything dies. Leaves, flowers, people. Actually, my experience was perfectly natural. That's why we go on searching for a love that doesn't die. If we find *that* it defeats the plague of brevity. It even, yes, suggests we might

233

not die or rather that there might be something beyond this endlessly dying fall of life.'

They were in the dappled, light-patterned shadows of the horse-chestnut. Outside its circle the weeds grew long and languid in the flower beds and ivy draped itself everywhere. The wild, climbing roses with their centres open to the sun had an abandoned and lascivious air. For some reason, Jennifer thought of Lucinda and her mulberry-lipstick mouth.

'Jennifer, Imagine yourself with anyone, any boyfriend, and think of death. Then with, say, a young man who loves you more than anything and everything. You see? It doesn't hurt so. Love's the cushion which catches you when your mind pitches down into death. And in adolescence you have no cushion yet. You're skydiving. Or I was. All alone. Without, really, even yourself to keep you company. Because actually you aren't yourself really. You're searching for that self. Perhaps we all are always. Otherwise we wouldn't care so much what others thought about us. We wouldn't need others to delineate us. And, Jenny, I seem to have lost my outlines in losing Sarah. Do you think she'll be back? She will be back, won't she?'

Two weeks later Sarah still hadn't come back. They hadn't even heard from her. Jennifer found that she missed her mother. She missed her firmness, her laughter, the relish with which she lived.

Jennifer's O level results arrived and were excellent but neither Jennifer nor Edward paid them much attention. Edward found he now had little interest in his book on the trial. He refused to discuss it with Geoffrey, and did not reply to anxious letters from his agent. Often he took the phone off the hook for days on end. Charles wanted to come round to thank Edward personally but Edward would see no one.

The days of Jennifer and Edward began to fall into a pattern. Edward was at home instead of at the library. He found, without Sarah's presence, that the house was amazingly peaceful. They saw practically no one. Jennifer said she liked the timeless feel of the house without news to jolt it into the unpleasant present. Edward had acquiesced partly because he couldn't be bothered to argue. Nowadays Edward wasn't bothered very much about anything.

They got up late, about ten thirty, every day and Jennifer cooked them both a boiled egg and toast. After breakfast they had a walk round the garden, but seldom down to the wild part. They chatted, mostly about Shelley and Aphra and sometimes Rebecca, whom Edward remembered quite well. Jennifer would then return to the house and wash up and tidy. She had told Maureen not to come for a while, until Sarah returned. Edward meanwhile pottered in the garden doing a spot of digging, of weeding, of picking the dead heads off the rose bushes. Or else he stayed inside, in the drawing room, reading old novels. He kept saying to Jennifer, 'Sarah will be back soon. I'm sure. Then I'll be able to get on.'

At about two in the afternoon they had a simple lunch of soup or salad and cheese. When the weather was good, they ate it out in the garden on the white wrought-iron table. Otherwise in the dining room. Jennifer enjoyed preparing the meals. She'd never known how capable she could be. After lunch she sometimes phoned and ordered more food from a local shop which delivered the following morning. In the afternoon and evening they worked, stopping only for a rather elaborate dinner prepared by Jennifer. Occasionally she made him a syllabub, once they had potted lobster. She tried out Fowls à la Mayonnaise from her mother's *Modern Cookery for Private Families,* but the mayonnaise was not a success.

In his study, when Jennifer thought he was working on his book on the trial, he'd often just pace up and down over and over again. He remembered a bear in London Zoo whose feet had worn two great holes in the stone floor of his pen. Always he spun round at the same points. The narrow space between the two hollows marked the dimensions of his world and his misery.

For the first two weeks after Sarah's departure he had kept quite busy. He had moved relatively rapidly through the days, trying to keep up his momentum so he could jump over the chasms of memory and despair. But now he was slowing down. He tried to deflect his thoughts from Sarah but they returned to her. He walked the square one day, saw droplets of rain on a

235

black railing, and suddenly he was describing them to Sarah. A weekly journal was delivered and he read it wondering what magazines and papers Sarah read now. The phone rang and it wasn't her. A woman outside, in the street, with her hair, wasn't her.

Every evening Jennifer brought him up a mug of drinking chocolate and kissed him on the cheek.

In the past he'd considered her sulky, now he realised she was just very vulnerable and affectionate. There was something very engaging about the vulnerable, they made one feel strong. He had never really felt strong with Sarah but it hadn't mattered because, in a way, her strength supported him. Jennifer was also, most of the time, very good-humoured.

One night Jennifer had come down and woken him up, saying she'd had a bad dream, a dream about Shelley, and she wanted a chat. She'd looked so scared and big-eyed beneath her helmet of russet hair which clashed with the pink of her long nightie. He realised he loved her. He'd advised her against being so obsessed with Shelley. It was unhealthy, he said. She had looked concerned. 'Do you *really* think so?' she had asked.

Sometimes Jennifer could imagine the evening of the thirtieth so vividly she could see the silver cutlery on the dark table, the candles flickering in the two candelabra. Ready. Waiting for the moment when she and Mr Davidson made the impossible possible. The curtains drawn. The clock ticking. The high-backed chairs. Would they see Shelley? Would they all see him? She was sure she would. She knew it now. They would eat and talk together. She would be the hostess. It would be the greatest evening of her life.

There would be syllabub in the fridge, the grandfather clock would chime nine o'clock, Mr Davidson would arrive. To her dinner party, her seance. Cut-glass wine glasses, thin-sliced brown bread to go with the potted lobster, decanted wine, moist butter and plain white plates with just a faint gold rim. The clock and the drawn curtains and the smell of the lobster and the chill of the white wine she sipped as she waited until she and Mr Davidson overcame time, watched, with respect, by Edward.

236

It was on the Sunday before the Saturday that she asked Edward if he would join her small dinner party. He shuffled coins around in his pockets and looked uncomfortable but said what a surprise, yes, of course he'd love to come.

She was so relieved he'd said yes. She wanted him to be there very much. Everything was leading up to this one evening. The brooding stillness of these last weeks without Sarah were, like the silent heat of a greenhouse, ripening her dreams into reality.

Edward would realise what all her hints and talk of Shelley and Rebecca had been leading towards and would respect her for the success of her plan. He would see that she too could arrange things, and on a grand scale. In his eyes, in her eyes, she would be somebody remarkable. A creator, a controller, a hostess to his beloved Aphra, to one of England's greatest poets, and to darling Rebecca.

On Monday morning a letter arrived from India addressed to Edward and Jennifer. The address was typed. She hoped it was from Paul. She put the letter in her pocket because Edward was having breakfast in the adjoining room and, if it was from Sarah, she wanted to see it first.

'Any post?'

'Two eggs or one?' replied Jennifer.

Edward was in the garden when Jennifer opened the letter. It was from Sarah. Over three weeks had passed since she left.

Dear Edward and Jennifer,

It might comfort both of you to know I'm not having an affair with Paul out here. I'd sent him a telegram and he met me off the plane but immediately explained that it had all been over with us some weeks ago. News to me. Oh Lord, I sound so chirpy, don't I? But after Paul telling me the news that it had been all over even before he left I was, you can imagine, broken-hearted.

But these last few days I realised something. In a way I didn't leave you, Edward, for Paul, I left you for a new life and not because I was unhappy in the old one. I wasn't, whatever I said to you that horrible night. I was comfortable. Too comfortable. Buried in comfort. Now I can't say

I'm happy but it's all new and exciting and, I don't know, I feel so alive. I've arranged for the restaurant to be sold and the money sent out to me here, to be used to improve conditions here at the hospital. I've told them how much I'll be donating and they all think it's magnificent. That I'm magnificent. Even Paul is quite impressed by the changed me.

So you have my address and can contact me if you think I deserve it.

But for the moment I shall stay here, administrating and generally helping out. Paul was just the trigger, you see, who shot me off into my new life.

I'm sure you'll both be able to cope with everything. I was going to give you a list of Things to Do but now I can't remember anything. Isn't it odd? I must stop now as we're being called for dinner. Will write again at length soon.

Love,
Sarah

P.S. But I do love you *both*, really, very much. Dear Jennifer, I know we'll be such friends when you're older.

Jennifer threw the letter in the rubbish bin, washed up and, watching Edward's gawky frame topped by his Christopher Robin hat, couldn't deceive him. She ran out with the letter, stained with egg splotches, in her hand.

'The letter. It's for us both.'

'Ugh. What a smelly thing. Who's it from?'

'Sarah,' she said in a dull, toneless voice.

With a garden fork in one hand and gloves on both, he read the letter over and over again with a puzzled expression rumpling his face. Jennifer winced to see puzzlement change to naked pain.

'How can she treat us like this? How can she? And she admits she wasn't even unhappy,' he said, and folded the letter in half, ripped it in two, folded the two halves up and ripped again and again until the letter was no more than a pile of confetti which a breeze carried off from his outstretched palm.

The fragments of paper danced away in the cool summer breeze.

After the letter Edward became a robot, moving mechanically through the days. He couldn't be bothered to do anything but sit in his study or in the drawing room just staring. The bookshelves no longer interesting, life at a halt. The wind rattling the windows of his mind. There was nothing else to do. Jennifer was a comfort but not enough. Edward had never before known unhappiness like this. He had thought sometimes in the past that he was unhappy. He had been wrong. This debilitating, bottomless despair was something so terrible he found it hard to imagine bearing it for long. It was so absolute. It infected every moment. He couldn't escape from it. He couldn't even sleep.

All week Jennifer prepared for the party. She hummed and sang as pots of mayonnaise appeared in the fridge, lemons in the vegetable rack, packets of sugar in the cupboard. Edward's wine cellar was ransacked, silver polished, best glasses washed, flowers bought. Edward thought he'd never seen Jennifer look so radiant. He wondered who she was inviting to dinner. Perhaps a boyfriend and, all at once, discovered he was jealous. She was all he had now and would she leave him as Sarah had left him?

By Saturday morning the house smelt and looked gorgeous.

Edward came down late that morning and, in the kitchen doorway in Sarah's apron with the smell of entertaining and polish all around her, Jennifer was so much like Sarah that for a moment he felt his knees kicked from under him and, weakened, he held on to the banisters. He was chalk-white and Jennifer couldn't help but notice.

28

Slowly she plodded through the day's preparations, pausing to make just two telephone calls, until at eight thirty that evening in the kitchen she sat all alone. It took so long, so many minutes, until the grandfather clock chimed nine. When it did she stood up, plunged her hands deeper into the pockets of her jeans, and waited.

A minute later the doorbell rang and here was the first guest. She walked slowly to the door and opened it.

Aemilia stood there, looking up the stairs to Edward.

'Hello, Jennifer,' she said to Edward.

'Aemilia! I didn't know ...' And he was rushing down, his face alive. It froze Jennifer but she still smiled

He strode down the corridor and kissed Aemilia on the cheek which at once turned red with pleasure.

'Gosh,' he said, stepping back and staring at her. 'I am pleased to see you. I don't seem to have seen anyone for so long.'

Aemilia said, shyly, 'Oh Edward, it's well, it's so nice to see you and it was such a surprise when Jennifer rang this morning. I thought ... well I didn't know what to think. Geoffrey said you wouldn't see anyone.'

'Surprise to me, I can tell you. Hey, Jenny, who else is coming?' His eyes were gleeful and mouth suspicious. 'Hey, young lady?'

He pushed open the dining room door and there was the long table laid, silver cutlery on the dark wood, candelabra, brown bread, lobster and polished glasses, for just two.

'Nobody. It's for the two of you. I've changed the plan.'

'But ...'

'I'm going out, actually. Last-minute arrangement.'

After she had closed the front door behind her, she stood for a moment on the steps. She had cancelled the seance for the sake of her father. Her childhood was over and there were tears of loss in her eyes. What was she to do now, she wondered, shivering slightly.